WHAT I DID ON MY SUMMER VACATION...

Thea Devine
Debbi Rawlins
Samantha Hunter

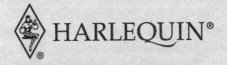
HARLEQUIN®

TORONTO • NEW YORK • LONDON
AMSTERDAM • PARIS • SYDNEY • HAMBURG
STOCKHOLM • ATHENS • TOKYO • MILAN • MADRID
PRAGUE • WARSAW • BUDAPEST • AUCKLAND

ISBN-13: 978-0-373-79409-6
ISBN-10:   0-373-79409-6

WHAT I DID ON MY SUMMER VACATION...

The publisher acknowledges the copyright holders of the individual works as follows:

THE GUY DIET

LIGHT MY FIRE

NO RESERVATIONS

This is a work of fiction. Names, characters, places and incidents are either the product of the author's imagination or are used fictitiously, and any resemblance to actual persons, living or dead, business establishments, events or locales is entirely coincidental.

This edition published by arrangement with Harlequin Books S.A.

® and TM are trademarks of the publisher. Trademarks indicated with ® are registered in the United States Patent and Trademark Office, the Canadian Trade Marks Office and in other countries.

www.eHarlequin.com

Printed in U.S.A.

Look what people are saying about these talented authors...

Thea Devine

"Thea Devine gives her fans exactly what they desire."
—*Romantic Times BOOKreviews*

"[Devine] pushes sexuality
to the limits of the genre."
—*Library Journal*

"The Queen of Erotic Romance..."
—*Romantic Times BOOKreviews*

Debbi Rawlins

"Debbi Rawlins has created characters rich in depth
who will tug on readers' heartstrings."
—*Romantic Times BOOKreviews*

"Debbi Rawlins scorches the pages."
—*Romantic Times BOOKreviews*

"Well-developed characters and humor,
as well as heart, make *If Only He Knew...*
by Debbi Rawlins stand out."
—*Romantic Times BOOKreviews*

Samantha Hunter

"Wonderful characters, vivid setting
and steamy romance."
—*Romantic Times BOOKreviews*

"Sensuality explodes on the pages!"
—*Romance Junkies*

"A wonderful new voice in today's romance."
—*A Romance Review*

ABOUT THE AUTHORS

Thea Devine has written more than twenty steamy historical romances, as well as a dozen sexy contemporary and historical romantic novellas for Kensington, Leisure and Harlequin Books. In that secret life her readers always imagined she lived, she was also a freelance manuscript reader over the course of many years for several major mass-market publishers and she's been married to the ever-patient and much-adored John for about that long. They live in Connecticut with three resident cats and one beloved mini-doxie.

Debbi Rawlins has written more than twenty-five novels for Harlequin Books. She lives in central Utah, out in the country, surrounded by woods and deer and wild turkeys. It's quite a change for a city girl. Of course, unfamiliarity never stopped her. Between her junior and senior years of college she spontaneously left home in Hawaii, and bummed around Europe for five weeks by herself. And much to her parents' delight, returned home with only a quarter in her wallet.

Samantha Hunter lives in Syracuse, New York, where she writes romance full-time. When she's not plotting her next book, Sam likes to work on her garden, quilt, cook, read and spend time with her husband and their dogs. "No Reservations" marks her tenth Harlequin Blaze story to date. Sam often chats on the Blaze boards at eHarlequin.com, or you can check out what's new, enter contests, or drop her a note at www.samanthahunter.com, and www.loveisanexplodingcigar.com.

CONTENTS

THE GUY DIET

Thea Devine

Always, to John. Nothing more needs to be said.

1

OKAY, I CONFESS. The whole thing started because I decided to go on a Guy Diet. Call it what it was—removing myself from the dating food chain altogether. Tossing out those superchunk hunks. Refusing to be seduced by those devil dogs. I was tired of the same old fast-food sex and I was ready for change.

My roommate, Paula, says penises are nonfattening and I'm a fool to give them up. I say there's nothing about them that doesn't bloat you and make you crazy, especially an unforeseen, unplanned pregnancy.

Paula says men are an all-you-can-eat buffet.

Enough with gorging myself on fast-food sex. It was time for a cleansing fast.

I wanted to find someone who could commit to more than just which shirt he'd wear the next morning.

So I came up with the idea of The Guy Diet.

Which I dreamed up because I write about food. You may even have read my column, The Grab-and-Go Gourmet.

I'm Lo Cavallero, Lo being short for LoAnne, which everyone thinks is Lou-Anne. So I ended the confusion and made it easier on everyone by dropping the Anne part.

In my real life, I share a minuscule one-bedroom apartment in the far West Eighties with the aforementioned Paula—Talcott— who was my college roommate.

Let me tell you about Paula. Paula is not me. Paula is tall, model thin, designer obsessed, blond, gorgeous, savvy and smart. I am tall and lanky with a mop of dark-brown unruly hair that matches my born-in-Brooklyn unruly mouth. I'm pretty smart, not that savvy, and I couldn't care less how I look.

Paula gives me glam and I give her good advice. She makes me seem sexy; I keep her grounded.

Paula graduated six months ahead of me, got her ideal job in an international ad agency and worked her way up to assistant account executive in what seemed like the blink of an eye, and ultimately found the apartment she invited me to share.

Although one-bedrooms can be dicey, we have twin beds so neither of us has to sleep on the floor or the couch, as friends do when they're crashing or when one of us gets lucky.

Which means Paula. Paula lives the life most of us fantasize about and there was always a little part of me that wanted to be that adventurous and cavalier about sex and life. Though, given my fairly strict upbringing, I preferred living that life by proxy until I met Paula.

In no time at all, I became Paula's confessor and her coconspirator, and I lived that single city life for the six years that we've known each other.

Still, I'm the super-responsible one. Goes right back to being a latchkey kid. My mom married young, was widowed young and raised me with no husband, on not much of an income and under the critical gaze of a houseful of censurious relatives. That made her even more determined to prove she could raise a kid, work and never ask for help from anyone.

Except me. When I was old enough.

I did the dishes, dusting, vacuuming and cooking from the time I could remember. I made sure my bed was made, my wash got done and my homework never suffered. And I got straight As because it would have hurt her if I hadn't.

I did whatever I could to alleviate Mom's burden until the golden day she got a computer-studies certificate from community college and a job that provided medical benefits and a pension.

It was strictly understood I was going to college and I was not to get sidetracked. Because she'd disown me. Period. For my part, being my mother's daughter, I was determined to make her proud, graduate with honors and find a secure job that would provide me with the wherewithal to help mom and assure her I would never go hungry, married or not.

Any other dreams I might have had, the evanescent ones—like being an artist, a writer, a chef, getting married—I didn't believe were possible. My goal was a concrete-steady paycheck because nothing could be depended upon—especially a man.

I actually should have chosen to study premed because when I was rooting around after graduation for the perfect job, I discovered the high-paying world of medical transcription. I took a course, got a certificate, decided to be an independent contractor and solicited my own clientele, consisting of two dozen physicians and an ad agency specializing in pharmaceuticals. So I have the freedom to set my own hours.

And then, the point I was getting to, I write this little cooking column for a small local independent Upper West Side shopper, the *WestEnder.*

The *WestEnder* started as just a small give-away booklet and grew into an on-the-newsstand-and-by-subscription tabloid. To entice readership, the publisher decided to add features and columns spotlighting local businesses and events, and, given the demographic, a book-and-movie review column, and eventually a cooking column.

I'd always done the cooking for me and Mom since I was old enough to learn how. Mom basically liked her food fast and hot because when she came home from work she was wiped. So I began concocting recipes for her, never dreaming my reach could extend beyond Mom's kitchen.

But—and this was where the whole thing started—Paula had been dating Jed Costigan, the publisher of the *WestEnder* and she invited me one evening in late March to join her and Jed for dinner at a newly opened restaurant that the paper's food critic had praised the week before.

It was jam-packed that night and I was a half hour late. I blew into the restaurant like a tornado, but that wasn't what stopped me midmotion as I barged in the door. Nor was it the restive crowd. Or the luscious smells. Or the harried waiters. Or the fact it was immediately apparent that the restaurant's much-lauded fast-food, fast-service promise had gone by the board.

No, it was something more intangible: the odd sense I had that Jed Costigan was immediately, wholly aware of *me* the moment I came in the door.

Odd because I'm not that kind of girl. And over and above that, I knew immediately that Paula sensed it, too.

Except, what did she know? Her guy had looked up when someone walked in the door? A perfectly natural response.

Paula sent me a glittering look as I approached the table. "And here's Lo," she said to Jed, who, with the best of manners, stood up and shook my hand.

"Good grip," he murmured.

"Oh, they all say that," I said, slipping my coat off onto the back of my chair. Now I was facing him and looking for something intelligent to say. "Wow, it's busy tonight."

A real conversation starter.

"I'd like to think it's in response to our review," Jed said serenely.

"It was a good review," I said as I was reviewing *him:* he was tall, well built, brown hair with reddish flecks in it, intent dark-blue eyes, a serious expression and an even more serious Armani suit. His impeccable manners hiding the soul, I thought, of a slick predator.

"Frankly," I went on, nearly stumbling over my own words, "all these people who live at warp speed think gourmet means tossing a handful of spicy Thai chicken in a container of by-the-pound salad greens. They could make this stuff at home a lot faster, better and cheaper."

Jed said, "Really?"

He was just being polite. Nevertheless, for some reason I pushed it. "Really."

"We've ordered already," Paula intervened. "You're having what I'm having."

"That's fine." I looked around the dining room because I didn't want to look at Paula or Jed because I knew Jed was covertly studying me.

"Okay," Jed said abruptly. "Here's the deal. You replicate what we eat tonight—the faster, better, cheaper part—and you write it up for me, and we'll see if we can make you into a food columnist."

THE SILENCE that followed his offer was deep as an ocean.

Man, that was a desperate shot, Jed thought ruefully. He couldn't tell at all how Lo would respond to an on-the-spot offer that he didn't know he was going to make. He just knew he wanted a reason to see Lo again and there was no better excuse than business. He'd been thinking about some kind of food column, anyway, so it wasn't quite an on-the-fly idea.

And, hell, why run the show if you can't do whatever you want.

He wanted *Lo*.

Instantly, ferociously, the minute she came in the door with her wind-tossed hair, her sparkling eyes, that long coat flaring out to reveal her form-fitting turtleneck, her legs that went on forever, encased in knee-high riding boots, and the endearing rosiness on the tip of her nose.

He'd thought, from everything Paula had told him, her roommate would be someone as slick and pulled together as Paula. A corporate vice president at least.

He hadn't expected someone like Lo.

One thing he knew immediately: it was going to complicate everything.

It didn't matter.

Lo blew in the door and everything changed.

He changed.

He knew it and he didn't intend to fight it. Not with Lo acting as if he'd given her a Christmas present. It just meant things were going to get messy.

So be it.

Lo liked a challenge, he saw, and she was just intrigued enough that she wouldn't turn it down. But she sure had to think about it— a lot. So he just folded his arms and waited patiently.

I WAS SO DUMBSTRUCK it took me a moment to respond. Finally, I slanted a long, disbelieving look at him. "You're kidding, right?"

"Dead serious," Jed said.

"That if I can replicate this dinner in my own faster, better, cheaper way, you'd take it as an audition to write a column."

"Yes."

"In the *WestEnder?*"

"Yes," Jed said.

I was speechless again.

Paula wasn't. "Start taking notes," she said. "Our waitress is coming now."

I could barely choke down dinner, I was so disconcerted, both by the offer and by him. I tried to take mental notes of what we'd eaten, but my brain was too scrambled to retain anything.

In the end I thought it was politic to invite Jed to witness the faster, better, cheaper cooking way.

Nerve-racking in and of itself, to say the least. Our kitchen was tiny, and he filled that space just with his unflappable male aura. He made me nervous because I knew he was watching me in his very intent way.

"So I'm envisioning that I'm leaving my office." I started my pitch. "I don't have a lot of time to shop. There's a convenience store where I grab a box of pasta, some chicken breasts, a precut package of stir-fry vegetables, and I'm gone. I have soy sauce and canola oil on hand. Rice, a can of chicken stock. And that's it."

I set the ingredients up on the counter, methodically heating the oil, cutting the breasts into cubes, putting them in the frying pan. I added some onion, the vegetables, the soy sauce. Made the rice with the stock, and fifteen minutes later, after the formal tasting, the consensus was my fast-food dinner was as good or better than the version we'd had two nights before.

"I like it," Jed said. "Grab and go. That's what we'll call it. You write it up and make it personal just the way you outlined it to me."

And that was how I morphed into the Grab-and-Go Gourmet.

Grab and go. I had aptly titled my work life as well as my love life. I continually repeated the same pattern, attracted to guys on the fly, yet hoping something would change.

Then, I had that revelation when I was doing a column about a grab-and-go diet a few months later: I'm a grab-and-go girl. I've been the free ingredient in every one of my relationships, and the guys have all been feasting on *me*.

Okay. You could blame me and my predilections for that. You actually could say I barely have a dating life at all. I have a bed-hopping life, which undeniably has its moments. It would be much more efficient if I ran my dating life more like a business.

But forget the idea of positioning, advertising, résumés, interviews, hoping your prospective guy likes you. Forget waiting for the phone to ring or hoping you're a good fit.

I had an epiphany: Why not just eliminate the guy factor altogether?

What do they have that your friends don't? Besides the obvious.

I couldn't think of a thing. I decided it was time for a healthy request—like, no more free sex.

When I suggested this to Paula, she said, "You are out of your freaking mind. What do you mean, no guys? Like, totally celibate?"

Now, I love Paula dearly, but she has a hard-shell finish that's as shiny as lacquer and as perfect, and since she broke up with Jed in early April, and observed a proper period—about a month—of mourning, there hasn't been a crack in that armor that I can see. And she's been anything but celibate.

So, did I really mean totally *stone-cold* celibate? Right on the cusp of summer fun? What was I thinking?

Still, I was staunch in my defense of my position. "I mean hard-core celibate."

"Well then, I'm not hanging out with you," Paula said pointedly. "No hard-core sex, no hard-core fun. What are you going to do with yourself all summer if you're not having sex?"

"I'll be having self," I said airily. And then I saw the look on her face. "For God's sake, not *that* kind of self. Like, getting-to-know-myself self. Like, being happy for a change, and not hanging on a hope, a prayer and a maybe he'll call. Like not being disappointed all the time. Like…"

I think at that point I decided she was right: I was crazy. Yet I couldn't back down since I'd made such a meal deal out of it.

"I'll find things to keep me busy. I'm not that shallow."

"Ha," Paula said. "You're as toe-deep in the Evian as the rest of us."

She was probably right. Still, work kept me busier than a hospital full of doctors. And there was the column, which took up a fair amount of time. It wasn't as if I couldn't find distractions.

Of course, summer wasn't exactly the best time to undertake a Guy Diet. But it's practically built in that, at my age, you don't want anyone to see you really skimpily clothed the first days of summer, let alone high, wide and naked.

And then, it's hot. So when you think about sweating and overheating, you're not thinking about sex at first sight or finding the man who will change your life. You focus on changing your own life.

Only, does it really make sense to take my cupcakes off the menu when every second guy is putting his beefcake on the counter?

I'll just ignore them. I'm determined. I'm going organic instead of orgasmic. I'm talking willpower. Hold the spice. Portion control.

Hmm. This is going to be harder than I thought.

Besides, I can't renege on The Guy Diet now because I've been so vocal about it. I just have to prove to Paula it can be done.

Maybe I could write a book about it.

Chapter One. Setting up The Guy Diet. Become a hermit.

Chapter Two. Negotiating The Guy Diet. Have all your groceries delivered and never go out of your house, watch TV or read a magazine, newspaper or the back of a cereal box.

No. That doesn't work. I have to work—everybody has to work. You can't avoid guys at work. You just have to develop a different mind-set.

This is my mantra: you can't continually be a target for any old guy's heat-seeking missile because the odds are you're going to crash and burn while he just brushes himself off and walks away.

There. My missionary position.

Damn, I mean my mission statement. I'm going to write it down, keep it over my computer.

Distill it: grab and go, crash and burn.

Story of my dating life.

And look at it this way: Jed's having given me the opportunity to write this food column was an incredible gift—even if it was only for a local paper.

I couldn't help it if I wanted some dessert. The problem is the best grab-and-go dessert is cake, and that always crumbles when you take a bite.

Kind of like relationships. All voluptuous, seductive and yummy to look at, and nothing substantial underneath.

That cake analogy did it for me.

I *need* someone substantial to sink my teeth into.

I mean—something. *Something* substantial.

On the other hand, sometimes cake melts in your mouth—

Check that. I am not allowed to think like that.

Crash and burn, remember. It never works out, no matter how high you fly.

Okay. It's the first of July. Perfect. I am now officially on The Guy Diet.

The first thing I did was order myself up a platter of healthy exercise regimen.

Since I walk a lot, I haven't needed a specific exercise program. Now to keep myself occupied and entertained, I decided that twice a week I would bike ride in Riverside Park plus do a weekend walk, as well.

I planned to live a simpler life: forget dressing up, forget makeup. Forget my usual haunts. No clubs. No bars. No drinking, no sex, no dates.

Yeah, on the surface, that sounds like a *really* fun summer.

On the other hand, there might be a method to this madness. If I wasn't at the usual places, I wouldn't meet and sleep with the usual grab-and-go guys. If I reverted to the jeans-and-T-shirt-clad, minimal-makeup me, I'd learn to appreciate myself all over again, and maybe then the right guy would appreciate me, too.

Whoa…*how* long is this going to take?

Say…one week?

I'm girding myself, can't you tell?

It'll probably be easier than I think.

So I went bike riding.

I like Riverside Park; it runs right along the Hudson River so you have that great view of the water while you're riding, walking, running.

Downside: pretty much everyone who's not in Central Park is riding, walking or running there every evening. If I wanted to avoid bare-chested guys and sexy six-packs, I should have gone bike riding in the subway.

The testosterone level was off the charts.

Not a good move to be moving your muscles while bemoaning lost opportunities. Exercise is good for the thighs, the soul and the mind. If I let myself think about sweaty bodies, I'll backside.

I mean back*slide*.

Paula was watching all this with a skeptical eye. She'd gone with me Saturday morning just out of curiosity. Paula never exercises except on the dance floor, so this was a great sacrifice on her part.

"The Guy Diet is never going to work. The guys are too tempting."

They sure had tempted *her*. Paula had met a week's worth of dates on that walk. Because she didn't walk, she stopped and talked to every guy who looked single and likely and took cards as if they were hundred-dollar bills.

I shrugged. "So? What would be the point if it's the same old strut?"

"You know what the *point* is."

I'd been on The Guy Diet for exactly three days. Paula was not making it any easier with her salacious jokes.

"And besides, what would happen if you met someone?" Paula went on. "What if there were this one perfect guy who wanted right then, right there to be the perfect person in your life?"

"You're joking, right?"

"What if?" Paula pressed me. Probably because it was Saturday night and, unusual for her, she had nowhere to go, no date, nothing to do but harangue me.

So I'd made dinner, one of my grab-and-go specialties—fast fajitas, with top blade steaks, fresh veggies and the usual accompaniments.

Love those little top blade steaks.

The point? That damned point. What if?

"It's inconceivable. And besides food is better than sex right now."

"You think? Nothing is better than—"

"The usual? No, anything is better than sex with a get-it-up-and-go guy."

"You protest too much."

"And you can't tell quality from quantity anymore. It's just one big-bang theory with you."

Ouch. I should not have been so blunt with Paula.

However, since I had transmogrified myself by virtue of The Guy Diet, I figured I had become pure in thought, deed and body.

"Saint Lo," Paula muttered sarcastically. "You're really going to drive us all crazy with this, aren't you?"

"No, I'm just giving up guys. Not your problem."

"Oh, you think you're not going to get cranky like the rest of us on a diet?"

"I will have lost a minimum of 170 pounds this first week by not having contact with a guy. I'll be all sweetness and light."

NOT.

"I'm praying for a devil to tempt you beyond all reason," Paula said.

"That, too," I murmured. "Finish the steak."

"Full speed ahead and damn the fajitas?" she retorted.

"I'll find a movie. *In or out?*"

Oops...sorry I said that.

"That was a movie," I said defensively.

Paula raised one brow. "*In and Out* was the title. In *and...*"

I can't get away from it. "Don't go there."

"I'm already there," Paula said lightly. "And for the record, I always prefer *in*."

I can't win.

Damn—there's even an *in* in win....

2

MY SCHEDULE: work, bike ride, work on column. So, on the weekend we'd eat really well because that was the time I allotted to experimenting with recipes. Or read it another way: busy work.

Oh, and entertain self…there was always a museum exhibit, a speaker at the Ninety-Second Street Y, a concert, theater, a gallery opening.

I deliberately excluded Paula, who the following week was busy pointedly going on dates. Can you stand the negativity?

Who needs friends? Who needs men?

You can be your own best company—except you wind up talking to yourself.

I talked to myself a lot. It turned out it was a great icebreaker because people always think I'm talking to them. Men think I'm coming on to them. Like the guy at the gallery opening down on Broadway last weekend.

"Did you say something?" The kindest way to initiate a conversation or a letdown.

And I just can't not answer. "Sorry. Just talking to myself."

"The show is that bad?"

"No, no, I'm enjoying it."

"Me, too. I came in from Jersey. I love this artist…"

Oh my God—Jersey? *New* Jersey? That's so over the bridge! Forget that. New York women do *not* bed bridge guys.

That was an easy out. I got away without a bruise to my ego and my Guy Diet intact.

"You can't keep doing this," Paula said for the hundredth time when I told her what had happened. Not much had happened. He'd caught me at a weak moment. If I'd been concentrating, I wouldn't have spoken to him at all.

Really.

And besides, he reeked of "over the bridge."

"Especially this time of year," Paula continued.

"I have plans," I said stringently. "I can talk to people. That's not disallowed on The Guy Diet."

"Did you even make a list of forbidden food?"

Honestly, I never thought about the forbidden part. Wasn't giving up guys *forbidding* enough?

Hey, wait a minute. Was Paula suggesting I have a sell-by date? "You are trying to undermine a very serious experiment in personal power here," I said finally. I didn't like the fact I was veering deep into distraction when I should have been fully focused on *me*.

Paula would say I'm always fully focused on "me."

"I'm trying to make you come to your senses," Paula said. "You're voluntarily giving up parties, night life, friends and sex. And not necessarily in that order."

"Yes," I said emphatically. "I am. And do you know why? I'm tired. Aren't you tired? Don't you want a relationship not to be tiring? And crazy making? Don't you want a relationship, period? Forget the jokes. I'm tired and I'm not having fun. That's why I'm doing this on my summer vacation—I'm giving up one-shot gratification. I'm giving up one-nighters, bad boys, no calls, desperation do-overs, disappointments, missed appointments, clubs and bars—in other words, I'm giving up the dating scene."

"Oh, well. That explains your crazy Guy Diet."

"Doesn't it?"

Paula sent me a skeptical look, that smug "yeah, sure" look and I burst out: "Okay, I'm going to flat-out say it. I want to find that love-you-forever, got-your-back guy."

What? The words sounded way strange. I hadn't meant to say that. Not out loud. I wanted to take the words back immediately because that was something no one was ever meant to know.

This *wasn't* about finding the forever guy. Or was it?

"He doesn't exist."

"Well, if you nitpick everything about every guy you meet and you're looking for guarantees and perfection, then, yeah, he doesn't exist."

Paula gave me a long, deep look. "I never thought you were a romantic. You're not bio-ticking are you?"

"No."

"Just tired."

"Yep. And trying to figure out why I'm continually following all the other lemmings and diving off the cliff."

"It's exciting. It's a rush. It gets the adrenaline going."

"Until you fall headfirst and hit the concrete."

"Recreational relationships aren't like that," Paula said. But then, she was pretty acrobatic, limber *and* adaptable.

"Aren't they?" I thought so. Recreational sex worked out the body but not much else. And the pleasure was always evanescent, never transcendent.

Fly-bys were just not that kind of guy. They were never boyfriends—they *boyfriended* us for the time it took to add one more conquest to their résumés.

Men always leave; I knew that. My life was all about that. And I secretly hoped otherwise.

"And besides, you know what happens when you go on a diet. Guys come out of the woodwork and your head's going to burst open."

"Then I'll put on blinders. If I don't see them, they're not there."

"So this is, like, a one-week fast?"

Oh, damn. I had been no-guy for almost a week. Another consideration I hadn't thought about. How long did one do The Guy Diet?

Long enough to get a glycemic advantage?

"The whole summer," I said recklessly. "I'm giving up guys for the summer." God, that sounded like a long time. Still, if I was going to do it, I couldn't just do it in a grab-and-go way.

"Ha," Paula said. "I'm setting up a diet pool. You won't last two more days, let alone two weeks."

"I've lasted nearly a week already," I said back. "You are so *on.*"

That was all bravado, of course. The overlay of friends betting on my willpower meant I really had to get serious. I had to define what the diet entailed: like how much contact, or how little, what I would allow myself to do and to say, what was acceptable, what I would forgo.

Not so easy when you've been talking *diet* in general terms.

Not enough to just say, I'm giving up guys.

I mean, there are gradations of sacrifice. Did *giving up* mean no contact altogether? Responding to a come-on comment? Or only people I knew? Guys at work? Making general conversation? Listening to a pitch? Eschewing—I love that word—men altogether?

And then, I *had* to talk to Jed. Already there was a Guy Diet *but*.

"You have to have rules," Paula said, like she had sonar and could read my brain waves.

"Yeah, yeah, I'm thinking about that. How much, how little. Jed's the exception. I *have* to have intercourse with him."

"Huh?"

Oh, the look on Paula's face.

"I mean, I *have* to talk to him."

"Oh? *Talking* is intercourse now?"

I felt myself prickling up. "It always was," I said loftily. "Forget about Jed. He's my free safety."

"That's football. You mean safety net," Paula amended sarcastically.

"Right, he's my free ingredient. Okay, forget Jed. I get to make the parameters because it's my idea. So let me think."

And then I couldn't think.

On The Guy Diet I can't:
Date

That was about all I could think of. Just not date.
No, wait.

Have sex

Good. A little deprivation never hurt anybody. That's why there are diets. Oh, oh—I have another one:

Flirt

Not necessarily in that order.

Let's see: Flirt, date, have sex. That's good. That's enough deprivation.

But now I had to contend with the real dilemma.

On The Guy Diet I can only talk to:
Paula
All of my girlfriends
Jed (weekly only)
Any guy I meet as long as he doesn't ask for my card
The guy in line at the corner store
The guy whose foot I invariably step on in the subway stairs

There you go. No flirting, no dates, no sex.

Paula read the list. "You're kidding. You can't get involved with all those guys."

"That's not involvement, that's…that's—good manners."

"No, that's temptation. It has to be no more guys, period, or what's the point? After all that talk…" Paula shook her head. "You have to eliminate Jed."

That was too much to ask, since she knew I talked with him regularly. Her vehemence seemed a little disingenuous, maybe a little wary.

I girded myself for a fight. "Jed's the freebie—he has to be exempt."

I hadn't forgotten the odd moment in the restaurant the night I'd met Jed. Or the hum of tension between us every time I spoke with him. I'd just disregarded it.

I knew what he was: a charming trust-fund baby with too much money, even more free time and a boatload of arrogance that had gotten crushed to a pulp when he'd screwed up working for the family brokerage firm five years ago.

To his credit, he immediately transformed himself into a budding entrepreneur to show "them" that he could earn money, he could run something and that he wasn't going to run from anything.

However, the truth was, if you believed the gossip columns, he was always in pursuit of something, and continually leveraging his growing reputation and his profitable little newspaper into the mainstream.

He hadn't dated Paula for more than a month before they broke up. Frankly, it didn't surprise me, because Paula was just like that herself, bored after a couple of weeks and endlessly seeking excitement in the novelty of the new—the great new account, the first-to-try fabulous restaurant, the exotic vacations.

Jed never said a word about her after the breakup. There was never a "How's Paula doing?" or "Send her my regards." I decided that since I was reaping the rewards of their touch-and-go relationship, discretion was the better side of the road, rather than my losing either a great opportunity or a friend.

So I waited while Paula thought about it. Obviously, she didn't like it, but any of her doubts seemed irrelevant to *my* diet. Especially because this was specifically about Jed.

I wondered if it was a test.

"Isn't there an editor or someone you could talk to instead of Jed? I mean, since when does a publisher edit a columnist? I think talking to Jed is cheating. Well, it's your diet. It's your rest of the summer."

Rest of the summer…ominous words. How many weeks was it till the rest of the summer? Could I rest and wake up when it was over?

I was getting really leery of the fact that Paula was suddenly into the idea. I mean, a betting pool on whether I could make it through the day without talking to a guy? Vetting my list of guys not to talk to? Please.

"You'll see," I said, still in mother-superior mode, "I'll be a better person afterward. I need time to prepare."

"You don't prepare to go on a diet," Paula objected. "And you have to promise to adhere to it when no one's watching."

"I keep reminding you, it was my idea. I need some reining in. Some power procrastination instead of going for the quickie meal deal."

Paula snorted. "A gut check maybe. I never did like that Ron guy."

"Exactly." That "Ron guy" was my last relationship. The one that made me realize that being a free ingredient wasn't the first step to got-your-back. Or love-you-forever.

Paula was right—I truly am a romantic, and I think on some level, I was hoping that this branching off the food chain would lead to something more substantial than regrets eating me alive.

3

NOT TALKING TO GUYS was more difficult than I would have ever believed. They're everywhere. You're walking down the street—bump, brush, "Excuse me," and you're talking to a guy.

You go to the corner newsstand to buy a *New York Times*. A guy is right next to you, you both reach for the paper simultaneously. You're talking to a guy.

Do random guys count? Add them to the list. No, don't. How would Paula know who I talked to on any given day? Why does Paula have to know everything?

Answer: she doesn't, particularly since she ridiculed the whole idea in the first place. So why did she suddenly get behind it, anyway?

"Watch the light…" Nice guy, pulling me back from oncoming traffic on a change of light. Talking to a guy.

I could deal with that. I'd never see any of those guys again…except—what if I walked this exact same route tomorrow? I bet I'd see one of them and he'd smile at me. Then what? I'd *have* to acknowledge we've bumped elbows, wouldn't I? It would be horribly rude to ignore an overture of polite friendliness, wouldn't it?

I need to rewrite that list.

And then, Jed called.

Paula was out. There was something about the lure of the bed-head bar and the overripe sex that she couldn't resist. It was almost as if she felt she'd miss something if she didn't do the scene—like the one most-wanted guy, the best hookup ever, the heir to some fortune choosing *her* to bed down for a night. Maybe forever.

She was a gorgeous groupie, eternally on the hunt, and hoping that this night, she'd be *the* one to touch some equally gorgeous guy's heart.

They have no hearts though. And a free ingredient is, after all, free. Still another reaffirmation why I'm on The Guy Diet.

I just didn't expect a guy to call that night.

And yet, there he was, as unflappable as ever. "Hey, Lo—what's doing?"

"I can't talk to you," I said sharply.

"Why is that?" he asked calmly.

"I'm on The Guy Diet. While you are a designated free ingredient, nothing is really free, so it would be better if we don't talk right now."

"Whoa. Wait. Don't tell me. Paula."

You see? My instincts were absolutely on target. "No. Just my own good sense. I'm off grab-and-go dating."

He digested that for a long, silent moment. I thought he'd congratulate me on my fortitude, but all he said was, "Right. A Guy Diet. So that means…?"

"It means I'm not supposed to talk to you. You being a guy and all."

"And yet you are." He sounded vaguely puzzled.

"You're my free ingredient, except if you say something you shouldn't." Oh God, why was I flapping on like that?

"Like what?" he asked curiously.

"I couldn't begin to imagine," I retorted. "And yes, I'm on track to deliver on Monday. Anything else?"

"Where's Paula? No, don't tell me. Loyal friend that she is, she's behind this diet thing five hundred percent while she secretly revels in having nullified the competition."

"I didn't hear that." Because I didn't like what it implied.

"Well, you see? The loyal friend doesn't think in those terms."

"I don't even know what you're talking about. I think in grab-and-go terms."

"Precisely my point," Jed said. "And now you're not around to grab and go with her. She'll do something about that soon, too. Remember I told you."

"You're evil and I won't speak to you for at least a week for saying that."

"You haven't spoken to me this week as it is."

"I know that."

Oh, oh, there it was: the hum, the awareness. I felt it right through the cell. Or I was imagining it. Probably imagining it because Paula's putting her finger in my Guy-Diet pie had unsettled me. And now Jed's suggestion—not pretty.

Still, I hardly knew him, certainly not enough to trust him, especially after he'd proved to be a grab-and-gone guy with my very best friend.

"Okay," he said. "I'm serving notice. The Guy Diet does not apply to me and you need to talk to me."

You see? That's Jed. Nothing fazes him.

"*Need,* Jed?"

"Need," he said firmly, and disconnected emphatically.

I didn't have time to even dissect that. Or maybe I didn't want to know.

Honestly. *Need?*

I was working for the next few days, as I do sometimes, at the medical arm of an ad agency specializing in pharmaceuticals, transcribing test results and inputting them into a delivery system.

Isn't that what dating is all about? Sorting through the chaff, finding the guy that delivers?

Check that. I couldn't think about anything but the job at hand since it required full concentration, and in-depth handwriting-and-vocal-translation skills. Though somewhere in the mix, I began plotting the next week's quick-prep gourmet meal. In fact, I was a little worried that food was fast becoming my real focus.

Tonight, for example, I had some leftover chicken in the fridge. I could toss some cooked pasta with that, then add chick peas, onions, peppers—which I cut up and keep frozen—olives, artichoke hearts, oil and vinegar and I had what I called fiesta bowl chicken salad, ready in the fifteen minutes you could be stuck standing in the checkout line with your ready-made salad.

Right there is what the Grab-and-Go Gourmet is all about.

Then, there was the grab-and-go girlfriend. Paula was waiting for me when I got home that night.

I'd had a fine few days—if you didn't count that irritating phone conversation with Jed. I'd had lots of time to play with recipes, to take cold showers, watch hot TV and have nice, fast home-cooked dinners every night. Who needed a guy?

Obviously Paula did, and she needed to grab on to me for some reason, too, going from "You're no fun" to "Can't trust you not to cut and run" in one testy week.

Or maybe she was testing me.

"What's this?" I really felt befuddled now. "I've got some nice fiesta bowl chicken salad waiting for me. You're taking this way more seriously than I ever meant it to be," I said sternly. "I'm doing fine. I haven't thought about guys for more than thirty seconds during the day—" so I lied "—and that's only because I have to talk to them sometimes."

"Sure, sure, sure. I bet you backslid."

"Not even tempted." Big lie. And when did I tell her I spoke to Jed?

I didn't. And I didn't want to examine why.

"Yeah, yeah," she said, which was too noncommittal and made me even more suspicious as we set out.

"Okay, cut the garbage. Why are you really here?"

"I'm a secret romantic?"

I made a sound. Paula was about as romantic as a down bathrobe. And hardly as soft.

I wanted to think my rationale for the Guy Diet was getting to her and that somewhere under the skin, she wanted me to be wrong, she wanted it to fail, she wanted her way to be the highway.

Or—she didn't want me talking to Jed, it hit me suddenly.

That was my niggling suspicion. I mean, didn't we make that long list of *can't talk tos* and now, a week into it, Paula was giving me absolution to do just that?

Stop it! I was making molehills into tunnels. Jed was a guy on cruise control, chock-full of charm, charisma and ambition helped along by a little bred-in-the-bone business acumen. He had everything; he didn't need anything—or anyone—even Paula, and least of all me.

"What's the deal?" I said eventually, refusing to budge despite her insistence.

"We'll just go get a drink and I'll tell you."

"Oh, no. I need to know right now or I'm going home."

"Okay," she muttered. "I thought you should try testosterone aversion therapy."

"What? I'm doing great. As long as I keep a distance."

"That's the point. I'm bored. *I'm* keeping a distance. And I want my friend back. And the fun we used to have. So I thought if we eased you into a situation where you could practice no-go therapy, we could still have an after-hours life."

"That's *nuts*." Paula had no other girlfriends? I knew that wasn't true. And then I thought, this was exactly what Jed warned me would happen. So then I had no choice but to go out for that drink, just to prove that he was wrong. And not to mention to show Paula I was not going to succumb to the random, roaming guy, even though I knew that Paula would.

Maybe *she* needed *di*version therapy because the only thing that was certain about bed-head bar hookups was that you'd be alone the next morning and on the hunt again by night.

Some people loved playing the game. Paula was one of them.

"Well," I said finally, "*I* want The Guy Diet to be a success. I'm up for your throw-down. I am going to win. So where do you suggest we go?"

Paula knew all the best places—she'd hooked up in every one of them. The pool of men she hadn't tried out must be diminished to drought proportions by now.

Since I was perfectly content in my *no guys* guise, I was curious to see what Paula was up to.

This could be a test of biblical proportions. Wait—shouldn't that come way later, like after I'd suffered intensively and had been tempted beyond reason?

"Well, here we are. I found this place recently. You'll like it." The restaurant, on a West Seventies side street, was low lit, with wafting classical music and banquettes, but at the entrance was a long, heavily populated bar.

"Do I have to talk?"

"We'll suspend the *no talk* rules tonight. Make them *no walk* rules."

"I can do that for a glass of wine and some peace."

Paula started working the crowd immediately. She knew exactly how to make a casual meet look easy: she knew the precise right thing to say and it never sounded cheesy or like it came out of a greatest pick-up lines book.

Before I knew it, we were surrounded by guys. Bob. Ted. Taylor. Ron. Exchanging cards, gauging the "are you good-looking enough?" factor, the cost of everyone's designer clothes and earnings-potential scale.

I couldn't possibly survive that kind of scrutiny. I grabbed my drink and sat down alone by the window that fronted the street, glad to be out of the fray. Let Paula reign in the chaos. A sip of wine was enough for me.

Then this totally caloric guy bent over and asked, "Are you saving the seat?"

Oh, the chocolatey goodness of that voice. And a body that I'm certain was wearing a sign that said, Bite Me.

"Please, join me." I kept my voice nice and steady and this side of disinterested. Every nerve ending picked up and shouted hallelujah. My body spurted to life. My head clamped down on my hormones ruthlessly but it was too late.

"I'm Sean."

"I'm Lo."

"Short for?"

"Just Lo."

"Nice."

Shorthanding the conversation to get the essentials up front quick and clear. But he wasn't in any hurry to talk, and I was fine with the wine and the line, and so…we sipped at each other, drawing out the information in short staccato sentences.

"Work around here?"

"No, midtown. You?"

"Live around here?"

"Farther west."

"Me, too. Good restaurant."

I didn't know. "So I've heard."

This was going nowhere. Aversion therapy worked. Taste, but don't swallow, like wine you spat out after you rolled it around on your tongue to assess the complexities of the pour.

This guy wasn't wearing a suit, just a shirt and a nicely tailored pair of trousers, high-end sneakers.

"My place is pretty close."

Bam. Huge crushing disappointment, like a stone attached to my heart. Why had I thought he'd be different?

"Can't," I murmured.

"For real?"

"I'm on The Guy Diet."

"Forgive me—a...guy diet?"

"Off guys till the end of summer."

"So what are you doing here?"

I batted my lashes. "Aversion therapy."

He bolted up from the chair. "It worked."

"Well, you could've spent five minutes getting to know me."

He glared at me. Not so yummy anymore. "Why?"

There, in one word, yet another reason for a Guy Diet.

He stalked away and Paula took his place so fast it was like she'd beamed down there. "What just happened there?"

"Aversion therapy—him for me, once I told him I was dieting. After two minutes of monosyllabic conversation, he invited me to *his* place."

Paula was silent. She would have gone like a shot.

"It works!" I said, ginning up my enthusiasm. "All I have to do is mention The Diet. It's the best letdown ever. Nobody's feelings get hurt and you have a couple minutes' conversation to spice up the evening. I don't know why I never thought of it before. It would have saved so much grief."

"Huh," Paula said finally. "You could have introduced him to me."

"Oh, please, don't tell me you would have..."

"He looked pretty good from where I was sitting. And I know how to get more than a couple minutes' conversation out of anyone."

"Well, he's mixing and mingling as we speak," I pointed out, "so I can leave you and you'll be in bed with him within the hour."

"I am *not* that easy."

"Okay, two hours." I could almost feel her body humming with sexual tension. She wanted the *get*. It was all about the *get*.

"If you go home, I'm coming with you."

"You're not required to deny yourself."

"What are best friends for?"

I'm telling you, this was weird. I felt as if we were at cross purposes. She obviously wanted to hook up. I just wanted to unravel.

"I'll grab a cab so Momma doesn't have to worry."

She started to protest again, then looked over her shoulder to where Sean was standing, quite close to us, actually. Her eyes narrowed. Paula scented prey, someone who was commensurate in job, status, good looks, and—truth be told—stamina for the game.

I felt a glimmer of triumph. The Guy Diet was working.

JED WAS CURSING the damned Guy Diet as he paced in front of Lo's apartment building. He thought he'd timed it just right, breaking it off with Paula early April, giving her a couple of months to get over their relationship and to distance Lo from any suggestion that she was stealing something that was Paula's...

Only it wasn't working.

Because Lo was feeling leery and guilty, and Paula was in full predator mode, encouraging both the saint and the sinner in Lo.

And trading on her loyalty.

He couldn't let that go on any longer.

He was a patient guy—he'd learned to be during the debacle at the brokerage that had catapulted him into the real world of making a real living—and there wasn't much that could unsettle him now.

Yet this whole Guy-Diet thing, coming virtually the moment that he'd decided the time was right for him and Lo, seemed almost karmic in its potential to create trouble.

Or comedic. It was pretty funny that here he was pacing the sidewalk when he should have had a key to the apartment months ago. Hell. He should have had Lo months ago. He should have...

All in good time.

After all, what did she know about him? Paula's version, and what she thought she saw all on her own.

Lo was as wary as a deer in the headlights all the time. So clearly she felt something between them that she couldn't deny. That was encouraging. There *was* something between them, and she was just not giving in to it. Not yet.

But soon.

He just had to tempt her beyond her capacity to resist.

And, hallelujah, a cab had just turned the corner and was slowly inching its way down the street. Good. She was home.

Even if she didn't yet know it.

JED WAS UTTERLY ignoring The Guy Diet. There he was, sitting on my front steps, and I was just not prepared to deal with him.

"What are you doing here?" I asked, sounding cranky.

"Sit."

"I don't think so." It didn't matter. He took my hand and pulled me down onto the steps beside him.

"What do you think about ice cream?"

"Not much open at ten o'clock."

"I think we should go get some."

"Why?"

"Because it's hot."

He drew me to my feet and we turned toward Broadway. He was wearing a blue cotton dress shirt rolled up at the sleeves and jeans.

Sexier than I wanted to ever admit. Formidable, and I couldn't define why. There was just something about him. Ice cream, for heaven's sake.

"Where are we going?"

"Not too far. Maybe you'd like to talk."

"About what?"

"Anything."

I bit my tongue. "I don't know you that well."

"No," he said, and he was dead serious, "you don't."

I looked at the lights of Broadway rather than him. At least these lights couldn't blind you, like feelings and emotions, and wants, needs and sexual tension.

Who was Jed? A guy who liked ice cream at ten at night. A guy who'd dated my roommate for a month and inexplicably ended the relationship. A guy who was periodically in the gossip columns, who'd made mistakes, who had made himself into a success.

A guy who made me tense and crazy, that was what I knew about Jed.

And then we were there at the nuts and ice cream emporium near West Seventy-Eighth Street, and Jed said, "See, I'm not the only one who likes ice cream late at night. They're open till eleven. What will you have?"

I guess sometimes our choices define us, although this was not a Ben & Jerry's menu. I opted for plain vanilla, Jed chose chocolate.

"No questions?" Jed asked after we'd walked for a while. I

don't think he ate a quarter of the ice cream in his cup. He was covertly watching me not eating mine.

"One. Why are we doing this?"

"Why not?"

Well, let me count the reasons. Because…because…

"Because I'm on a Guy Diet."

"Then I won't mention the freebie part."

"Why are *you* doing this?"

"You know why," Jed said. "Just take it a spoonful at a time. It'll all go down that much easier. In fact—" He stopped and took the spoon from my fingers and scooped up some ice cream and fed it to me, watching with that unnerving intensity as my lips closed over the spoon.

"See? Smooth and creamy."

Right. Like him. Like I was feeling right then. Like I didn't want to feel about him right now. I could almost here the hum of tension.

Then he came in closer and just swiped my lips with his tongue—his hot, sweet, firm, delicious tongue—and my knees nearly buckled.

"Hey!"

"What?"

"That's—"

"Not a kiss," Jed finished for me, neatly cutting off my indignation. He nudged another spoonful into my mouth. "No kissing going on here."

"You call that no kissing?"

"I call that one spoonful at a time, Lo." Another helping, and again he licked the residue off of my lips, this time with a light, hot pressure that was almost too irresistible.

I didn't seem to be protesting. My body went liquid; darts of pleasure assaulted me. Time felt suspended. His tongue touched my lips again and I opened my mouth slightly, met him halfway and touched his tongue with mine.

Oh, no.

"Maybe," he murmured, "I should just kiss you."

"I thought there was no kissing going on," I managed to say.

"That was as close to kissing as you can get. Besides, it's time."

"Time we kissed, you're saying."

"It's long past time actually."

The tension escalated. I wanted that kiss. And I didn't—because I suddenly realized if he kissed me, I'd be haunted forever. He just wasn't a go-to guy, and I was no longer a get-go girl. And if I liked it too much, if I wanted him too much, I'd be lost forever.

And I was that close to wanting him. The taste of him, the feel of his tongue was already imprinted on my lips and inside my body and I wanted more. That feeling, that taste, the way I felt, I wanted more.

He tilted my head up. "Tell me you want me to kiss you."

The silence thickened unbearably. The heat had nothing to do with the temperature. His pull was nearly irresistible. The look in his eyes nearly convinced me.

I *wanted* him to kiss me. And I couldn't say it. I couldn't.

"I wish to hell you weren't on that damned diet," he said abruptly. "You don't have to be on a Guy Diet."

The moment broke open. I took my spoon from him. "You know what—it's not a joke—as much as I joke about it. I'm doing it for me."

That was both the truth and a lie. Because the covert not-to-be-admitted reason was to get some distance between me and all my past dating. I was protecting myself, trying to do it differently, and I just couldn't succumb.

"Okay, so I'm not going to kiss you tonight. You're going to regret it."

I did already. I found my voice. "This was a trial by devil."

"I'm definitely going to tempt you. And it will happen. Not tonight, but it will. I promise."

We were at the apartment building. He took my key, opened the door, let me in and then, in the ineffable way of devils, he disappeared into the night.

4

I LOVE MEN. I just know you think, from reading my scathing indictment of rut-and-run guys, and the fact I'm wary about Jed, that I really hate men.

But I don't. I could make a list as long as your arm of all the things I love about men. Start at the belly. No, wait a minute—not getting raunchy here. Yet.

The eyes. Hmmm. Yeah, the eyes, though guys always say they love a woman's eyes when they want to avoid sexualizing.

Everything is sexual.

What I haven't experienced is that one man who makes me think everything is possible, nothing is probable, and with whom I never run out of things to say because everything's important.

I know there are relationships like that. That's what I want. That's why I'm tired. That's one of the reasons why I didn't kiss Jed. *And*...because if this tension between us veered into physicality, it would be such a betrayal of Paula by both of us. That's why I've been considerate of her feelings, that's why I'm dieting.

The upside is, I've been feeling fresh, invigorated, and *not* sapped of all my energy trying to please a guy who isn't going to call me in the morning, anyway.

Guys with no substance. They're like commercial cake mix, they're dough boys; they melt in your mouth, they taste good and they're gone.

Maybe what I want is a fruitcake kind of guy. Rich, chewy, fruit laden, moist, tender...um, forget that analogy.

Where was I? Men. I love men, especially fruitcake men.

Even so, I didn't even want the distraction of men. Or Jed who is a whole separate category. He's distracting just because he exists and I almost kissed him. I have a feeling I'll be spending too many hours gnawing on the nuances.

However, life without sex isn't horrible. Or difficult once you've really wrapped your mind around the fact that for a limited time only there would be no warm body to heat up your hormones.

It's doable…

…except if you lived with Paula who lived for sex and hated the fact I was really sticking to The Diet.

Only, I didn't tell her about my ice-cream social with Jed. Or the almost kiss. Does that count as not sticking to…oh, never mind—and don't ask why I didn't.

"You know what? I think you're doing the bunny rub at that office you go to every week," Paula said accusingly.

"You know what? Remember when I talked about being tired? Well, now *you're* wearing me out. This is *my* diet. You're acting like you're the one being deprived."

"I am. I mean, it's diet, diet, diet. All you ever say is…I can't—The Diet."

"It's barely week three, there's maybe another two weeks to go. This is not onerous."

"I'm not liking you a lot right now."

"I know."

I was working on this week's gourmet recipe during this particular exchange. We glared at each other. I diluted some pesto sauce with some chicken broth and mixed it in with my spinach fettuccine and drizzled some cheese over it.

"Taste this. It's better than sex." It was delicious! I made a note to add another must-have to the grab-and-go pantry, pesto in a jar.

Back to the computer to add that to the sidebar. Then serve with what? Nice thick chewy bread to sop up sauce…kind of like—

Stop it.

Maybe a quick homemade-bread recipe for the next column? The fragrant and luscious fresh-out-of-the-oven kind you slathered with butter and just gobbled up like—

I knew I was making noises because Paula looked at me sharply.

"I love food," I said defensively. "I was just thinking about a French loaf you could prepare in an hour, say."

"Enough with food!"

Right, too much diet all the time.

And so of course, my cell rang.

"Hey, it's Lo."

"It's me." Naturally it was Jed, always there, hanging over Paula and me like a sonic wave. And with the tongue swipe, it was a deal. I was hyperaware of him now. Something had changed from the way it had been before I inaugurated The Guy Diet. I just hadn't told Paula about the other night.

"Hi. Just finishing the column. What's up?"

I wanted to be as brief as possible.

"I'm hoping to hear you gave up The Diet."

"Why should I? I'm feeling good. Everything's fine. Anything else?"

"Paula's there," he guessed.

"Nice of you to realize that," I murmured, as if that would fool Paula.

"Umm. Yep. Competition."

Loyalty kicked in. "I think this editorial conference is over."

"Unless we have phone sex."

No. He couldn't do that to me after pointedly not kissing me. And besides, I didn't know him well enough for stuff like that.

Although that had never stopped me from having random bed-head encounters. And a long, hot summer night's walk with *him* that nearly ended my resolve. Still…

"Talk to you next—" I said.

"Let's have lunch," he interrupted my sign-off.

"Why? Shoot me an e-mail. You can say whatever you have to say just as well in one. Probably a lot more."

"No. We'll schedule lunch," Jed said. "It's a long-term thing."

I had a quick-flash vision of *his* long-term thing and immediately I felt a funny little curlicue slither down between my legs and I shuddered.

And wouldn't you know it, Paula noticed instantly.

"Next week," I said firmly, eyeing her warily.

"Okay. You promised."

"So what did he say that horrified you so much?" Paula asked silkily when I hung up.

Time to lie. Big-tent lie to cover every lie I was going to tell her from this day forward about my dealings with Jed.

"I ran the idea of a grab-and-go cookbook by him. He says no book. Not yet." I tried to act indignant over an idea I just made up. "Damn it." It didn't quite come off because the forbidden thought of Jed's "long-term thing" kept getting in the way.

"A book? When did you even mention the idea of a book to anyone, let alone Jed?"

Oh, boy. So she kept track of our conversations, too? I should have stopped it right then. Instead I started embroidering the lie.

"Last week," I told her. "Just quickly ran it by him and he said he'd think about it."

"You didn't run it by me," Paula said, looking a little offended. "I didn't know you were even ready to think about a proposal."

"I only kind of mentioned it." Now I was grasping and desperate to end this conversation and cover up my lie. "He didn't think there was enough product."

"Product…?"

"Recipes." I tried the short answer, tried braking and ending the conversation, but the look on her face made me keep going like an SUV on cruise control. "You know—they're short and quick, and there just aren't enough of them to make a book yet."

No surprise, Paula didn't buy it. She knew too much about creative stuff and books in particular because about every third person in her agency was trying to write one.

"You definitely have enough for a proposal," she said in a patronizing, I-know-what-you're-trying-to-do and I'm-calling-you-on-it tone of voice. "You could sell on proposal, likely, pretty easily."

I couldn't even say I'd rather finish the damned thing because a) it didn't exist except in my imagination and b) who wouldn't want an advance in advance of having to finish a book?

"I guess I probably could," I said finally. "It was just a thought."

"That you e-mailed him?"

"I mentioned it during last week's editorial conference." Editorial conference sounded much more businesslike than our usual spiky conversation but that didn't help distance me from my lie.

"Oh, that's great. You call *that* an editorial conference? Did you do the column? Yes. Oh by the way, I want to write a book? Why didn't you ask *me* about the prospect of a book?"

Paula was homing in for the kill, so I thought for self-protection, I needed to go on the attack. "Why does it matter so much to you?" Oh, that was good. Now we sounded like three-year-olds on a playground. "And don't tell me how much you care about me, and you're worried about me, and The Guy Diet sucks."

"The whole idea of The Guy Diet sucks," she said succinctly.

"Thank you for your input. I don't care. It's working for me. Excuse me while I write my book."

I was so annoyed, I could have spit avocado pits, but of course, there were none in the apartment, and worse than that, I couldn't stalk off in high dudgeon because there was no door to slam except the one out to the hallway.

The Guy Diet was wreaking havoc with Paula's hormones, not mine.

And you know what? I didn't care.

Of course I cared, but each of us had set up straw men that we cavalierly burned to the ground and there wasn't much left except ashes in my mouth.

I hated it that Jed was right.

I should have just told her I wasn't interested in Jed. Only I didn't know that I wasn't.

The next day was Tuesday. I had a pile of tapes to transcribe about as thick as *War & Peace*. And I had to summon up some ingenuity for tonight's grab-and-go dinner.

I considered the contents of my pantry—one shelf of one cabinet in the teeny windowed kitchen of our apartment. I needed a bigger kitchen, I needed a bigger everything, more scope for my ideas and more room in which to expand.

I *should* write a book.

I had some canned salmon, the boneless skinless kind, pasta, broth, a half bag of spinach—enough. I could add mushrooms, zucchini, tomatoes, capers to the initial recipe when I wrote it up.

Meantime—

My cell rang. Yes, you guessed it. "Hi, Jed. What's up?"

"Hi. Terrific column this week. So, are you still dieting?"

"Which diet?"

"The guy one."

"Still dieting."

"Isn't that getting really h—difficult?"

"No," I said airily, thankful he didn't say *hard* which probably

would have led to some messy double entendres. I said it instead,
"No, it's not hard."

"Paula there?"

"Not yet. So what's up?"

"Me. And that lunch."

Uh-oh. A war between my cold clutch of fear and my irritation.
What was he going to dine on? Me? He took the opening.

"Just set up a time," he said.

"There's no time. I work, remember."

"How about Saturday?"

"Jed…" I said warningly.

"A business lunch."

"No business lunches on The Guy Diet. No guys, remember."

"I'm not a *guy*. I'm…I'm…"

"A guy. You know, it's tough enough avoiding guys at the
agency office, on the street, on the bus every day. Just don't put
any more guy temptations in my path, please, even if they're
wrapped in the guise of a business lunch. You have done more
than enough."

He whistled. "Wow. I'm a temptation. That's nice to know.
I never met anyone who'd turn down an expensive lunch on
principle."

"Well, then—I'm your girl."

"I like that thought, too."

He was scaring me. "Jed…I'm going to go now."

"Why?"

"Because it sounds like what I don't want it to sound like."

"It could sound even better if we had lunch."

"Don't do that."

"Do what?"

"Make it sound like there's some undue interest on your part."

"Does it have to be undue? How about real interest?"

"It's not interest. You just want to yank my chain."

"How about if I just want to have lunch with you?"

"Not possible, at least till the end of the diet."

"How about—"

I had to stop; I was enjoying this conversation, too. Nothing like
a little sexy repartee to grab your hormones and ready, set, go.

"Okay, I had a thought."

I couldn't picture Jed thinking for more than one thirty-second sound bite at a time. "I already heard your thought. No phone sex."

"That's another thought. I'd be happy to explore that over lunch, too."

Dear heaven, stop it! "Dieting, remember?"

"Impossible to forget. Listen, you should do a cookbook."

My heart stopped. "I can't do a book."

"That's crazy. Why not?"

How did I explain the big-tent lie? "Because I already told Paula you thought I didn't have enough recipes to make a book."

Long silence as he digested this. I pictured him going through the maze of trying to make any sense of the fact I'd said no before he'd even given me the opportunity to say yes.

"Got it!" he said finally. "Paula was giving you the third degree and you popped the first big lie you could think of. What is it with you two? We were over four months ago."

"Yes, well. I went on the diet. And you're a grab-and-go kind of guy. The two things aren't compatible."

Another short digestive silence, and then: "Me? Grab and go? That's another thing we have to talk about. Meanwhile, a book."

"I've thought about it."

"Good. Think about the phone sex, too. Could be fun on The Guy Diet, you know, no harm, no foul, no kisses, no calories."

"Let me brief you." Oh damn, wrong term. "I have only three real self-imposed diet restrictions, and they are—no flirting, no dating, no sex. Of *any* kind."

"Yes, but phone sex isn't fattening."

"It clogs the arteries to your brain and you say stupid things because you're not thinking straight and then the sex is gone and…"

"On the phone?" he interrupted me.

"I bet you could think of three things to do with a phone that have nothing to do with—" Oh my big mouth. I'm doing phone sex. "I'm hanging up."

"Don't leave me hanging."

"You're already very well hu—" I broke off the salacious sentence and disconnected. Cell phones are insidious; they're always with you and you can't get away from anyone or anything. And it's too easy to get into phone sex even when you don't think you're getting into phone sex.

With people you shouldn't be getting into any kind of sex with.

How did this happen? And with a grab-and-go guy.

Jed scared me all to hell, enough to want to extend The Guy Diet till winter.

No, check that. It's not easy to diet in the summer. However, now that I was biking every couple of evenings and walking on the weekends, I was seeing some interesting results: I was feeling pretty fit and trim.

Let me tell you, there's nothing like the feeling of your body toning and thinning. Just cut out the fast food, the fat, the frat— give it three weeks, four—and you're strutting out the door.

Downside: the attention, which flattered, distracted and deterred you from finding that got-your-back relationship if you succumbed to it for one minute.

I should print up a T-shirt saying, I Am Not Your Hard Target.

Oh, you thought I forgot about that? I never forget anything.

Neither did Paula.

"So how's it going with the book?"

It was just toward the end of the next week and I was feeling pretty good about the idea of a book and the fact that Jed had suggested it, too.

"I'm actually collecting the recipes so I can see exactly what I do have." There, that sounded coherent, grown-up, respectful of the fact that Paula had encouraged me when Jed had allegedly not.

I should have known better than to be that optimistic. Paula hated the fact that The Guy Diet was working. And that I was not miserable and she was.

Do you suppose she'd write the preface to my book?

My dear friend Lo created the Grab-and-Go Diet as
a blind for the fact that she wanted to grab and go through
life with the man I love. I hate her.

That would sell books. If it were Paula's guide to guys and sex.

"What *do* you have?" she asked curiously.

Oh, this was too much, as if Paula were now guiding the project to completion. *Why* couldn't she leave it alone since she'd already caught me in the lie and likely knew it.

"A dozen recipes I've already prepared, tested, tasted and written up for the column. Plus another fifty ideas for more. This isn't going to be an instant book."

"Too bad. Grab and go definitely sounds instantaneous."

"Well, it's going to be grab and test and jigger ingredients and test again, and then retest again, so we're talking minimum till the end of the year to get together enough recipes to make a book."

"I'll be right here to help you. I mean, what else do you have to do while you're on this insane diet?"

"You're not on it. You have a life to lead, places to go, guys to get laid by."

She ignored that. "I'm willing to sacrifice to see the project through."

I know I made a derisive sound. I know I shouldn't have. Or said, "What, one night?"

Spiralling into oblivion here. That was not a nice thing to say. Even if true. Paula didn't want to see about the project; she just wanted to oversee the incoming caller IDs on my cell.

I knew Paula. And I was on a slippery slope that was freezing under me even as I wondered frantically how I could stop my freefall.

She gave me a Mona Lisa smile. "How about we do takeout tonight while you re-jigger ingredients? My treat."

Her trick, rather. Stuck on ice, having to make artificial conversation for the rest of the night. And if Jed called, please God, don't let him.

I might freeze to death.

I exited my program as she clicked on her phone.

I DIDN'T EXPECT company.

Takeout came with take-me-to-bed. Paula had arranged for two of her recent bed buddies to bring the food and we'd all have a jolly time together playing date swap, while one or the other tried to get the willing one of us—Paula—in bed.

Too tacky.

"You can have your fly-by sex," I offered, which I thought was way generous given the ruse to undermine my resolve. "I'll take Skipper for a walk while you samba."

"Oh, come on, you're no fun."

"You keep saying that. I think I'm lots of fun. I'm just not flirting, dating or doing takeout sex."

"Let's eat, anyway."

It was a regular banquet. Had Paula really thought she'd get me fed and drowsy by nine, on my back with a missile aimed at my hard target and orgasm coming low by nine-o-five?

I didn't think so.

"You're no fun," Skipper said, repeating what Paula had said earlier to me. What? Were they in cahoots or something? You bet.

He was tall, pretty good-looking in a vapid-model way. He might have been twenty-five, he certainly wasn't a got-your-back type. He was more full-frontal assault.

"I am truly. I'm just on a Guy Diet."

I'd gotten him out and we were walking aimlessly.

"What the hell is that?"

"I decided I wasn't going to be a free ingredient anymore. Like tonight. So I decided no more guys for a while."

"I'm a guy."

"Yeah, I know." Well, I could've drummed up some more enthusiasm but I wasn't feeling the love, actually. And he was more like a brother or an eager puppy. And I was ticked at Paula.

"You mean I'm not a guy?"

"I mean, I'm serious, you're not. Paula doesn't think she is, but she would be in a nanosecond if the right guy wanted her back."

Skipper grunted, "Huh?"

"Exactly."

After a cup of coffee and explanations, we shook hands. Skipper exited stage left to subway. Heroine walked home alone. Bad-boy Bob, just leaving, gave heroine a jaunty wave, saying, "You should have stayed. That was some mind-blowing sex."

"So how come you're blowing out the door ten minutes after it's over?"

Paula was fuming that I'd spoiled her doublet, and off-the-wall furious because—of course—Jed had called.

That big tent had better be made of superstretch fabric because when you start to lie, it just doesn't stop...until you tell the truth.

Paula just wouldn't let it go.

I buried my head in my pillows, refusing to even talk about the guys, the sex, what Skipper had said, what I had told him, what Bob thought, how inventive he was—and why the hell was *Jed* calling me when it wasn't even the end of the week and the column wasn't yet due.

Remember, we shared the bedroom, now reeking of fast-food sex, making the whole rant that much more irritating.

Didn't she get that Jed played at everything, and was playing me, her, everybody in the process? That he didn't have a serious relationship-minded bone in his body if he couldn't maintain a relationship with her for more than a month?

I couldn't let Paula get the upper hand on this. If I didn't take it seriously, she'd become stalking girl and things could really get out of hand.

That led to the thought, why am I putting up with this?

Maybe Jed should flat-out tell her there wasn't a hope in Hoboken that he was interested in getting back together with her.

But he already had.

So...why *was* I letting things get this out of hand?

5

I NEVER WOULD have thought that going to the ad agency for a day would be a relief. But there I was, in the cafeteria getting coffee and breathing a huge sigh because I was finally alone.

What I meant was, Paula wasn't there.

I really loved Paula, and it was obvious she still had a thing for Jed, but this whole idea that because I'd taken myself off the market, I represented a threat to a relationship that was over four or five months ago made no kind of sense except to a crazy lady.

Paula was not crazy.

However, Paula might be desperate. And relying on the same old patterns because that was how she'd hooked up with Jed in the first place. So it seemed likely to her that somewhere down the sleep-around-while-she-waited brick road, she would find another guy like Jed.

And meantime, I'd gotten religion, I'd seen the light, and I was happy—with no guy. Paula was definitely confused by the whole conundrum. That was why she'd been so weird.

Maybe my mission during The Guy Diet was to help Paula find happiness.

Hmmm.

Conclusion: *Paula* should go on the diet.

Never. At least, I tried. I gave it five minutes of consideration. She's my best friend after all, but now it's every woman for herself.

What to do about Paula?

I never thought things would get so complicated just by my going on this diet. I never thought I'd develop such willpower. Or that not sleeping around would be so liberating.

I was now determined to see it through till the end—particularly because Paula had decided to make it more difficult for me to do so.

I would just avoid her.

So rather than going home that evening, I went to the Met. I didn't particularly want to go to the Met, but it was a place and there was a new exhibition everyone was talking about.

And what do you think happened?

Guys. Guys happened, swarming all around, because everyone was looking for a place to meet someone that wasn't where they used to meet people before.

Museums were so highbrow, so out of the box.

And you couldn't get away from guys.

"Ooops, excuse me. Sorry. Didn't mean to step on you." Well, yes.

Hope ruled: this could be the start of something big.

I talked to a couple of guys. Nice guys. Not particularly interested in the current artistic installations. Much more interested in installing themselves in someone's bed.

Write me up a violation—I enjoyed talking to them. I couldn't be rude, could I?

"You're late," she said, as I tiptoed into the apartment.

"I went to the Met," I told her.

"Didn't know you were particularly fond of Impressionism."

No, just my impressions of…oh, forget it.

"This isn't new," I reminded her. "This is part and parcel of the Diet—me, being independent, focused, interested in other things besides sex."

"Right. No flirting, right?"

What, had she been spying on me?

"Just polite conversation," I said. "No cards exchanged." Cards were like bodily fluids now?

I went to check my e-mail instead of getting into a verbal tussle about the finer nuances of The Diet. There was a message from Jed.

Lunch tomorrow. Must do. Have to talk. Pick you up—home or office?

Must do, huh? Go away, Jed. I started to type in something scurrilous, and then I reread the message. This was a no-joke message.

This was serious Jed. And this might not have anything to do with books or food or my column even.

Since I was scheduled to transcribe at the agency the next day, I posted back the address, cautioning Jed that this wasn't allowed under Guy Diet rules, but I'd make the exception because he was in the free-ingredient column.

And of course I didn't tell Paula.

I TOOK LUNCH from twelve to one. As I came out of the elevator and into the long hallway that led to the street, I could just see Jed beyond the revolving doors, leaning against a parked car.

I stopped for a moment because I was so taken by the sight of him outside the normal places where I had contact with him.

Like the apartment. Or a restaurant, because I think I remember double-dating for dinner one night after that famous day we met.

I'd always viewed him through Paula's eyes. Never wondered about his side of the story. Had always pegged him as a goodbye guy.

Today, though, he came across not as the playboy entrepreneur, but as a confident, self-assured man, a calm center in the midst of lunchhour chaos, waiting with great patience for something.

Or someone.

I wished, for him, it could be the someone he was *really* waiting for.

Instead he got me, swinging through the doors and greeting him like an old friend.

"Where's the nearest grab-and-go restaurant around here?"

We went around the corner to the Sixth on Seventh Café, which served a limited menu of good food really fast. We didn't talk much, we ordered, I kept looking at him, as if I'd never seen him before.

It felt different. Serious. Bad-news serious maybe. I hated bad news.

"You understand," I said after we'd ordered, "Guy Diet rules still pertain."

"I remember, I'm a free ingredient and all that. And there's no kissing."

"Exactly. No kissing. So this is business, right?"

His expression, apart from a certain light in his deep-blue eyes, had gone utterly sober. I'd never really looked at him beyond the surface. On his own, he was charismatic, formidable even. But then, he was a Costigan, something I had tended to forget before this moment.

Frankly, it shook me up a little.

"Totally business."

"Good." I shook out my napkin. "So what's up?"

"Okay, no sugarcoating. I sold the *WestEnder.*"

I heard the words but they didn't quite register. "You sold it?"

"I did."

"Oh." There wasn't much else to say. I had no idea what this might mean to me except the loss of an income stream.

I gathered my wits. "What exactly does that mean besides you made a lot of money?"

"It means that, for one thing. For another, nothing should change."

"You mean, nothing will change the first day. I'll bet my lunch, though, that inside of two weeks, everything will change. So, have you been taking all your staff out to lunch to break the bad news?"

"It's not bad news."

"It's way beyond bad news. It's…"

"It's deeper pockets that can pay more money and expand the paper beyond where I can go with it."

"Oh, fine. I'm happy you're walking away with a few extra million in your pocket. What about freelancers like me, who get paid by the column inch?"

"Hey…hey, calm down. Did you hear the deeper-pockets part?"

"No," I said angrily, levering myself up from the table.

He grabbed my hand. "Sit down, Lo." His voice was very quiet.

I sat. I couldn't make a scene, really. Too many people knew who he was, and now and again, the paparazzi caught pictures of him that were prominently displayed on Page Six.

Not to mention ubiquitous cell cameras. With the way my luck seemed to be going, someone had snapped me in that hellfire moment and was uploading the picture to some disreputable gossip column even as I slowly sunk back into my seat.

I muttered under my breath, then said, "I'm sorry. I didn't think."

"And you don't listen, either," Jed said mildly. "Let's eat," he added, as the waitress came with our lunch.

How he could be so cool when I was still seething, I couldn't fathom. This lunch alone cost what I would have been paid for a month of columns.

Then I looked at my casserole and wondered how I could do it cheaper and in under fifteen minutes.

And I looked at Jed who was watching me with the familiar intensity, and he smiled.

Nice smile. Not a rock-your-world smile, but still, I felt this little flutter of…what? It was different. It was without the scrim of Paula's needs and jealousy between us.

I smiled back, wondering what I was doing. But that was what he was like. You couldn't not respond to him. I needed to take it calm and slow. Plus this was serious business.

As the casserole was delicious, I mentally listed every ingredient and thought about prep while we ate. Easier on the temper than excoriating him for things he had no control over in a business deal.

Of course, excluding the profit he'd made.

He ordered coffee after. I sipped it and then he asked, "Have you calmed down?"

I nodded. "Just trying to figure out how I'm going to make up that income."

"You don't have to. You're going under contract and—they want a book."

My heart stopped. *"What?"*

"They're putting the columnists under contract. From you, they want to see a first-look proposal for the book we discussed."

"Oh." Not much I could say to that. Under contract meant way more income. By the week. Maybe an increase. An advance, perhaps even, for a book. Oh my God.

"Yeah." He didn't have to say much more.

"This is awesome," I said.

"This is good for you, Lo. And it's good for me, too."

"You got what you wanted out of it."

"I got most of what I wanted out of it," Jed said. "But now that I'm not running the show, I see an additional benefit for me."

I was curious. "Which is?"

"Now we can have phone sex."

He was kidding.

He wasn't.

He said the contracts had been looked over by his lawyer and would be waiting for me when I got home tonight. Any problems, his lawyer would address them. Anything else I wanted, call him.

What did he mean by that?

He *was* kidding about the phone sex business—wasn't he?

"This was a very nice lunch," I told him as we were parting.

"I'm not sure I like the idea of my continually being your freebie."

"But I can have all the free ingredients I want," I countered—honestly, I couldn't help it— and, as the expression changed in his eyes, I backtracked. "Let's just say I think of you like fiber—filling and good for the diet."

Whoops. I didn't mean that. Did I really say *filling?* Just walk away while you can. Contract legalities first, then smooth over the sex talk.

Because *that* was not going to last.

"I can be filling," Jed murmured.

I pretended not to hear him. I thought if I concentrated on the good news, on when and how to tell Paula, what I'd said would go away. Still, how could I tell Paula I had lunch with Jed?

But doesn't everybody get good news over lunch?

Besides, she was on a business trip.

Oh, Lord. I could barely concentrate on what I was doing the whole afternoon thinking about the reality of a "Grab-and-Go Gourmet" cookbook. I needed an agent. No, I needed to review the terms of the contract and discuss it with Jed's lawyer before I signed anything.

The contract was waiting for me, Paula had not arrived home from the airport, and for the first time in a long time, I had some privacy. I needed it to absorb the sixteen pages of every-contingency-possible exceptions. There was no money offered, only the right of first look and first refusal for my proposal.

This was more than I had expected. I felt as if I was inching toward something momentous, life changing, and it had nothing to do with guys or sex.

How refreshing.

The Guy Diet works in mysterious ways.

As did Jed. The minute I had read through the contract a second time and taken notes and written down questions, my cell rang.

Answer it or not?

I decided not—given that comment this afternoon. But then he texted: *They got you. See NY by Day.*

I rang him back as I booted up my laptop and pulled up the Website.

"I am so sorry."

"Why? It's a really awful picture of you and a fudgy blind item."

"You must have great spin doctors on retainer."

"The Costigans don't like negative publicity," Jed said gently.

I accessed the "NY by Day" column in the *News,* and yes, there I was, with my mad mask on and an innocuous line about the mystery nobody who'd just been rejected by the playboy scion of what socially prominent family.

"It's horrible," I said miserably.

"It'll go away," Jed said comfortingly. "Now, can we get to the phone-sex part?"

"Hello…Guy Diet."

"I'm not just any guy."

That was for sure. I didn't know this Jed, the guy-opposite-me-at-lunch Jed with the impeccably tailored suit, impeccable manners and the improbable aura of success surrounding him.

"Right—you're the playboy scion, with the millions tucked in your back pocket with which you can continue playing."

"What if I want to play with you?"

That was breath-stopping. "You couldn't possibly. We barely know each other."

"I like the bare part. We could get bare *and* get to know each other better. And throw in a few kisses while we're at it."

I swallowed hard. Jed didn't play fair. "Not on my Guy Diet."

"But I'm the free ingredient."

"Right, the one with no calories, no fat, that's nonfilling, with no substance," I retorted.

"That means there's always room for…"

"I'm not breaking The Diet."

"I don't see how phone sex breaks The Diet."

"It's no guys. Not some no guys, *all* no guys."

"I am *not* some no guy," Jed said severely. "Or just any old guy."

"I know," I said regretfully, "but I have standards to maintain."

"Me, too," Jed said, flipping my abrasiveness back at me.

Ouch.

"Talk to you soon," he added and the phone clicked off.

Code that "Why talk to you ever again?"

Why couldn't I keep my mouth shut sometimes? How important was this damned diet thing anyway?

I had to do some really deep soul-searching on that.

Took me about thirty seconds. Playing with Jed would not get me what I wanted: the relationship with got-your-back guy, which I was not willing, I discovered, to compromise for the momentary thrill of having sex with Jed. Or even kissing him.

And over and above that, it seemed as if the more I held him at bay, the more intense Jed became.

Well. Who would've thought I'd have principles, goals *and* standards? And be willing to stick to them? And keep Jed Costigan so stirred up?

This really *has* been a great summer so far.

THIS REALLY HAD BEEN a lousy summer so far, despite the fact Jed would pocket major money from the newspaper sale. Everything else was all to hell because he couldn't budge Lo from her damned diet and her ridiculous stance protecting Paula.

It was all about Paula. It made no sense, and he was a make-sense kind of guy. Lo made sense. Paula made nonsense and had since the moment he'd met her. Dating her was like constantly looking at a reflection in the mirror: see and be seen. Somewhere underneath the veneer, there had to be a real Paula with real feelings and maybe one who sometimes forgot to apply makeup.

All the same, he'd never seen that Paula, and near the end of the third week, he didn't much care one way or the other.

Yet Lo cared about her, for reasons that utterly escaped him. So it was time to play devil's advocate—time to dig into the dirty bedrock of their friendship and root out why Lo was so reluctant to even be with him.

Time, in fact, to finally kiss her and settle that part once and for all.

THE NEXT DAY Jed was waiting for me outside when I left for my weekly agency stint dressed for a hunker-down kind of day in an overly air-conditioned office.

"Hey," he said softly.

I was staggered to see him, an even more casual Jed, in sunglasses, jeans and a navy T-shirt. Read *muscular.* Read *unexpected.*

"Hey, yourself. What are you doing here?"

"I'm kidnapping you. We're skipping school today."

"No. You are skipping school. I'm going to work. I work for a living. Unlike some people I know. And," I added for good measure, "I'm on this Guy Diet…?"

"Oh, I know," he said, making a motion with one arm. "Nevertheless, we're playing hooky, both of us."

Okay, kabuki-dance time. "I can't."

"You can. It's ninety degrees and that is a beach-blanket-bingo day if ever there was one."

"Jed…"

A long sleek black car drew up beside us.

"Ah, here's Stecker with the car."

The car? The *car? And* a driver? You couldn't make a driver-on-call in Manhattan seem like everyday ordinary.

"I keep a car," he murmured. "Don't use it much. Once in awhile."

A car and driver on call? This was Jed's real world, the one with designer women, elegant living, perfect manners, on-call limousines and limitless bank accounts.

I felt my body go hot, cold. Paula was more his world than I was. Paula was high maintenance; she could do the clothes, the social scene.

Paula was high tea. I was instant oatmeal.

"I realize," Jed said. "You've got work to do, people to see, recipes to concoct, Paula to appease. Got it. Get in. You can call everyone en route. Paula doesn't have to know a thing, if you must, but I still don't get why."

I didn't get it, either. I didn't get him. He wasn't that kind of guy.

Or was he?

"Get in, Lo. I won't bite."

"Yes, but you do kiss."

"I do—and I will. Though don't let that scare you off."

It scared the hell out of me. I got in. I called the agency. I put everything on hold. I couldn't find a word to say as the driver maneuvered through the traffic over to the West Side Highway.

"Call the lawyer tomorrow," he said at one point. "And don't accept the first offer. He will tell you precisely what you need to do."

"Okay." My voice was stuck. I couldn't find words. "Thanks."

"Good. Now, wake up."

"I can't." The car was air-conditioned. There was soft music playing. The driver consulted a GPS device every now and again. "I thought you were more of an Easthampton kind of guy."

"That goes to show," Jed said. "You just never know."

He meant, I didn't know. "Where are we going?"

"I asked Stecker to find a beach. I'm assuming it will be a very nice beach where we can have a picnic lunch and where, in the course of events, I will finally kiss you."

Stecker was heading toward Brooklyn. And my childhood playgrounds—the schoolyards, the city parks and now scruffy little beach areas down near Sheepshead Bay and farther out to Manhattan Beach. Oh my God. He could not have known—he couldn't.

I didn't say a word. When Stecker exited at Shore Parkway, that did me in. Jed was taking me home, and it was nowhere near Easthampton.

The beach parking lot was half full. Stecker drove us to one of the far gates and then took out a blanket and a backpack from the trunk.

Jed was watching me with that same intense gaze, then he nodded to Stecker and said to me, "Let's do it."

You never remember, as an adult, how the sun really beats down off the water, or the smells, the noise, how hot the sand is, the crunch your sneakers make as you make your way to the ideal place to sit and watch the water.

Those childhood memories, retrieved on a hot summer's day when you've run away from responsibility, do make you feel like a child again.

Jed even had a collapsible umbrella. We set up just beyond the wet wash of the shoreline, spread out the blanket, removed our sneakers, rolled up our jeans.

Everything familiar, everything strange. Jed was a stranger. I knew nothing about him and it seemed as if he knew everything about me.

Or—this was the devil doing his homework and trying to tempt me again. I disregarded his comment about a kiss.

"You are scared to death of me," Jed said suddenly in the midst of laying out the food, which had been neatly packed in the backpack.

"You think?"

"We're just having a day at the beach."

"Nooo—we're avoiding work at the beach. And then there's the small matter of a kiss."

"Oh, don't even think about it. It will come."

"Jed—"

"What?"

"I'm serious."

"Me, too. Try that salmon sandwich. It's wonderful."

I bit into the sandwich. I wanted to bite into him because he was so intractable. Instead I stared at the horizon where there were sailboats drifting along.

Jed rummaged in the backpack for a moment and then held up a tube. "Sunblock. Brace yourself because I'm going to touch you and put it on you and you're going to rub it on me," he said. Firmly.

I didn't stop him as he levered himself onto his knees to get closer to me, or when he took one arm and began to massage the cream into my skin. And then my other arm, my calves, my neck. So serious, so intense, rubbing the cream all over every inch of exposed skin in the most erotic, irresistible way.

My insides melted. A whorl of desire slithered through my veins. I couldn't stop it. Didn't want to.

This was time off the books. We were playing hooky. Who would know? Who cared?

And then he touched my face. Tilted my head slightly toward his. Stroked the cream on my cheeks, my jaw, my chin, his eyes so deep, so blue, so serious, his touch not erotic at all, and yet— I caught my breath, I grasped his wrist to stop him, to help him, to— He met me halfway, he touched my lips, licked them, he cupped my cheek and he settled his mouth on mine for the barest instant and then pulled away, inches away…just to watch the spiraling pleasure in my eyes at that breath of a kiss.

He took my mouth again, fast this time, hard, deep, probing—
the kind of kiss where time stops, arousal is instant and uncom-
promising—and there's nowhere to go when you're out in public
with mothers and children all around you and you desperately want
a room and some privacy.

Jed drew away reluctantly. "Your turn." He could barely rasp
out the words. He handed me the sunblock, but my hands were
shaking so hard from the force of the desire I felt for him, I could
barely grasp the tube.

"Now I get to kiss you?" I murmured, squeezing the cream into
the palm of my hand.

"Only if you want to."

I got to my knees and started at the back of his neck because I
knew if I looked into his eyes, I *would* kiss him again even though
I hadn't absorbed what that first kiss meant.

I didn't think the pure sense of his maleness would hit me in quite
the way it did as I applied the sunblock. I was suddenly conscious
of the texture and fairness of his skin, the shape of his body. I felt
the raw power of him, even quiescent, under my tentative stroking
fingers. And the sexual alertness just under the skin, and the thing
in him that called out to me, I felt it as intensely as the sun.

Or it was a combination of that, the sand, the endless horizon, the
taste of the forbidden, the feeling of liberation, or just the fantasy…

"Hey…" He twisted around to face me, pulled me down beside
him, positioned the umbrella to shield us, and came in, slowly and
deliberately for the kiss.

Now I felt like a teenager, hot, urgent and grinding in the dunes.
No stopping me now.

I don't know how long it was before Jed pulled away again, and
when he did, he was in total control of his senses because he could
actually speak.

"I think there's going to be a lot of kissing from now on."

Trying to behave like a sane adult, I said, "I think we have to stop
now." We couldn't go all X-rated on a beach full of kids and moms.

"I don't think so. Talk to me."

"I can't talk," I whispered.

"That's good." Another long, drowning kiss. "I like kissing you."

I made a sound.

"Still can't talk? Excellent. Then you can't protest and there can be more kissing. Because that's how I envisioned today—a good lunch and lots of kissing."

I made another sound but he stopped it with his lips. "You talk too much."

I didn't talk at all; he stonewalled every attempt with a kiss, deep kisses, tiny kisses, nipping kisses that made me squirm and my body liquefy with molten lust.

"I really like this kissing business," he murmured against my lips at one point. "We have to do this more often."

"You're really okay with just kisses."

"Absolutely."

"Liar."

"Maybe. Maybe I want more. At some point. Talk to me, Lo. Tell me why you're so protective of Paula?"

That came clear out of the blue, and yet we were lying there in such intimacy, him braced on his elbows, me just to the side of him on my back, accessible for kisses and truth and dare, that whatever I said would feel like a confession.

I couldn't avoid his eyes or that intense expression I always saw when he looked at me. I couldn't tell him anything, especially my feelings about him.

"You can guess," I temporized.

His expression hardened for a fleeting instant, almost so I thought I imagined it. "Okay. Here's what you need to hear—I was never in love with her. She was most definitely not in love with me."

"Maybe—" I swallowed the rest because he dropped a kiss on my lips. "Maybe she thinks she still is."

"No."

"Maybe she thinks you're in love with her, and that you'll come back."

"Never."

You couldn't get more definite than that.

He waited for my next conclusion, which I chose not to air, and he finished it for me, "Maybe you don't ever want her to think you stole something from her."

I just closed my eyes because that was part of the truth, one of the things I had avoided coming to grips with. And I knew that Paula *did* think, on some level, I had taken him away, just because of that moment in the restaurant all those months ago.

"Maybe," I whispered.

"What are you going to do?"

"I don't know. What would you do?"

"I'll tell you what *we're* going to do," Jed said, wholly avoiding an answer, "we're going to walk on the beach holding hands like we're lovers, maybe get our feet wet, and then I'm going to make out with you all the way back to Manhattan."

I shivered. All those miles, all those kisses. I didn't think my body could take it.

We packed up and walked. The sky was impossibly blue, there was a slight breeze stirring the air and the sun was blazing hot.

Or maybe that was me, coming down from the ignition of Jed's incendiary kisses. And we did make out all the way down the highway.

I didn't let myself think, feel guilty, make assessments. I could barely walk when I got home, and I was swooning with gratitude that Paula wasn't there.

And relieved that I and my secret were safe.

6

It TOOK a hefty amount of willpower not to dwell on those kisses and the whole rest of the day. I distracted myself by calling the lawyer to discuss the contract, the details of which we painstakingly went over until we both were satisfied.

Then Jed called.

"I'm assuming after yesterday, you've explored *all* your options?"

"I'll bet you were right in the lawyer's office when we were talking."

"I just want to know about exploring options."

"Which ones did I not cover?"

"Mine," Jed said soberly.

"And they are?"

"Dinner tonight and see what happens."

This was so not fair. "It's not the see-what-happens part that concerns me. It's the *what happened* part. Like, yesterday."

"Okay, that could happen. I definitely promise more kissing. There's nothing wrong with that. I enjoyed that happening."

"Nothing more *can* happen because I'm not exploring any more options…yet." I added that tentatively because this was going someplace I hadn't even thought was on the radar.

"You know, you *did* prove your point about the diet," Jed countered.

"And now you want to prove yours," I said back. Oh, my mouth should be fined for indecent exposure.

"You want references? I knew it. A hard-nosed dieter like you…"

"You don't have references. And I know how hard-nosed *you* are." His tone changed subtly. "Oh, you absolutely do, don't you."

"Jed…"

"You don't have to imagine it anymore, You don't have to hear about it from *her.* You have firsthand experience and now you *know.*"

Oh God. I resorted to the age-old denial that sounded false even to my ears. "It's not like that."

"Right. Paula didn't talk about me—us—ever."

I wouldn't confirm or deny that. "I don't want to talk about Paula, unless…" Genius idea. Kind of like sending Jason after the Golden Fleece. "Unless you know someone we can hook her up with."

"I know a lot of someones," Jed said cautiously. "But they'd ask me for references and I'm a gentleman and…you don't want that."

"No, I just want—"

"Me. You want me."

My breath caught again and there was a long silence as I frantically tried to define a response to that.

"I want—okay, this is what I want. I want…"

"Me," he interpolated again.

"Okay, now I think The Guy Diet has made me delusional, because I could swear you said…"

"Yeah, I said it. You want me. No denials. Not after yesterday."

"That's off the wall, Jed. And besides…"

"What? What objections could you possibly have? You don't report to me anymore. I'm not with anyone, you're off guys altogether, other than talking to me. No one can have any objections…"

I started to open my mouth and closed it. "I'm still on The Diet."

"Okay. Phone sex till you end the ridiculous diet. When is it over? You have to be ready to have sex by now. Especially after yesterday. I tasted that hunger in you. And I sure want to have sex with you."

He was right; the diet could be over anytime I said it was, but I decided not to tell him that.

As for sex—I was still holding out for got-my-back guy. And that wasn't him. I knew too much about him as he'd so easily intuited. And I was too vulnerable to him.

Beyond that, there were too many things working against our even having dinner together, let alone anything else, that I thought I'd better not say another word. Especially not the *P* word.

"Tell me you're done with the damned diet."

I made a sound, stuffing back the words, *I could be.* This was temptation in its purest form. This was the suffering and penance part and there just wasn't any middle ground. Not even for Jed Costigan.

"Not," I managed to squeak. "I'm not done yet."

"When?"

"End of summer. About another two weeks."

"Is anyone really keeping track?" Jed asked. "Dumb question. Of course someone is."

"I made such a big deal of it…"

"*Did* you?" Okay, sarcasm not lost on me. He went on, "Honest to God, Lo. It's all about the big deal you made of it. And you're pushing this thing beyond everyone's limit. But—it's your diet. You do what you have to do. I'll call you tonight."

Was that just a little abrupt? This was exactly the moment you could read things into a conversation or a quick turn-off that could make you crazy.

Since Jed wasn't got-my-back guy, and this wasn't that relationship where all things are possible, I decided it was safer not to read anything into it at all.

For about ten minutes. Then I thought—did he really say what I thought he'd said? *Why* did I go with him yesterday? *Why* did I let him kiss me like that? For so many hours?

I groaned, thinking of the ride home in the luxury limo with his body on mine, and his endless, mind-blowing kisses softening my body, my heart, my desire…and his iron-man restraint in not demanding anything more.

That could screw up an afternoon's worth of work, parsing the *did he means* and the silences in between.

Enough of that. The Guy Diet was now officially not cost-effective. It was running my life and maybe ruining it at this point.

Maybe I'd missed meeting a great guy in my effort to avoid the get-go guys. Maybe I really had to rethink the whole idea of saving myself till I found *that guy.*

I was pretty certain Jed wasn't that guy. Jed was the intrigued gets-everything-he-wants guy who'd bumped into a wall he couldn't breach. Guys like Jed either went around or climbed over obstacles. Or knocked them down. And God, he knew how to kiss.

He wasn't a stand-still kind of guy, either, for all his great qualities. He liked variety. He was easily bored. Wait, wait, wait—check that—he wasn't bored yesterday from hours of sand surfing with me.

That was something I knew from Paula. I knew other stuff, too, which made it problematic that I would ever succumb to his idea that I wanted him. In spite of those kisses. In spite of the fact that we were so combustible.

Because before he'd ever put his hands on me, I knew how large they were, how firmly he could touch, how delicately he could find the places you didn't know existed that you wanted him to discover. I knew what he looked like naked, how much time he took to arouse and enfold you, and sometimes how raw and primitive he could be. I knew the things he said. I knew how long he held you in the aftermath.

I knew—I knew too much and I knew it all solely from one person's experience. And I never let myself even for a moment remember.

Until yesterday.

You want me.

How could anybody *really* want anybody before they even knew each other in a deep-pored, beneath-the-skin kind of way?

I meant the kind of knowing where you're accepted for your flaws and wanted in spite of and because of them.

Like when you were in l—

Oh God, I was actually *thinking* the *L* word.

And all the way on the ride home from Brooklyn yesterday, in the midst of all the kissing, I kept remembering the details. Paula loved to dwell on the details because they were so juicy and good even as their relationship had gone sour.

By her account, *he* was in it for the sex and nothing more, but now I didn't know if that were even true, or just wishful thinking on her part. Or maybe *she* was in it for the sex and he had wanted more—but just not with her.

Whose truth was the reality?

What *was* the truth of any relationship if each partner told a different story? All this time it was Paula's story, and I had seen Jed only as she had defined him.

Yesterday afternoon had rocked my foundation. His kisses *were* a foundation—and I didn't want to discover there were any cracks.

And, adding to all that was on my plate already, Paula was due home soon.

"Yes, I had a good trip. Yes, the client is happy. Yes, I had sex.

Anything else you'd like to know?" she asked cheerfully before she'd been home for five minutes.

"Tell me about the client part," I said, backpedaling around the obvious.

"They liked the new creative direction. And Washington is really cool—especially at night."

Good. She was so buoyant, the sex must have been great.

"So what's up with you?"

So I told her. "Big news, maybe. The *WestEnder* was sold to a new block of investors who, among other expansion ideas, are bringing on the columnists full-time. People like me."

She sobered instantly. "So Jed's out of it?"

Silly me. What other detail would she be interested in? But no. I said as little as possible to corroborate that. "That's my understanding. I signed my contract yesterday."

"That's great. More money, right?"

"Regular money, anyway."

"So no more Guy Diet."

"I'm thinking about it."

"Could you just end it so we can go out and have fun? Maybe we could eat out once in a while? In fact, how about we celebrate the new management by having dinner out tonight?"

Distract her. It was the only thing I could think of. Anything was better than talking about Jed.

"Okay. Let's do it. And we'll celebrate the fact that tonight I'm officially off The Guy Diet."

Only I'd had no idea how liberating it had been to be on The Guy Diet, because the minute I came off it, I was not a happy camper.

We went to the bar-restaurant we'd gone to for my so-called aversion therapy. I was still feeling pretty averse, and a scan of the crowd didn't reassure me.

Still I decided to play along because I wanted Paula to be happy. I just didn't know how far I was willing to go because she obviously was on the hunt, and a one-night stand in Washington couldn't even hold her for one day.

You see how complicated things get? And I hadn't even added in the possibility of Jed's phone call.

I tried to forget about all that and concentrate on enjoying the dinner and Paula's company. I flirted a little bit to ease her mind and prayed, to ease mine, that Jed hadn't meant what he'd said.

Right now the important thing was that Paula and I were out together surrounded by guys, and we could have our choice of any of them that night.

I didn't want any of them for five minutes.

This had to be a residual effect of The Guy Diet. Major impatience. Irritation with small talk. You started to be very particular about the things with which you chose to nourish yourself.

So I was just going to whip out food analogies every time I didn't like someone?

I had changed.

That realization hit me right in the gut.

I had changed—mentally, philosophically, physically. Radically.

But nothing around me had changed, not my friends or their after-hours habits, or my recreational pursuits, because why would I choose to be here if I wasn't enjoying myself?

It was a staggering moment.

I had changed. And the old ways weren't going to work for me anymore. I felt as if I had taken a quantum leap beyond all this and that The Guy Diet had gotten me there.

Whatever it was, I was finished here. I might have even been finished with Paula as a roommate, but I didn't want to negate that so fast. There weren't all that many reasonable, albeit tiny, one-bedroom shares in Manhattan.

At least I didn't have to leave her there. Bill or Andy or Tim—I don't remember his name—told me she'd already left with this guy, Red, who knew about some party happening down in NoHo.

Just what Paula loved, being among the A-listers at some exclusive party event.

Perfect. No excuses needed. I grabbed a cab, flipped my cell from vibrate to ring and immediately it rang.

A lot of missed calls, I saw. All from Jed. "Hey."

"You've been off call for a damned long time."

"So I have." Treading lightly here. He was a man of his word, after all. He had called.

"And you're where, now?"

"Almost home."

"Good. Meet you there."

The last thing I wanted. "Jed—" But it was too late. And the cab was just turning onto my street, and damn it, there *was* someone waiting.

This is going to spoil everything.

That was what I thought. Crazy, right?

I almost said, Don't stop. Take me to…oh, down to NoHo…but, I mean, Jed was no threat. He was just a sweet treat on which Paula had overindulged, who might just send me into sugar shock if I even tasted what he was offering.

He was right there to pay for the cab the moment it stopped, and then he held out his hand to me.

I knew too many things. His hands…

I didn't want to remember, not the warmth, not the feeling of fitting, not anything to do with…anything that had happened between us, anything about him that I could…*like.*

"So invite me up."

I couldn't get out of it. I had no reason to refuse after those kisses, that afternoon. I wasn't too happy that he had taken the choice out of my hands, but I said dutifully, "Would you like to come up?"

There was absolutely a smile in his eyes, and I knew this was going to be one hellacious trial by…liking him too much.

He knew the apartment, of course. And of course there was the abominable, awkward, getting-acclimated moments. God, I hate those moments.

"Wine?"

"Nope." He was ambling around the living room looking at the books.

"Coffee?"

"Nope." He swiveled around to look at me. "What do you think?"

"I'm trying not to think."

"It's there in your face, Lo, you are thinking."

Oh God. "It's that obvious?" I moved farther away from him. I knew what I was doing. "Do you want to sit?"

"Nope."

Now I was getting jittery. *Don't ask the question. You know what the answer will be.*

"Talk?"

"God, no."

"Jed…" I knew too much, and all of it was welling up inside me like a symphony.

I wanted it so badly I could scream. "You should go."

"No. I should stay. I want to stay. You want me to stay."

I took a deep calculated breath. "I know too much," I said—no, I blurted it.

That didn't faze him in the least. "Me, too," he said simply, leaving me to wonder what exactly *he* meant by that.

I wasn't going to ask. I *wasn't*.

"What do you mean by that?"

"You know."

I hate games. You see? This was why The Guy Diet worked. You get impatient with crap because there were more important things to get to.

Like getting Jed out of my space so that I could breathe.

Because I knew what he meant by, *me, too*.

"So I'm finally standing here in your living room," Jed said at length, as he stared out the window, "and here's the thing. I don't give a damn about Paula."

"Well, that's good," I muttered.

"Don't you think?"

He was the cat toying with Miss Mouse—*me*.

"I think it would be nice if you leave."

"Maybe I should get to the kissing part. That was pretty effective."

That stopped me. I couldn't breathe. Just couldn't…breathe.

Because I knew things. Because I loved his kisses. Because I wanted him more than I wanted to admit…

And because I'd have regrets whatever I chose to do.

He watched me so carefully, I knew he saw all my feelings play all over my face. Including the knows-too-much part.

But then, there was, *me, too*. And that scared me to death.

I suddenly realized that the minute he touched me, all my crutches would be gone, all the jokes and food allusions in the disposal unit. No protective covering, no rights of refusal prior to the act.

Tonight he was the wall, and I couldn't get over, around or under—no, check that—I could be under him for this one night in one minute with just one kiss. I knew it, deep in my bones. I wanted to, badly—but I couldn't let myself. Somewhere a little voice reminded me of the betrayal part.

He waited, I waffled and the silence thickened unbearably. Finally, he held out his hand. "Come to me, Lo."

My body felt explosive. My body wanted him, the kisses, the sex, *everything*—with him.

It felt as if I'd been in suspended animation, waiting for him; as if I'd suppressed and denied every piece of evidence that he was truly perfect, and the knowledge that once I reached out my hand, I could never go back.

I took his hand. He drew me against him and touched my face, my lips, my hair. He kissed me then, a light, testing, seeking kiss, no rush, no hurry, no urgency, just feel, feel, feel. I felt my heart accelerate, my body give as heat sparked all over me, enveloping me in the heat of him from those raindrop kisses that slowly, sensually went deeper, more controlling, driven by the hard edge of restrained lust, violent need and something more.

And then he drew away—again just inches—to whisper, "This is even better than yesterday."

He felt a little moue of denial on my part.

"Why are you so surprised?"

"Why aren't you?" I retorted, instantly on the offensive. *Be* offensive. That would reveal his true colors. Or mine. "Why was it long past time?"

He gave me a long, considering look. "You really don't know."

"I really don't," I said, softening my voice, because there was something here above and beyond the inevitability of the moment.

I couldn't stop looking at him then. It felt as if I'd never seen him before.

I wondered what he was thinking, because he obviously was in no rush to answer my question or amplify anything he'd said previously.

"Actually," he said after a pause. "I've been waiting for you."

For the second time with Jed, I was speechless.

"Don't say anything. Everything's been said."

I found my voice. "When? When was everything said?"

There was a sparkle of humor in his eyes. "When you kissed me at the beach."

How did he know, *how?*

"I just wanted you to know," he added softly.

"Oh." Wait, what did that mean, *just wanted you to know?*

"'Oh' is very eloquent," Jed murmured. "Tell me more." He drew me close and I knew it was going to happen now. I wished for a moment that it wouldn't, because I wanted it to be perfect, and not here, in my shared living room, where anyone could walk in and catch us.

It didn't matter, though, because all the questions were answered.

I could have kissed him all night, but the urge to touch, strip and feel my naked flesh against his was way more powerful than the idea of restraint and taking my time.

I had wasted too much time already. Still, I took my time, anyway, slowly removing his shirt, then sliding my hands all over his chest, feeling the substance and power of his body. Fed by his kisses, his murmuring encouragement, I took the lead and he let me.

He was so beautiful, his body so strong, muscular and taut, I almost couldn't bear it; his belly, his narrow hips—my favorite parts—his penis, so perfect, surging into my hands.

I felt a hunger to know him everywhere as he slowly undressed me. Everything I wanted, he wanted—to touch, to feel, to know every part of my nakedness, everything he'd denied himself all these months, I gave him now. No holding back. No doubts, fears, intrusive memories, no what *ifs.*

I couldn't wait to get him in my bed. I crawled over him, with my mouth, my tongue, my hands, up and down his body and between his legs. I wanted to eat him up every way you could think of. I wanted to imprint him with my touch, my tongue and my sex forever.

My body was so ripe and moist, I thought I would burst. I felt myself dissolving all over him; I couldn't get enough of him; I wanted to take him deep inside me forever and keep him safe.

It was only when we lay body against body, and I couldn't tell if what I felt was my bare skin or his, that I understood the appeal of waiting so long for this moment. And then when he lifted himself over me so I could protect him, and he mounted me and thrust his penis deep inside my body, I felt such a connection I nearly cried.

The knife edge of a too-long-suppressed need fueled our first ferocious joining, blotting out everything. The surroundings, the past, the future were all subsumed in the heat and fury of his pummeling thrusts and my voluptuous response to him.

We made love for hours. I think there was a point at which we stopped and rested, even though I couldn't bear not to feel his penis inside me.

"More." It didn't matter who said it, who wanted it. It was enough just to be joined, gently rocking, lightly kissing, erotically touching and feeling the heat and texture of his body. And the power.

Especially the power. It got to me, deep in a primitive place where it was all about the heat, the mating.

And he made me feel safe, and I didn't expect that, either.

"I told you," he murmured, as he stroked my hair.

"I knew," I whispered. But I couldn't have known how much I would love having intercourse with him. I wanted to stay in our tight little bubble where we would be naked, coupled and wallowing in sex forever.

That was my Garden of Eden. And *love* was a tricky word, not to be spoken lightly in the daze and haze of such incandescent pleasure.

"Come home with me tonight."

A reality bite. "I don't think I should."

He looked at his watch. "Hell. It's nearly three, and Paula could be rolling in any moment."

Paula. I hadn't given one thought to her. My focus was solely on Jed and how much *not* a surprise it was how perfectly we fit, how we meshed and matched. How much I wanted him. Now, again. And again, after that.

Forget what's-her-name. *Why* had I put everything on hold because of her?

I sat up and he levered himself to his knees to kiss me again. He was raring to go and I grasped his penis and kissed him, mutely begging for him to take me again.

"Come with me."

I was desperate to say, *Stay with me.* The pull-tug was awful. I wanted so much more of him, to explore the new beginning of *us*...and more than anything, to make up for lost time with him that could never be done over.

It was always about time, most urgently it was almost time for

Paula to return, who would be unnecessarily devastated if she found us together.

I wanted to mount him again and damn the consequences, but he knew he had to leave. In between hot, arousing kisses, he dressed as I watched, and I reveled in the fact that that beautiful male body, that ferocious penis, those erotic kisses were all *mine*.

And nothing more needed to be said.

Except it was time to say something to Paula.

7

THE GUY DIET was so over.

"Did you hear me?" I demanded of Paula, who was in bed, moaning, groaning and heaving, not necessarily in that order. "The Guy Diet is over."

Paula gave me a blurry look. "I don't care. Where were you when I needed you?"

"Being rational. That's why I'm done."

Paula sat up suddenly. "I thought you were done last night. Something happened after I left the bar."

God, she had radar even in the throes of a hangover.

"Yeah, I came home."

She had gotten home around 4:00 a.m., slept for about an hour, and I'd been ministering to her hangover since then.

"Why?"

"Summer's almost over."

It wasn't. It felt like it because I was in heat and I so wished I had gone back with Jed. I could be naked, on my back cradling his body instead of making up more lies to pacify Paula.

Why did I even say anything? Where was last night's resolve?

"You've got that right," she muttered. "Why do I do this to myself?"

"Yeah, why do you?" I asked rhetorically. "You're a masochist. You want a relationship, yet you sabotage every possible chance of one because you want guarantees, you want perfection. So how's that working for you this morning after?"

"Ooof—nasty this morning. Maybe something happened last night that was bad, so you're snappy today."

Something happened? Everything happened. You have no idea how much I didn't want to be in that apartment with Paula and how much I wanted to be in bed with Jed.

"Okay, shower time."

She fell back on the pillows. "I'll call in."

"Don't. Please don't. Because then I'll worry myself to death about you all day."

"I love that you care."

Maybe that was my huge flaw, that I did care, that on some level I loved Paula like a sister—and she treated me like a sister, sometimes, telling me things I shouldn't know and letting me see her at her worst.

"I care enough so I don't want you to get fired."

"I want a job like yours, you know, writing. About marketing or men or both or none, or something."

Definitely still one sheet to the wind.

I pushed her into the shower and turned it on.

"You can't fool me," she shouted over the roar of the water. "Something happened yesterday."

Well, she did it, whether she meant to or not—I felt the guilt.

And you know what made it worse? I realized I had no excuse to go out overnight. That meant no nights with Jed. Not yet.

Why should I care about Paula's feelings at this point? I should do what felt good, right? I should be with Jed.

Well, lying even more to Paula wouldn't feel too good, especially about Jed, and particularly at the outset of wherever last night would lead. So I couldn't have gone home with him last night, or tonight—or any night until I dealt with Paula.

Okay, for one minute I thought about extreme measures. After all, it was my sex life, not hers. Jed wasn't her property. I wasn't her conscience or her soul. In this shark pond of competition for guys, I should view it as every woman for herself.

So I guess this was where the "maybe I owe her" part got to me. Or maybe I thought *she* thought I owed her. For the grab-and-go gig. After all, if she hadn't been dating Jed, I never would have met him or opened my mouth or—had over-the-moon sex with him last night.

This was nuts. The Guy Diet had thrown everything out of kilter. Everything that should be right felt wrong, and everything that was wrong just got magnified into a bigger problem.

Which could be easily solved if we—I—could find Paula a guy. A nice guy with no flaws, no quirks and lots of money.

Easy. Now I was off The Guy Diet, *I* could troll the bike paths and the outer reaches of the park. I could talk to guys and take cards and make introductions, we could go to the beach on Saturday and ogle the bodies.

Oh God, I was tired just planning it. What was I thinking?

I had to get real: I'd gotten no sleep last night and I wished it had been because I'd gone home with Jed and he'd made love to me until I was delirious.

The *only* solution was to get her a guy. I didn't know how. I didn't know who. One thing for sure, he had to be as slick and as corporate as she was, had to look good with money to spend and could drink her under the table.

Piece of cake.

Wasn't it true that if you projected yourself a certain way, like a magnet, things would come to you? Like money. Jobs. Friends. Guys.

"Tell Paula," Jed said when I spoke to him later.

"It's not that simple. She's already suspicious of my giving up the diet—if I tell her about you, she might go off the deep end."

"Forget her deep end. What about your deep end?"

"You can dive in anytime."

"What time?"

"You name it—time and place."

"I'll see you at six, here."

"And while you're at it, think of someone for Paula."

"Not going to happen, Lo."

"You're not helping."

"You'd help more if you'd just tell her."

"Not until I find someone for her."

"You'll find someone for yourself sooner."

"Nonsense."

"Test it out. Don't say I didn't tell you."

Well, he obviously didn't want to put himself out. Fine. I would find that perfect someone, someone just like Paula, starting from point zero, even with my *available* antenna atrophied due to The Guy Diet.

"We're going out tonight," I told Paula, "and you're going to get your act together. No drinking, no picking up and leaving with random guys. You're going to behave yourself and maybe you'll attract the kind of guy that sticks to relationships."

"You're dreaming. There's no such thing."

"*And* you have to stop the negative thinking."

"Something happened. You've gone 180 degrees around from where you were even last week."

I ignored that. "We start tonight. I'll pick you up at nine."

"Why so late? What are you up to?"

If only she knew.

"Not every hour of every minute of my day is your business."

"I knew it—something happened. I bet you had sex. I bet you cheated on that dumb diet and that's why you're done with it."

Now I had to get out of the apartment. "Nine o'clock," I said firmly before I bolted out the door.

Phew. Now I had to factor in time with Jed—minimum, something hot and hard for lunch. And then max him out for two hours after work.

God, I made him sound like a credit card. I didn't want things to go that way—grabbing snatches of Jed in between trolling with Paula.

That made it so not perfect.

I might just as well be back on The Guy Diet.

I called Jed immediately. "Can we meet for lunch?"

"Come to my place."

"I don't mean that kind of lunch."

"I do."

"I can't. I have to go back on the diet if I'm going to survive the hunt for the perfect man. So we need to talk about…"

"Just get over here," Jed said, emphatically disconnecting.

Well, that tore it. Why were Paula's problems getting in the way of sex with Jed? I couldn't get out of the building fast enough to grab a cab, which in Manhattan at lunchtime required major battle strategies even to get to Central Park West where Jed owned a big old-fashioned apartment overlooking the park in a prewar co-op.

He was at the door as I emerged from the elevator, and I felt my breath catch. I hesitated a step before I continued down the short hallway.

"We have to talk," I said.

"No, we don't. We have to kiss. We definitely have to kiss. Anything else can't be that important."

Funny. "I know where kissing leads," I said severely. "And…"

"I like how you think," Jed said, backing me against the door after he closed it. "Kissing first, details later."

"O-okay…" I couldn't say much more than that because he settled his mouth very precisely on mine and that was the end of any coherent thought.

"We have about a half hour," he whispered at one point. "Do you really want to waste time on anything else?"

Anything other that getting his penis immediately between my legs seemed superfluous.

"I…" Close quote, close quarters, don't think, just feel, let him feel every inch of your body as he strips off your clothes and you tear off his and take him in hand, take him in your mouth, devour him every which way you can think of, then protect him so he can mount you and hold you naked, hard and tight against the door, and he fills you with his lust and his desire—and what more is there in life than the rhythm of his thrusting, the length and feel of his penis and the exquisite unfurling of your orgasm when he spews hard into his own. The first of many.

"Don't move…" His lips barely moved against mine a long while later.

I couldn't. More kisses, dizzying kisses. No more of this. Had to talk, had to get back, had to have more kisses, more sex, more of him, more wasn't even enough.

"Jed."

"I know. I ambushed you."

"I just have to…"

"God, I hate *just have tos*." He eased away from my body and immediately I felt bereft.

I bent to pick up my clothes. "You're going to hate the rest, then."

"Does there have to be a 'rest'? Because I can guess what 'the rest' is about."

"You tell me, then."

He gave me a flashing look that had a trace of humor. "No sleeping together until Paula is hooked up."

I tried to recover as I slipped into my clothes. "Well. That doesn't mean no sex. It just means no overnights." I heard what I was saying and I thought, this *is* nuts. He's going to think *I'm* nuts, and this will be over before it even gets a toehold.

Okay, moral choice—sex with Jed for however long it lasts— or lose a dear friend, for however long it takes her to forgive me.

God, moral choices are so hard.

At least he wasn't watching all my anxiety play out on my face, because he'd gone into the bathroom.

I stared at myself in a nearby mirror. What did I see? I was nearly naked, my hair in disarray, my body, my face all soft with sex and satiety. What I didn't see was the tension that always surfaced when I was feeling out a new lover. What was unspoken was my loyalty to Paula.

You are crazy. Give this up for Paula?

He came back into the hallway dressed in jeans and a tee. "Okay, my worker bee, back to the hive. Do what you have to do. I'll call you tomorrow."

"You're kidding."

"No kidding. Doorman will get you a cab."

"Jed?"

"Really."

I didn't believe him. I decided to test him. "I'm taking her out tonight. Dinner at Tresco's."

"Nice. You can tell her about me and live happily ever after."

"But you're not an 'ever' kind of guy, are you?" I murmured, under my breath. I thought.

He gave me an enigmatic smile. "Why*ever* would you think that?"

I actually didn't know what to think. Who cared about work when I could have been in bed all afternoon with him?

I needed to focus on *my* sex life. *My* love life. Only, I didn't yet see how I could.

8

I FINALLY WENT HOME at eight-thirty so I could shower. Paula was there waiting for me.

"You are acting so weird," she said.

"You're acting like a hormone-clogged teenager," I retorted, feeling great irritation I'd given up my overnight for a night out with Paula.

Forget the shower—I decided to just freshen up because I didn't want to wash away the scent of Jed. I wanted to remember it, every last second of what we did and how he felt inside me and how much I wanted him inside me right now.

"You still haven't confessed that you had sex."

"Okay, I had sex."

"I knew it." Triumph supreme. Paula's rut radar never failed.

I ignored that. "Are you ready?"

"Ready to hear juicy details," she countered.

I bribed her. "At the restaurant. While we have dinner, I'll tell you everything."

Did I mean that? I didn't know. We took a cab uptown where new-wave restaurants were starting to make incursions and draw clientele.

Tresco's occupied the duplex of a brownstone near the Cathedral of St. John the Divine.

We opted for the rear parlor where there were fewer patrons and a cozy atmosphere of intimacy.

"So here we are," Paula said, setting her wineglass on the table. "I don't have a hangover, I'm on my best behavior and I'm being nice."

"I'll be on my best behavior, too," I said, "but I have to say some things before we get into my rehabilitated sex life."

Paula stiffened. "What kind of things?"

"Things you don't want to hear."

"God, I knew it. Ever since you invented this Guy Diet nonsense, you've been like a sanctimonious crusader for truth in dating. What don't I want to know that I already know?"

"You can tell me," I said.

Paula's lips tightened. "You're going to say I have to stop my wild and wicked ways."

"Pretty much."

"I don't want to."

"Because…?"

"Because why should I? I'm not looking for a relationship or marriage…"

I gave her a skeptical look.

"Or marriage," she repeated emphatically as a waiter approached with menus. "I'm looking for good times, a few good sex partners and making lots of money at what I do."

"Okay. So what was the thing with Jed all about?"

Paula shrugged as she scanned the menu. "He's a Costigan, he's social, he's rich, he's nice."

"You were hoping," I interpolated. "You were more than hoping."

"Well, there *was* no hope." Paula looked at up at me, her gaze skewering. "He broke it off because of you."

My heart stopped, my hands started shaking. That couldn't be true; that was Paula needing an excuse for why things ended between them, and a place to vent her disappointment and rage.

I could barely look at her. "That can't be so."

"*So.* He didn't put it quite that way. He didn't say that the instant he saw you that day—that time we had dinner together when you played up your faster, cheaper, better cooking? He didn't say 'I took one look at Lo and my insides just melted.' Maybe two weeks later, he said words to the effect of, 'I met someone and I need to get to know her and I can't do that to you or with you.' You were the reason, Lo, and it just about killed me."

"I didn't know," I whispered. "I didn't—not until…not then, not at the beginning at that dinner, at that moment." I knew my face showed all my emotions—regret, guilt, hope, sorrow.

"Are you ready to order?" The waiter had held back until there was a long moment of silence that could not be filled with excuses or lies.

"Not yet," Paula said edgily, and as the waiter turned away, she added, "Maybe I did want something more with him. But what he did only proved once again it wasn't possible. And the only thing I cared about after was that I didn't want you to have it."

I swallowed hard. "He never said a word."

I waited for you, he'd said. *I just wanted you to know...*

"No. Because a couple of weeks later you started that crazy guy diet."

"But he did wait, Paula, in deference to you. And he never talked about it. Never said a word—"

I wanted her to say it. I didn't want to have to tell her.

She filled in the blank. "And then you had sex with him."

"I didn't quite fall into bed with him. I had reservations. I didn't want to hurt you."

"So The Guy Diet was all a sham to cover your poaching him."

"God, it was so not that. It was real, and it had nothing to do with Jed. I didn't know then. I can't even wrap my brain around it now."

"Oh, I think on some level you knew."

That was true, too, but I didn't want to examine the thought further.

"I'm not hungry, and I don't want to be lectured to."

"I wasn't going to do that. I was going to tell you about Jed."

"You didn't really have to."

So nothing needed to be said. So odd. It was as if we both had some kind of sonar that picked up the clues.

I didn't know what else to say, or how to make it better for her and less fraught for me. I should have told her sooner.

"So happy we're friends again," Paula said sarcastically.

"Can we not be?"

Paula got up from her chair. "I don't know." Her voice was shaky with emotion. "I have to think about it now that I really know."

I heard the sound of her heels across the floor and going downstairs through a blinding wash of tears. I heard the distant hum of conversation. I thought, Jed was right, I should have listened to him. And I thought, I'll call and ask him to come have dinner. It'll be okay.

I didn't think it would ever be okay. This had been more hurtful than full disclosure a week or two ago would have been. Paula wouldn't have been so vulnerable. It would have been a swift strike and over.

So instead my ill-considered plan had made things worse; put her in a one-on-one setting, in a public place, where she couldn't do anything but walk out the door.

"Lo?"

That, inexplicably, was Jed's voice and Jed's body in this restaurant, standing inches away from me. I looked up to see that Paula was with him, and talking with another man.

A nice-looking man who was pulling out the chair for Paula, who sedately sat and sent me an inscrutable look across the table.

"This is Brian, a colleague of mine."

Brian acknowledged me, and Jed went on, "Glad we caught up with Paula downstairs. Do you mind if we join you?"

I swear I could barely see him through the haze of my tears. This wasn't T-shirt-and-jeans Jed. This was dressed-to-the-nines Jed, all authoritative and socially powerful. And taking back his hands-off stance in terms of Paula. Acting as if we were all old friends, and easing the way for comfortable conversation that never let up all through dinner.

That had to be from years of training in good manners. No one could walk into this situation and make lemonade out of it.

There was this glint in his eyes every time he looked at me. He knew. And I don't know how; I just understood that it didn't need to be said. He just knew.

And over and above that, Brian was a really nice guy, projecting that same air of confidence and self-awareness as Jed. There was something about him that reminded me of Jed. Maybe it was that they were cut from the same cloth. They'd had the same upbringing, background and the mandate to make sure that everyone else around them never felt uncomfortable.

It was an astonishing insight for me, watching the two of them operate like a well-oiled machine. There was nothing fake about it. This was how they were with a stranger or a best friend. I was certain of it.

But better than that, Brian seemed to like Paula, and she certainly responded to him. I didn't think there were any guarantees that anything would happen beyond this dinner. Though Brian wasn't Jed, he wasn't focused on another woman, either. And maybe if Paula gave it a chance, Brian might turn out to be the guy with whom she could envision that "something more."

In any event, it became a really nice dinner, literally stirred up from the ashes of a terrible moment between friends.

I laid it to the fact that there were no expectations and not a single hint indicating a slide toward the bedroom afterward. There was respect in the way both Jed and Brian handled the situation that was almost old-fashioned.

It was so refreshing—at least to me. I couldn't tell what Paula was thinking.

Did it matter? Something was broken between us, and I wasn't sure it could ever be repaired.

But to look at Paula's face, soft with an openness I hardly ever saw, and to watch her body language with Brian, I thought that maybe getting things out in the open had been worth it.

The evening sped by. The conversation never lagged. Jed ordered coffee, espresso, sambuca, a tray of *petites fours,* gelato.

There wasn't a shred of tension in the air when he signaled for the check and discreetly tucked it in his pocket.

Brian rose then, saying, "I'll see Paula home."

I felt Jed's hand on my arm and I looked into his warm gaze, and I stayed put until Brian and Paula were out of sight and down the steps.

"I thought you weren't going to do anything about Paula," I murmured, conscious of that look in his eyes.

Jed sighed. "I wasn't, but the thought of waiting for Paula to find a sex life wasn't too appealing, actually. I'd rather have one of my own."

"Speaking of that…"

"No, we're not speaking of that. We're not talking about any of this tonight."

"We are, too—we need to have the *when did you* conversation," I said.

"Do we have to? What else do you need to know?"

Good question. Because he was right. The sequence of events from the time I'd first met him to this moment encompassed everything I needed to know.

If I wanted to list it all, I could start with him putting up with the whole Guy Diet thing. And now I knew the considerate way he'd broken up with Paula. The fact he made certain his people were taken care of in the wake of a potentially disastrous-for-them business deal. The way he didn't let all my other nonsense deter him. How tonight he turned an untenable situation into something very positive. And the singular idea that, by his own admission, he'd waited.

For me.

He wasn't going anywhere.

That was important in a way that I didn't quite know why it was—yet. I knew he was watching me figure it all out as he sipped his espresso.

I threw up my hands. "Okay."

"Good." He put down his cup. "So I'll add this much to your list. You're funny, you're loyal, you're fearless, and you talk too much. Is that enough?"

"Yes." *No.* "But…"

"Enough." He got up and held out his hand. "Come on."

It was only after we left that I remembered him taking the check and that there hadn't been an Amex in sight before we exited.

"Jed…?" I know there was panic in my voice.

He read my mind. "It's taken care of."

"How? When?" I demanded. Oh, plebian me. In Jed's world, these things never needed to be spoken about. He'd likely arranged it before he and Brian had magically appeared at my side.

"Ah, the car is here."

You know what I was thinking. I'd forgotten about the car. The car was important. On top of everything I'd understood about him tonight. It was almost midnight and Cinderella was about to be left on her doorstep.

I instantly went into panic mode.

Give him up now.

I took a deep breath. "Maybe you should just take me home."

"And why should I do that?"

Good question. Because I was scared, because it was all too much, because there was something that I wasn't admitting and that scared me even more.

More than that, the realization hit me like a ton of bricks that he lived in a world beyond mine, and that whatever time we had together would be short-lived because his world would eventually require that he find the socially marriage-appropriate partner.

Who most assuredly wasn't me.

"Umm, it's been a really emotional evening with Paula and all."

"Don't give it another thought. She's over it by now."

I prickled up. "Really? Why? Because between you two frat guys, you decided he was going to seduce her and give her a diet of him for a couple of weeks to build up her self-esteem?"

Jed whistled. "Wow. You make us sound like Neanderthals."

"I just don't like what I'm thinking right now."

"I think you just want to pick a fight and I can't figure out why after such a pleasant dinner."

"So take me home," I said stubbornly.

"I don't think so."

See? He was putting up with my nonsense.

"Come on." He took my hand again as I got out of the car. Instead of heading up to his apartment to go at it like bunnies, we started walking toward Fifty-Ninth Street.

Central Park West was magical at night—the lights from the apartment buildings glowing, the streetlights glittering overhead, the evening balmy with a slight breeze, people out strolling, nodding to each other.

Something about a summer night that was as good as leisurely sex. There was no hurry, no tension, no time constraints, no need for superfluous words.

Maybe that was the point.

Because when he finally kissed me, on the corner of Central Park West Fifty-Ninth and Central Park South, where everyone could see, I didn't care about anything but him.

Maybe I needed to write a column about what I learned on my summer vacation. A walk on a summer's night is sexy. A kiss under a streetlight is as arousing as an hour of foreplay. That Jed is not a fly-by guy. That I don't know what I'll do when I have to let go.

Tonight I hung on. Tonight was a wild ride, wholly fueled by my high-flying emotions and my lust to subsume his essence into me. I stripped naked the moment we entered his apartment. I meant business; I wanted as much as I could have in whatever time there was left. I undressed him and took him to bed in a fever of lust.

Anything we'd ever done before didn't seem like enough. I wanted to invent new things to give him pleasure. Everything I thought of didn't seem enough. I wanted something far beyond anything he'd experienced before. Beyond me, beyond sex, over into forever.

And yet, all I had to do was burrow between his legs and suck at that narrow band of flesh under his scrotum to give him that beyond-forever pleasure. It was such a simple thing. I aimed to suck at it all night, but I felt his hands subtly directing me toward his penis, toward his mouth.

I didn't need his kisses tonight, I needed his penis, long, strong and penetrating. I wanted to feel him, hard, primitive, rocking my world.

I protected him and mounted without foreplay, arching my body to give him the deepest connection, the utmost fill. The thought of his penis so completely embedded between my legs nearly sent me into spasms. I wanted to sit on him like this for the rest of my life.

He cupped my breasts, he squeezed one nipple and I nearly had an orgasm. But I didn't want to come, not yet—I'd barely begun my ride, and I didn't want to move.

He wanted, he needed motion. His body beneath mine was restive, rippling with the need to thrust, and my desire to feel him driving me to climax overrode my lust to keep him rooted, hard and quiescent, between my legs.

My emotions felt raw, utterly primeval, propelled by a force outside myself as old as time. That was what it felt like to lose myself in his relentless possession of my body. I lost time, I lost thought, I lost myself to the insensate pleasure I pulled from his body.

This was not making love; this was pure animal mating, older than time. I drove him, I claimed him by the pure force of my violent hunger for his sex.

And when I could bear no more, he rolled me on my back, and just let me feel the heat and heft of the most indomitable part of him planted deep within me still lusting after my pleasure.

This time, he kissed me. This time, kisses that were slow and languid, rocking and rolling. This time, the full awareness of every inch of him was overpowering, turning my body molten, and sending hot rills of pleasure swirling through my veins to explode between my legs.

How could there be more than this? And then that encompassing feeling afterward—how could I even describe it?

And yet I lay still, so wide-awake, wondering when and where it would ultimately end.

"So," Jed whispered, sometime deep in the night when he sensed I was still awake and trying hard not to rouse him, "here's the one and only *when did you* part. Don't say a word. The only reason I feel comfortable telling you this is that we're in the dark, and it's a secret. It was that evening you came to have dinner with Paula and me. That moment when you paused in the doorway, all tall and windblown, stamping off the cold, and wearing that long camel-hair coat, those jeans and boots and that turtleneck sweater. You were so fresh, so full of life and energy, so beautiful, and in that moment, I saw…" He paused, as if he were seeing it all again. "I saw myself with you."

I let that sink in. That evening. If I closed my eyes, I could see it. The three of us in that crowded restaurant talking about harried lives and fast, cheap food.

"And my *when did you*," I countered, "was before that lunch when you told me you'd sold the paper. I was watching you from inside the building and it struck me suddenly that I was seeing someone who was wholly different than the guy I'd known only through Paula's eyes."

"Definite epiphany," Jed murmured. "It changed everything, obviously. Diets, attitudes, everything."

"Actually, it did."

"Well, *now* I can see that."

And everything would change again, I thought, but that was okay. I had tonight, and however many more tonights there might be with Jed's magic hands coaxing me to arousal, to climax. It didn't take much; all he had to do was play with my nipples and I was gone.… He could take me anywhere the whole night long— and again, tonight, he did.

I WENT BACK to my real life, where a paycheck was paramount, my roommate hated me and impossible deadlines loomed.

How could I concentrate when sex occupied my thinking all day long now. When you have it, you can't get enough of it. There really was a good reason for a Guy Diet—at least you could focus on the important stuff.

Though, what was more important than sex? And Jed?

Maybe Paula and me on speaking terms?

I tiptoed into our apartment that night but she'd beat me home, and she actually was in the kitchen puttering around.

She held up a forkful of spaghetti. "Does that look done?"

"Taste it."

"Ewww. With no sauce?" She sipped a strand. "It tastes wet. Slimy. Firm."

"Good. Drain it. Please don't tell me it's jar sauce."

"It's jar sauce because I didn't know if you were coming back here tonight."

"I didn't know if you were," I countered.

"I took a day off to think about it—Brian, I mean…about everything."

"Was it good for you?"

"He's a nice guy." She poured a whole jar of sauce into a saucepan and set it to heat. "That was nice of Jed."

"I thought so."

"He did that for you, you know."

"What?"

"Brian—he did that for you."

Oh, oh, oh…I felt her words reverberate. I thought about my all-encompassing list of what didn't need to be said. He did it for me.

"He did that for you," I said carefully.

"No, you don't understand. He didn't know if Brian and I would click. He just wanted to make it better…for you."

Omigod. Don't examine that too closely. Distract her.

"But did you like him?"

"Brian? I liked him. I liked that there was no pressure, that he was easy to talk to, that he was a gentleman, that he called today. Yes, I liked him. Yes, I'm going out with him again. And yes, I'll have sex with him if he asks."

"Good."

"What are you going to do?"

I am not going to let myself fall in love.

I didn't say that. I was halfway there already. Because *he did that for me.* All of it. Even deliberately giving me the chance to write the grab-and-go column.

Got-my-back guy. That was what it boiled down to. Maybe not love-me-forever guy, but—oh my God. *Jed* was my longed-for got-my-back guy. And he never gave up. And I never saw it coming.

It shook me up. Made me think about things that were impossible to dream about.

Or talk about. So I said, "I don't know what I'll do. I guess, just enjoy it while I can."

"What do you mean, while you can? You think this is going to be over and out by tomorrow?"

Damn. I really didn't want to ruminate on the reasons why I didn't think it could last. "Don't you? I'm not exactly in his stratosphere."

"No. But you make those rockets go off. Don't discount the power of phytochemicals."

"I think it's so funny you're giving me advice about Jed. You're more qualified to navigate his world than I am."

Paula gave me a long look as she served the spaghetti and sauce. "Something spooked you."

"It's all too much. Knowing he has that kind of money, connections and the on-call car and driver? Isn't that enough?"

"That's for your conscience to decide."

"My conscience wants to know if we're friends again," I said.

"If you eat my spaghetti."

I sighed. "Okay, but that's a stiff price to pay."

DOESN'T THE GUY DIET seem like it was forever ago? I was on it for about five, nearly six weeks.

I was out biking that next very, very hot afternoon. Jed had gone out of town for a couple days on business, and I felt at loose ends and as if nothing had been resolved except my epiphany.

I'd gotten what I wanted. The guy who had my back, with whom I had supersonic sex, whom I couldn't tell I wanted to be with him forever.

You can't have everything. I kept trying to convince myself that was enough. Exercise helped. You could look around at all the other potential guys who might be available eventually. You could hope and dream. Still, the thing I discovered was you can't help wanting the one you love to want to love you forever.

You just can't turn off that Niagara Falls of yearning.

Let me update you.

I'm almost finished with my proposal for my grab-and-go cookbook.

The management now running the *WestEnder* is happy with the column and a nice chunky regular paycheck now comes in the mail.

Jed turned his profit on the paper into another venture, with Brian as his partner. That was why he was out of town this week.

And Brian is dating (read sleeping with) Paula. So Jed is a genius matchmaker, as well.

As I was riding my bike, I saw swarms of guys looking for someone to love them for a night, maybe two, depending on how hot your friends think your partner is.

I headed toward the boat basin where at least I could get a bottle of water at the end of the ride. I was looking really trim and thin with all the exercise I've been getting, and all the sex has just enhanced my natural glow. Not that I've had any this week, but— I'm just saying.

Everything actually was wonderful.

Except—I was in love with Jed. The worst kind of love—the forever kind, with no reservations, no nitpicking, no warrantees—the still-be-with-him-when-I'm-old kind of love, and I can never tell him.

It was really awful. And wonderful.

So I needed this strenuous exercise, otherwise I'd be mooning around the apartment devising all kinds of sad strategies to finally let go. Like, after he came back from this trip.

Exercise was definitely good for clarity, so you can come to those important life-changing decisions that will make you miserable for the rest of your life.

There was a café at the boat basin with a great view of the Hudson River. It is also a hive of predatory singles. But for me, it was just a place to take a breath and grab a drink.

And not think about tomorrows.

So I hopped off the bike and wheeled it over to the café.

And there was Jed, in jeans and T-shirt, a bike at his side, sipping lemonade, right in my line of sight.

I stopped breathing.

He looked up and saw me and I started slowly toward him. This was not one of my best hair days. I had pulled it back into a shaggy ponytail, I wore no makeup, my oldest rattiest jeans, a T-shirt and sneakers. Not my best look. And not the girl-of-his-dreams look. Or the dream I wanted to be for him.

"Hey." That was about all I could think of to say.

"Nice views." He motioned to the chair next to him. That he had just gotten back home and was here, of all places, didn't even surprise me for some reason.

"How're you doing?"

"Getting exercise. Where did you come up with a bike?"

"Lo—I own a bike," he said reprovingly, handing me the cup so I could quench my thirst.

Of course. He wasn't above or beyond mortal pursuits. I didn't want to ask how he'd known I'd be here—maybe he was on his own bike ride for his own purposes.

I felt myself flushing. Or maybe that was the aftermath of the exercise. I needed that water. I didn't think I could swallow.

"Paula told me you probably came down this way."

He'd read my mind. "Now she's your ally?"

"*Our* ally. So, since I'm here, and you're here, and it's damned hot, and I wouldn't mind getting out of Manhattan, let's go for a ride."

At which point, Stecker magically appeared in the off-ramp roundabout, and in minutes we'd loaded the bikes into the trunk and were heading north in air-conditioned comfort.

"And how was the trip?" I asked, rooting around for something to say so I wouldn't say that one big forbidden thing.

"It was good," Jed said, as if that explained everything.

"And so…?"

"It was very good."

Maddening. Or maybe it was just too hot to talk business. Already we were passing the George Washington Bridge, toward the Cross County Parkway.

Jed kept looking at me. I kept looking at the road. I finally got that we were heading toward Rye Playland, an amusement park with its own beach and boardwalk, about forty-five minutes outside of Manhattan.

It wasn't all that crowded, since it was Friday. Stecker went off to park, and Jed paid the admission while I looked at a map of all the rides, and then we went on through the front gate.

Before us was the ice rink and miniature golf course. Beyond that, the boardwalk and beach. To our left, arcade games and concession stands, and against the sky, the towers of the water rides, and roller coasters.

Jed took my hand and we strolled toward the boardwalk, the view of the beach and the glimmering water of the Long Island Sound.

"I love amusement parks," Jed said. "Look."

I turned and looked. I could see the highest curve of the roller coaster, I could see the tower of a ride called the Double Shot and hear the shouts and screams of kids as they plunged down the tower after a breathtaking lift up. I could smell food, feel the hot sun, feel myself loosening up.

I felt really calm, suddenly. This could be the place and the way to end it.

"This is kind of how I picture my life," Jed said. "Kind of like…life is a land of play. You get choices about which ride to take, and you know beforehand that each one comes with its own excitement, lulls, highs, lows, up, downs and the occasional crap shoot. That's how *I* see it anyway…"

He took my hand and we stepped onto the beach. I looked at the water, which seemed to merge with the horizon—endless, limitless.

I knew he was looking at me with that familiar intensity. And then he said, "Do you remember when we briefly mentioned the whole *when did you* thing?"

I remembered.

"I have a confession to make."

I swallowed hard. Maybe he'd make this easy for me. "Okay…"

"I didn't quite tell you the whole *when did you* truth."

Oh God. I braced myself.

"The part when I said what I saw when you entered the restaurant that night? Okay, this is the confession part. What I really saw." He paused, one of those long torturous pauses where he gave me a deep, knowing look.

And he said, "I really saw SUVs and puppies."

"What?"

"And just before, when you were rolling your bike into the café? Family summers in Maine. Do you sail?"

I thought I would faint. "I don't…"

"Sure you do. Or you'll learn." He was so confident. "So this is what I want to say—come play with me, Lo. The ups and downs and highs and lows have to come with puppies and SUVs and stuff like that…because that's what I saw the first time I saw you, and that was what I wanted right there and then—with you. And that's what you want, too."

This time, for real, nothing more needed to be said.

And then he kissed me. Like, really kissed me, and who cared who was watching. It was a glorious orchestra-playing, movie-ending kind of kiss, on the beach, with the sun shining, a faint little breeze waffling off the sound, a catcall or two in the background, applause.

The kind of kiss where all questions were answered and everything was known, acknowledged and complete. It was perfect.

"There definitely has to be more kissing," he whispered against my lips.

Definitely.

So I guess you could say The Guy Diet worked. I got my guy and I know he's got my back. And my front. Forever.

If you want to know what I did for what was left of the summer—need you ask? I fell even more in love with Jed.

* * * * *

LIGHT MY FIRE

Debbi Rawlins

This is for Kathryn and Brenda.
Their patience, kindness and understanding
mean so much to me.

1

MOST PEOPLE looked forward to their vacation. Not Jordan Samms. The advertising business didn't sit still just because she took a week off. But her boss insisted that she needed the break, and the truth was, maybe he was right, because her most precious commodity, her creativity, was on the wane. Which terrified her.

"Hey, Jordan, you have a call on line one," Lisa said as she passed the break room.

"Got it." Jordan finished doctoring her coffee and hurried with it back to her office. She'd been waiting all day for a call from one of her New York clients. With the three-hour time difference between the east coast and L.A., she'd begun to think they wouldn't connect today.

Since her University of Southern California coaster was buried under an avalanche of paperwork, she set the mug down on a stack of discarded illustrations in the middle of her desk, and pushed the button for line one. "Jordan Samms."

"Hey, Jordan. It's just me." It was Sonya.

Jordan's gaze went to the oversize calendar on the far wall. Of course it was her soon-to-be-ex friend, two days before they were supposed to go on vacation. What a surprise. "Please do not say what I think you're going to say."

"Don't be mad."

"Damn it, Sonya." Jordan yanked her chair away from the desk and sat down.

"It's not like I planned on meeting anyone."

"This is so unfair."

"Come on, Jordan, at least we haven't prepaid for anything."

She shook her head. The woman really didn't get it. This was the third year in a row that she'd backed out of their vacation plans at the last minute. Always because of a new guy. "The reason we haven't prepaid for anything this year is because I knew you'd pull this stunt again."

"Exactly. So you shouldn't be upset."

Jordan closed her eyes and shook her head. Her friend's logic astounded. "Fine. Go. Do whatever."

"You're upset."

"Damn right. I've got to go."

"Wait, Jordan—"

"I'll see you in a week." Jordan hung up the phone before she said something she'd regret. This situation was as much her fault as it was Sonya's. Every year she expected Sonya to grow up. Keep her word. Every year Jordan ended up disappointed. She knew better than to set herself up like that.

She looked at the popular Breezy detergent slogan sketched out on the board on the red wall opposite her desk. That stroke of genius had earned her this corner office and a hefty salary. Unfortunately, that was nearly two years ago and the pressure was on to perform another miracle.

She abruptly turned away. Thinking about that right now was professional suicide. Panic had already set in. The well was dry, but the deadline wouldn't go away. Maybe Sonya's call was fate. Just the excuse Jordan needed to postpone her vacation. Surely, Patrick would understand that in this particular instance it was more important for her to finish the ad campaign.

It was nearly two. Her boss would be back from lunch. She got to her feet, knowing a face-to-face with him was much better than a phone call. He'd give her a hard time at first. No matter how busy he was, the man always made time for lunch and vacations, and he expected his employees to do the same. But since these were extenuating circumstances…

"Got a minute?" she asked, poking her head into his office. His door was always open, giving everyone in the company total access any time. She liked that about him.

"Sure," he said, looking up with a smile in his pale-blue eyes and laying down his pen. "What can I help you with, Jordan?"

She entered his massive office and plopped down on one of two chrome-and-leather guest chairs facing him. The guy had owned the company for nearly forty years and had made billions in advertising, and he had a reported personal net worth of over fifty million, but he'd never once acted as if he thought he was better than the pair of janitors that cleaned the suite of offices each evening. He'd even made the time to take Jordan under his wing and teach her the ropes. In the five years she'd worked for him, Patrick had been more like a father to her than her own had been.

"I have a problem," she said, and then added brightly, "Or maybe it's one of those blessings in disguise."

The corners of his mouth quirked as if he knew what she was going to say. Which was impossible. But he did have this annoying way of reading her. "You know my vacation starts in two days…"

"Yes," he said evenly, his gaze fixed on her in such a way that she knew right then he wasn't going to give an inch.

She sighed. "My friend cancelled again."

"That's too bad. You need to find someone more reliable with whom to make plans."

"Yeah. Think I would've figured that out by now, huh?" she said, and noted the slightly patronizing glint in his eyes. "The thing is, though, I could really use an extra week on this campaign, so—"

Patrick shook his gray head. "I'm surprised you'd even ask."

"I don't want to cancel my vacation. Just postpone it."

"You know what my answer is, so why bother?" Patrick's smile didn't erase the concern in his eyes. "You're tired, Jordan. You've been working too many hours." He put up a hand when she opened her mouth to protest. "Apart from the obvious health ramifications, your work is bound to suffer."

Jordan looked away so he couldn't see the fear in her eyes. Was it too late? Had her creativity dried up to the point of no return? Even worse—her greatest fear of all—had the whole thing been a fluke? Coincidence? An odd stroke of sheer luck? No brilliance involved?

Uneasy, she cleared her throat and got to her feet. "I'll figure out something."

"Which, I trust, will not mean staying home and working from there."

She hesitated, the thought having occurred to her. "I can always go to the beach."

"What had you and your friend originally planned?"

"After having gone on two cruises by myself I kind of left it open."

"Ever considered an action vacation?"

"You mean, like being outdoors with snakes and mosquitoes?"

He smiled. "Step outside of the box, Jordan. It might do you some good."

Her heart lurched. Did he mean professionally? Did he know she was drowning? Spending half her nights panicked that she would never have another original idea again? "I'll look into it."

He picked up his pen again. "You should be able to find something on the Internet, if not, I'll give you the name of my travel agent."

Jordan forced an appreciative smile. Action vacation her foot.

SHE SIGHED at the computer screen. Skydiving was out of the question. She'd only accepted her forty-second-floor office with a view because it was a matter of prestige. The perfect trophy to show she ran with the big dogs. But she never got close to the window, and God forbid she actually look out unless she was at her spiffy blue-tinted glass-topped desk a solid fifteen feet away. She hated heights. Which definitely left out rock-climbing, too.

Moving the cursor to the next listing, she considered exploring the beginners' white-water-rafting trip. At least that meant she'd be sitting, albeit in a canoe thingy. How strenuous could that be? Plus, the guide wouldn't let her drown. Bad for business.

She checked the dates. No availability until the end of August, two months too late. She skimmed through a variety of other offerings, finding the barefoot windjammer cruise the most appealing. But that was totally booked, too.

Well, she could lie. Stay home and work on the campaign, and invent some fabulous vacation touring the Amazon or something like that. She could probably even lift pictures off the Internet to show around the office.

Nah, Patrick knew her too well. He'd get it right away that she was lying. Plus she was horribly bad at it. She leaned back in her chair and stared at the computer screen. Maybe she should try Patrick's travel agent. With such short notice, if they were unable to find an excursion for her, maybe then Patrick would give in.

The thought lifted her spirits, and logging off, she started to get up. Patrick walked into her office.

"Ever been camping?" he asked.

Her gaze went to the piece of personal stationery in his hand. "Once. A zillion years ago, when I was a Girl Scout."

"Good." He handed her the paper. "This will be perfect for you."

Two boldly printed words immediately got her attention, and made the hair on the back of her neck stand. "Extreme camping?"

"Don't worry. You'll have a personal guide. And, just so you know, you can go for one week. Which doesn't mean you get to skip the second week, but if you do this, you can make up week two at another time."

Jordan opened her mouth to jump on the deal, then thought about it. "Define *extreme*."

Patrick smiled. "Sounds worse than it is."

Easy for him. Even in his midsixties, he was fit and trim from playing tennis and golf and occasional rowing. Other than bicycling twice a week, several daily trips to the refrigerator was the extent of her exercise routine.

"Actually, I was thinking about a windjammer cruise."

His eyebrows rose. "Aren't those booked up to a year in advance?"

"I was hoping for a cancellation."

He gave her a long measuring look, and then took the paper from her. "You're right. You probably couldn't handle this, anyway."

"I didn't say that."

"It's all right, Jordan. I'll give this to Tom in the mailroom. His vacation is coming up and I think he'd be interested."

"Tom?" The little twerp who'd hit on her his first week on the job? Definitely not the outdoors type.

"Yes, he's quite the athlete. Ran four marathons in the last two years, and I believe competed in one triathlon."

"You're kidding!"

Patrick shook his head, and then started to go.

"Wait." She held out her hand. If Tom could do this camping thing, she sure as hell could manage a week without a microwave and blow-dryer. Besides, Patrick said it was guided.

"Good for you, Jordan," Patrick said, returning the paper to her, a spark of triumph in his eyes.

"Right." She wasn't stupid. She knew she'd been hoodwinked. Patrick knew she was too competitive to ignore the challenge. But so what? How much choice did she have?

She stared at the writing on the piece of paper. One week, just her, the great outdoors and a seasoned guide. Maybe this was just what she needed to start the creative juices flowing again. How bad could it be?

2

Zach Wilde normally didn't meet the clients at the airport himself, but it was an unusually busy season and the company was down two employees this month. That put pressure on everyone, from the woman who took reservations to the shuttle driver who made the airport runs.

Since he had only one pick-up, he took one of the small Jeeps, parked it in the lot and then jogged to the terminal. He got to baggage claim just as a stream of passengers arrived at the turntable. One woman wearing jeans and a designer polo shirt stood out in particular, although why he couldn't say. Maybe because at first glance she reminded him of Sandra Bullock. Average height, maybe five-five, with nondescript straight shoulder-length brown hair, dark eyes from what he could see.

Or maybe what had gotten his attention was the confident way she seemed to lead the pack. Going straight for the moving bags and plucking a medium-size black, leather duffel-style one out from the jumble of plaids and canvas. She seemed to be traveling alone, which meant she could be Jordan Samms. Oddly, he hoped so.

He wore a white T-shirt bearing The Great Beyond logo on the breast pocket, so as soon as he approached her she lit with recognition, and made no bones about sizing him up.

"I think you're here for me," she said, and transferred her bag from her right to her left hand. "I'm Jordan Samms."

He nodded. "Zach Wilde."

"Wilde?" She grinned as she accepted the hand he offered. "Appropriate." And then she frowned. "Are you my guide or just picking me up?"

"Your guide. Any more bags?"

"This is it."

That left him pleasantly surprised. People tended to bring

double that amount of luggage and then he had to be the bad guy and remind them they could only take what they could carry on their backs.

"Good." He took the bag from her and she didn't protest. "The Jeep isn't parked too far away. Is this your first time extreme camping?"

She fell into step beside him. "Does it show?"

He smiled. "Hope you brought lots of sunscreen."

She grimaced at her milky-white arms. "I don't have much time to dawdle out in the sun." She transferred her gaze quizzically to him. "The ad said seasoned guide."

"And you expected Grizzly Adams?"

"Well, yeah."

"Sorry to disappoint."

"Oh, far from it."

He slid her a sidelong glance, but she didn't look back. Just smiled. A sly, sexy smile that got to him in a way it shouldn't. This one was trouble. Maybe he should find a female guide for her. No, everyone else was booked. That was one of the reasons he'd agreed to take this on himself. The other was that the travel agency that gave them most of their bookings had called in a favor for an important client. He didn't think it was Jordan, personally, although she gave the air of someone in power.

He stowed her bag in the back of the Jeep, and then they both got in. As light as her luggage was, she was going to have to downsize the contents by a third. He'd break the news when they got to base camp.

"Is this your first time here?" he asked as they left the parking lot.

"Yep. Never been to Idaho before."

"Beautiful country."

She nodded absently as she dug into her brown expensive-looking leather purse. A second later she produced a cell phone. "Excuse me, I have to check in with my office."

"Sure." Zach just smiled. That was probably the last time she'd be using that phone for a week. She wouldn't be happy about that, but tough. He knew her type. Too well. He'd been there once. A mere four years ago. Working so many hours that one day spilled into the next. No more. Not him.

"I'm not getting a signal," she said, frowning at her phone. "That's not possible."

"You will in about three minutes."

She kept trying, groaning in frustration.

Fine. He'd told her it would be another three minutes. Let her make herself nuts. Him, he was enjoying the scenery even though he'd seen the acres of fir trees thousands of times. He'd paid for most of college spending summers renting out kayaks and guiding rafting trips three miles from here. Still, he never got tired of it.

She finally gave up and looked around. "That wasn't much of an airport."

"No, but it serves its purpose."

She fidgeted for a minute, and then glanced at her watch. "We leave first thing in the morning, I assume."

"We still have six hours of daylight."

"We're leaving today?"

"Why not?"

"No last meal, or anything?"

Zach laughed. "I take it this was not your idea."

She went back to feverishly looking for a signal. "This isn't good. If I'm having trouble here, what happens once we're on the trail? Oh, here we go. Thank God."

A trail? Ms. Samms was in for a big surprise. Zach kept driving, trying not to listen to her conversation and seriously thinking about asking Rachel to switch clients with him. The problem was that her couple was a repeat and had specifically asked for her as a guide.

"Damn it. I got cut off."

"Jordan, why don't you try to relax?"

She looked at him as if he'd cursed at her. "You don't understand. I can't be out of contact."

"Then you have a decision to make," he said, pulling over to the side of the road. "Either you give up your cell phone, or I take you right back to the airport."

JORDAN STARED into his vivid blue eyes. "You can't be serious."

"I am."

"I'm paying for this thing. You can't tell me what to do." She didn't care if he was just about the most gorgeous man she'd met in forever.

"I'll give you a full refund, which is against policy, by the way."

"Just because I won't give up my cell phone?" Now, she was angry. Who the hell did this guy think he was?

"Ms. Samms, we'll be rafting for thirty-two miles, then we'll hike through a canyon into the mountains and not return for a week. How much reception do you think you'll get?"

"I figured that much," she said, avoiding his pointed glance. Actually, she hadn't thought that through. This wasn't good. She needed to check in at least once a day.

"So the problem is what exactly?"

She hesitated. "Telling me I have to give up my cell phone is not the same thing."

"You're right. I made my point badly, but if you're going to be miserable and worrying about what's happening at the office the entire week, this isn't the right vacation for you."

Jordan looked away. She couldn't even use the lack of phone service as an excuse to cancel. Knowing Patrick, isolating her was exactly what he wanted. "Okay, I get it. No phone."

"We're good then?"

"We're good."

He pulled back onto the highway, and she slid a look at the way his thigh muscles bunched when he worked the clutch. His skin was a healthy golden bronze she envied, and his light-brown hair was streaked from the sun. Damn him, but he had a perfect nose. If she could pick one out of a catalog, that would be it. He had to be the poster boy for the company. If The Great Beyond were one of her clients, she'd use Zach for the advertisements in a heartbeat.

"I might as well tell you, too, that you won't be able to take everything in your bag."

"I purposely packed light."

"I'll admit you did an admirable job, but remember, you have to carry your own pack."

"Oh."

"In addition to a couple of items of clothing, you'll want sunscreen, of course, and bug repellant and small personal hygiene products."

"Who carries the food? You?"

He laughed, and she didn't like the sound of it. "We'll eat whatever we catch or find."

"You're kidding, right?"

He cocked a brow at her before returning his gaze to the road. "Did you read the Web site at all?"

She cleared her throat. "Actually, no. Not all of it."

Zach smiled. "You'll enjoy it, Jordan. There's no feeling like it on earth."

"What?"

"Being one with nature. Relying on yourself to survive. Knowing you can overcome any obstacle set before you."

"Oh, I don't know. Sitting on a beach, sipping a cocktail at sunset ain't too shabby." She sighed. That's exactly what she should've done. Booked a suite in San Diego. Get a little sand between her toes. Soak up some sun. Overindulge in piña coladas, and maybe find a willing partner for a couple of nights.

"Having second thoughts?"

"Actually, I'm on about my fourth thoughts."

He looked over at her. "It's not too late to turn around."

"Trying to get rid of me?"

"Nope. Actually, I'd hate to see you wimp out."

Jordan glared. "Save the psychology for someone who'll buy that crap."

He chuckled. "Okay, I'd just hate to see you miss out."

"Why? You don't even know me."

"True." He started to say something else but apparently reconsidered. Instead, he said, "We're here." And then steered the Jeep down a dirt road in the middle of a forest of conifers.

"How can you tell?"

He ignored her sarcasm. "You'll have one last time to use a real bathroom, make a phone call and I've reserved a locker for you to store the things you won't be taking."

She saw a clearing and then they came to a couple of buildings. Two large vans were parked off to the side, as were several more small Jeeps like the one they were in. Beyond that was a river with kayaks lined up along the side.

"So this is it, huh?"

"This is base camp, yes."

She couldn't help but laugh. "With all the amenities of home."

Zach opened his door. "One night sleeping out under the stars and you won't even think about home."

"Wanna bet?"

He smiled. "Let's go get you checked in."

"Never mind the stars," she muttered as she got out of the Jeep. "Sleeping in a tent is roughing it enough for me."

"Well, that's going to be a problem." He hefted her bag out of the back. "We're not taking a tent."

3

ZACH SMILED as he carried her bag toward the office to get her checked in. A step behind, nose wrinkled, she hadn't commented over the lack of a tent. Probably too busy wondering if she should turn tail and run. Naturally, he wouldn't talk her out of it if that's what she wanted, but he would be oddly disappointed.

She had a certain spark that appealed to him. And although it seemed clear this vacation wasn't her idea, at least she wasn't a whiner. He looked over at her. "Who twisted your arm to come?"

She gave him a lopsided smile. "My boss."

"Ah. What would you say your fitness level is?"

Her eyebrows rose indignantly.

"We ask everyone. In fact, you'll be given a waiver to sign."

"So that if I keel over halfway through the week, you won't be held responsible?"

He smiled. "Something like that." They got to the office and he opened the door for her. "You look like you're in pretty good shape. We don't have a problem, right?"

"Good enough to keep one foot in front of the other. Rock-climbing? No."

"Fortunately, that's not on the schedule."

Jordan entered the small, cramped office, turning to meet his gaze. "A schedule? Good. I'd like to see it."

He'd walked in behind her. Sally, one of their most tenured employees, was manning the desk and she looked up, trying to hide a smile. "That was a figure of speech," Zach said, shaking his head. "Here you go, Sal. Got one fresh off the boat."

"Funny." Jordan gave him a dry look, and then turned to Sally. "You look like the person in charge. Please explain why there is no tent involved in this trip."

Zach put down the bag near the door where he waited. This was going to be an interesting week. He didn't say anything, just let no-nonsense Sally handle Jordan while he got a good look at the way the light-blue denim stretched across her backside. Nice and round. Good to hold on to.

He forced his gaze away, surprised at himself. Not just because she was a client, as good a reason as that was to stay clear of her, but because he'd had little interest in women since his divorce.

"If you weren't going to be out for a week," Sally was saying, "then you'd have more room and weight allowance to pack a tent." She passed Jordan the standard agreement and waiver forms. "As it is, you'll be carrying a forty-pound pack with your clothes and sleeping bag and personal items. You'll need to read and sign these forms, and of course, if you have any questions…"

"He carries the food?" Jordan asked with a nod in his direction, otherwise barely acknowledging his existence.

Sally's amused green eyes briefly darted to Zach. "I'm going to let you two figure that out. How about a bottle of water?"

Jordan murmured a thanks and skimmed the forms, frowning occasionally. She signed each of them with an illegible signature and then pushed them toward Sally and picked up the bottle of water Sally had set down.

Between the desk, two chairs, a filing cabinet and a small refrigerator, the office was crowded. The staff took turns checking people in. None of them were the type who wanted to be cooped up indoors. Sally normally handled the kayak maintenance and scheduling, and hadn't guided since she'd had her second child last fall but for a moment Zach thought about asking her to take Jordan for the week.

With a weathered hand, Sally pushed the short, choppy blond hair away from her tired face. "Zach, would you like me to show Jordan to her locker?"

"I've got it." He picked up her bag. "See you in a week."

"Good luck." Sally grinned. "Both of you."

Jordan sighed loudly. "Why do I feel like a lamb being led to slaughter?"

SHE WAS definitely out of her league. Nodding congenially to two passing athletic-looking blond Amazons wearing really cool hiking boots, Jordan switched the bag from her right to her left hand, swearing it hadn't been this heavy after she'd packed it last night. It was all her fault for allowing Patrick to bully her into taking this vacation. She didn't deny her part. He'd brought up the supposed prowess of wussy Tom in the mailroom, and she'd taken the bait—hook, line and sinker. And now she was thinking in really bad puns.

Vacations were supposed to be fun, not torturous. Especially when you paid a small fortune for the pleasure. What a racket this extreme business was. Marketing genius, really. Tack the trendy word on and hike up the price of the package. Wished she'd had thought of it.

The locker key Sally had given her making a painful imprint in her palm, Jordan took an extra step to keep up with Zach. Yeah, he had great buns and normally she'd be enjoying the view, but right now all she wanted was to dump her bag. She knew full well why he'd let her carry it and why the locker room was clear across the parking lot. Made a person think twice about how much they wanted to lug on their back for the next week.

"Here we go." Zach opened the door to a huge room, the walls lined with lockers, and then took the bag from her and swung it up onto a large table set up in the middle of the room. "Sort the things you're taking, and I'll go get your pack."

"Yes, sir."

A faint smile lifted his lips, and then he headed toward the back of the room and disappeared through a door. But not before Jordan got her fill of his sculpted thigh muscles. The man was a god. He had to be in his midthirties but he'd compare favorably to the fittest twenty-year-old. She sighed and unzipped her bag. Her, not so much. Too fond of potato chips. Movie popcorn was nothing without butter.

Peering into her bag, she groaned. Here she thought she'd done pretty well minimizing, but she could see that she needed to be more ruthless. Obviously all the makeup would stay behind. But not the mascara. That would be insane. She set aside an oversize bath towel that she would take and then considered the three pairs of jeans and running shorts.

"No shorts," Zach said, making her jump because she hadn't heard him approach. "You'll get too scratched up where we're going."

"Yeah, but jeans are heavy. Besides, you're wearing shorts."

"Just today and tomorrow while we're kayaking. I'd suggest you do the same and then take two pairs of jeans with you."

"For a week?"

"We'll have a wash day."

"Some vacation," she muttered, and stuffed all but one pair of shorts and two pairs of jeans back into her bag. That's when she spotted the two emergency candy bars she'd tucked in the bag's side pocket. She quickly pushed the shorts back to conceal the treats. She didn't know why. None of his business if she wanted to take them, but nevertheless…

"Let's see the boots you brought."

She eyed the pack and sleeping bag he laid on the table before pulling out the boots.

"Good choice," he said, nodding. "Lightweight and waterproof."

She didn't deserve any credit. The woman who'd taken her reservation and credit card number had been quite specific. "Is that sleeping bag going to be enough?"

"Trust me." He smiled, totally disarming her.

For the next week, she didn't have a choice but to trust this man. Twenty-four-seven. Geez, it was going to be a long week. Her gaze briefly strayed to his muscular legs, before she turned back to sorting her things. When it was all over, she had her hidden candy stash, two changes of clothes, a T-shirt to sleep in, big wooly socks, a towel, basic toiletries—including toilet paper, which she didn't dare think too much about—and some first-aid stuff and water-purification tablets Zach gave her, along with her sleeping bag, stuffed into her pack.

She traded the tennis shoes she'd worn on the plane for the hiking boots, pulled her hair back into a short ponytail and stuck a red ball cap on her head. Everything else that she'd brought, she jammed into a locker.

Too late, she realized she'd forgotten to change into the shorts and T-shirt she'd left out. Zach had disappeared into the back for a few minutes, and she quickly peeled down her jeans, the denim getting stuck on her boots for a few seconds before she kicked off the jeans. The running shorts were stretchy and not as tricky and she pulled them over her pink bikini panties pretty quickly. Changing from the expensive polo shirt to an oversize T-shirt she'd picked up in Acapulco last year took another couple of seconds.

Behind her, Zach cleared his throat.

"No use worrying about modesty," she said, as she bent to scoop up the jeans, not quite as blasé as she tried to sound. "I'm sure you'll see more than you'll want in the next week."

She turned around in time to meet his eyes, and her heart skipped a beat.

His eyes had darkened to a midnight blue. Heat spread between her thighs and she really wished she weren't wearing Spandex.

"Right," he murmured and turned away to slip the pack he'd carried out with him onto his back. "One last bathroom stop and we're off."

"Wait a minute." She stared at his pack, the heat of a moment ago cooling significantly. His backpack wasn't much bigger than hers. "Is that all?"

"I don't follow."

"Where's our food, a stove, eating utensils…" At the growing amusement on his face, Jordan's voice trailed off. No matter what kind of waivers she'd signed, she was pretty sure starving her was against the law.

ZACH GRABBED her pack off the table and then steered her toward the ladies' room, while trying not to stare at her shapely legs. She looked great in jeans, but in shorts, well, damn, he couldn't think about that. He kept his gaze at shoulder level, and noted that with her hair up, the graceful curve of her neck was someplace else he shouldn't be concentrating on.

Better to think about that moment of recognition on her face when she realized he wasn't exactly packing an assortment of gourmet meals. The truth was, he did have a compact fold-up stove and some dehydrated pasta and veggies, some oatmeal, a few protein bars, packets of nuts and some jerky, but mostly they'd catch their own fish and the occasional rabbit.

He wanted to get a head start before the sun went down. "I promise you won't go hungry," he said finally, and pointed to the ladies'-room door. "Last chance. This is it for a week. Enjoy." He couldn't hold back a chuckle. Not with the dirty look she gave him.

She stopped to shove the jeans and polo shirt into her locker and then shuffled into the restroom. She took hardly any time inside, and then came out with a white-cream-slathered nose. After she'd tucked the tube of sunscreen into her pack, he helped her secure it to her back.

"Comfortable?" he asked.

"Peachy."

"Good." He led the way to the waiting tandem kayak and then stood back to see how she handled herself with the backpack.

She did a pretty good job of climbing into the front, long, lean muscles defining her calves as she awkwardly balanced herself into a sitting position. At least she hadn't landed on her backside or in the water. Not yet, anyway.

"Here." He threw her a life vest that had been tucked in the back of the kayak. "You'll need to wear this while we're on the water."

She glared at him. "So why do I have my backpack on?"

"Practice."

She muttered something he didn't quite catch, but he figured that was just as well. He got out his vest and followed suit.

Almost everyone had either left yesterday or this morning for their white-water rafting trips, which represented most of their business. Only Jeb, one of the newer guides, a first-year law student whose agility made Zach feel old, had just walked out of the office with his clients, a family of four. Zach acknowledged the group with a lift of his chin before pushing off and then getting in the kayak.

The Great Beyond hired a lot of college kids for the busy summer months. Most of them came back each season until they graduated, and then they disappeared among the sea of starched shirts and BMWs. Zach didn't have a problem with nice cars, in fact, he had a brand-new blue Beamer himself. Top of the line. Cost him a small fortune. It was all the rest of the stuff that he hated and avoided. The pressure and long hours and the insatiable craving to make each professional success greater than the last until you lost sight of everything that was important.

"Am I supposed to be paddling?" Jordan asked, and he realized how far his mind had wandered.

Stay in the present, he reminded himself. Getting ahead of himself had gotten him into enough trouble to last a lifetime.

4

FOUR HOURS LATER, Jordan's arms ached like crazy. The current wasn't horrible but she wasn't used to the upper-body activity, and she was tired from paddling, hungry and cranky. The only saving grace was the gorgeous scenery. Ponderosa pine and Douglas firs and a couple of kinds of trees she didn't recognize started a few feet off the shore and blanketed the mountains on either side of the river.

About halfway from base camp, a fire had destroyed several hundred acres, leaving blackened stumps and charred earth, but already the forest's resiliency was evident in the resurgence of tiny trees and clusters of orange and white wildflowers.

"Getting hungry yet?" Zach asked.

"Are you kidding? I'm way past hunger." She glanced over her shoulder at him, but only for a moment. She'd already met her paddling mishap quota for the day.

"Another hour and we'll set up camp."

"Great."

"Or we can go two more hours. Gotta make sure you get your money's worth."

"Uh, no. One hour and that's it."

Zach's throaty chuckle seemed to crawl up her spine and seep deep into her skin, almost as if he'd reached out and touched her. "Okay, I'll be gentle."

She briefly closed her eyes, glad he couldn't see her face. She didn't blush often, but heat stung her cheeks and it had nothing to do with the hot, toasty sun that she'd pretty much had enough of for the day. It was kind of curious that she'd been paired up with a man. Hard to believe that there had never been a past problem with a sexual harassment complaint.

Oh, damn it, he was probably gay. The sudden thought explained a lot. But then she remembered the look on his face when he'd caught her undressing. No, definitely not gay. He lightly touched her arm and she nearly jumped into the water.

He pointed, and she scanned the area of interest and saw a bighorn sheep. The animal appeared to be headed for the river, traveling nearly perpendicular to the mountain. With effortless grace it leaped down the rocky cliff area where no trees dared to grow.

They moved past the majestic animal, and after that, the rest of the hour went by agonizingly slowly, giving her too much time to think about the advertising campaign that awaited her back in L.A. As soon as the thought of the lagging new slogan crystallized, the familiar fear clawed at her throat. She had to come up with something brilliant and fast or her career was over. And then all the people who'd thought her early success was a fluke would either laugh or regard her with pity that she couldn't bear.

"You're quiet," Zach said after a while.

"Ah, just thinking about work."

"You should be checking out the scenery. You just missed a black bear and her cub."

"Where?" She jerked around, her heart thumping when the sudden movement of the paddle momentarily threw them off course.

"Too late. They were up on the ridge."

"Oh."

"Look, I'll give you another hour to unwind. And then no more thinking about work."

"That'll happen."

"It will. Trust me."

Jordan sighed. No use arguing. A guy like Zach didn't understand the pressures of the business world. His life and job obviously blurred. How could he even tell them apart? He didn't even have to commute, for goodness sake.

"Hey, after this week," she said, watching a fish flip out of the water in front of them. "After you've gotten me back in one piece," she added. "What do you do? Turn around and take out another customer?"

"Sometimes. Depends what's on the schedule. We all take turns maintaining the kayaks and the equipment, and manning the desk. And for the record, I haven't lost anyone yet."

"Good to know." The water started getting a little choppy, the rapids swifter than they had been for the last couple of hours and she had to concentrate on her paddling.

The good news was the next hour flew by, but by the time they beached the kayak, the tension in her shoulders caused the area between her shoulder blades to burn. Big-time. Made getting out of the kayak awkward, but she managed to help pull the boat safely onto the shore, wincing only a couple of times when the pain got too intense.

"You okay?" Zach asked, eyeing her with concern as he secured the kayak by tying a line to a tree.

"Fine."

His lingering look said he didn't believe her, but he didn't press the issue. He pulled off his life vest, waited for her to do the same and then stowed them both in the far end of the kayak, while she tried to stretch out the painful kinks in her upper back. He grabbed his pack, and then, bless him, scooped hers up before she had the strength and energy to get it herself.

"Don't get used to the service," he said, winking. "This is first-day courtesy."

Her pride and competitiveness almost got in the way. But screw it, she really was one sore puppy and she had another six days to prove herself. So she meekly followed him to a clearing at the edge of the woods where he dropped both packs.

"How does this look?" he asked.

"Hard and rocky."

"We'll get some tree branches to put under our sleeping bags. You'll sleep better than you do in your own bed."

"Never doubted that for a moment." How was she going to be able to move tomorrow? Not much didn't ache. "What's for dinner?"

He knelt beside his pack. "Again, since it's the first day I figured we wouldn't rough it too much."

"Thank you, Lord." She lifted her gaze heavenward. "Hey, look." A rainbow arched from one peak to the other, the red, blue and yellow vivid against the emerald-colored trees. She adored rainbows. The same way she'd adored her grandmother. After Gramms had passed away when Jordan was thirteen, she'd decided that every time she saw a rainbow, Gramms had sent it to her. "It hasn't rained."

Zach stared at the colorful display, an appreciative expression on his face. "Up there it has. That's why everything stays so green."

She decided he had a good profile. Strong, prominent chin with just the right amount of stubble. Thick lashes any woman would kill for. "As long as it doesn't rain down here."

"If it does, we build a shelter."

"Build? What about dinner?"

He chuckled. "I'm on it."

She toed her pack, moving it to the side, loathe to actually try and pick it up. Now that she wasn't clutching the double-bladed paddle she thought some of the pain between her shoulder blades would ease, but it hadn't much.

Watching Zach pull out a compact stove and set it up, she really wanted to offer to help. She did. But that would likely require moving and she didn't know if that was even possible at this point.

"How about filling this with water while I get a fire going?" He held out an aluminum bowl. Not that big. It couldn't hold more than a couple of quarts.

But aye… "Sure." She took it from him, and gingerly retraced her steps toward the river, doing a couple of neck stretches. Good thing she faced away from him because her contorted and undoubtedly hideous expressions would either scare the life out of him or send him into hysterics.

Squatting to dip the bowl into the ice-cold water was a whole other matter. Her thighs were in no better shape than her back after she'd sat in one position for over five hours. She grunted and groaned, softly so he couldn't hear, and that somehow seemed to help. Straightening again required deep, even breathing and a few mental curses.

"Everything okay?" he called as she labored back toward him.

"Terrific."

He'd not only started a campfire but had another flame lit under the stove.

"Don't tell me you rubbed two sticks together." She handed him the bowl which he placed on the stove and then added the purification tablets.

"Flint." He grinned, showing off his perfect, straight white teeth, and then nodded at the stove. "Sterno. When we run out I'll show you how to start from scratch."

"Oh, goody."

He dusted his hands together and then rose fluidly without even a single wince. "Let's figure out where we're going to bed down."

"I vote for the Ritz Carlton."

Amusement glittered in his blue eyes, making them impossibly more beautiful. "If you can find one, you're on."

"Don't underestimate me," she muttered and then followed him as he inspected the ground, occasionally kicking away a large rock.

"This isn't a bad spot," he said, using the side of his boot to push aside a dead branch and level the ground.

"If we were deer I'm sure it would be perfect."

"Are you going to make wisecracks all night?" he asked, with raised brows and a sidelong glance.

"No, I'm hoping to get some sleep."

He shook his head with mock disapproval, his gaze lingering on her. "From L.A., you said, right?"

"Born and raised. A true native. Why?"

"I bet you get mistaken for Sandra Bullock."

"Yeah, a few times. But I'm younger."

Zach laughed at her hasty qualification, and then he looked serious, his eyes meeting and holding hers. "At any age, that's a compliment."

Jordan felt the surprise warmth fill her cheeks and she quickly turned away. She hardly ever blushed, and now twice in one day. Frankly, she wasn't sure why she had now. Maybe because she hadn't expected that kind of comment from Zach. Not that he'd said anything too out there.

"So this is the spot, huh?" She focused on the ground, still unconvinced that a few branches under her sleeping bag were going to make a comfortable mattress.

"Feel free to choose another area, but I would suggest staying close. To me and the fire."

No problem there. She had no intention of getting too deep into the trees. Who knew what lay in wait? She kicked at the hard ground about six feet away from the opposite side of the campfire. This didn't seem so bad, after all. Especially since she was dead-tired.

Zach continued to clear his area, prying a few good-size rocks from the ground with his pocket knife until he had a smooth place to lay his sleeping bag. She on the other hand, sort of shuffled her feet until she'd kicked most of the large rocks and dead branches away. Anything more would've meant stooping down without any assurance that she could get back up again.

"Let's gather more wood and some branches while we wait for the water to boil," he said, springing to his feet, which really annoyed her.

Of course it wasn't his fault he was in so much better shape. That was part of his job. But jeez...

She trudged along behind him, tempted to tell him she needed to sit this one out, but pride kept her moving. Besides, she was getting stiff now and keeping mobile was probably in her best interest.

Nearly an hour later they had enough wood for the rest of the night, their sleeping bags were laid out and something that looked incredibly unappetizing simmered in the pot. She hadn't asked what it was. If it was too nasty there were always her emergency candy bars.

"Dinner will be ready in five," Zach said, peering into the pot. "You can go ahead and wash up if you want."

"Where?"

One side of his mouth slowly lifted. "Where?"

She glanced around. "I guess the river is it, huh?"

"Yep, and the temperature is going to start dropping so you might want to take that into consideration."

"Right." Jordan sighed. She already knew the water was cold. No help for her aching muscles. But she'd feel better once she was cleaned up.

Slowly, she hunkered down to her pack, the short journey a torturous one. She got out a towel and loofah and the shirt she planned on sleeping in. Briefly debated a sports bra, and then decided against it. Just one more thing she'd have to wash. She was quite certain she wouldn't be the first braless woman Zach had seen.

After grabbing a couple of other basics, she started to straighten. Pain shot across her shoulders and both thighs cramped. Her entire body seemed to freeze. She tried to move...oh, but the pain...

"Um, Zach, I think I'm gonna need your help."

5

ZACH LOOKED OVER AT Jordan, all hunched over, her face pale even with all the sun she'd gotten. Immediately he got to his feet and went to her. He knew what was happening and it was his fault. She'd done too much. Used too many muscles she didn't normally use. She'd said she was fine, and he'd let her push herself.

"Give me your hand," he said, and she did without objection. "Easy now. I won't pull. Just get up slowly."

"This is so embarrassing. Ouch." She gripped his hand and raised herself a fraction. "Damn it. Ouch."

"Take your time."

"Not that I have a choice," she said, grimacing as she got halfway to a standing position. "For the record…ouch!" She shot up the rest of the way.

"You okay?"

"I hurt." She released his hand and blew out some air. "Though not half as much as my pride."

"Never mind pride. I knew better than to let you go so hard. I'm sorry."

She frowned, curiosity lighting her brown eyes. Color returned to her face. Up close he could see a light smattering of freckles across her nose. "Why did you?"

"I admire your drive. You're competitive, which isn't a bad thing if you channel it correctly, and I wanted to see how hard you were willing to push. I figured you'd know your physical limitations."

A slow, knowing smile curved her lips. "Then it wouldn't be your fault, would it?" She rolled a shoulder, winced and added, "Admit it, you wanted to humble me. Break me before we got started so I wouldn't give you too much grief."

"Not consciously." He'd have to think about that one. "But I do know I don't want you useless for the week. Speaking of which, if you want dinner, we have some more preparations. You have five minutes to get cleaned up or you'll have to wait until after we eat."

Her mouth opened, indignation flashing in her eyes, and then without a word, she took her towel and toiletries and went back to the river.

He berated himself again as he watched her move so tentatively. At least he knew there was something he could do to help. It might not be enough, if the sound of her gasp was any indication of her pain. In his own defense, she sure looked as if she were in good shape. He should have known better than to trust that.

Five minutes later, she came back to the campsite. She dropped her things, then joined him by the fire. "Okay, what do you want me to do?" She peered into the pot, wrinkling her nose and then pushing the hair away from her face as she turned to look at him.

"Sit here." He indicated a small boulder he'd been using as a stool while he'd started their meal.

She hesitated. "Why?"

"Trust me."

"If you say that one more time—"

He gently took her by the shoulders and sat her down. She groaned a little but she'd see that the effort would be worth it. He got the tube of muscle unguent from where he'd left it, then, positioning himself behind her, he pulled the neckline of her shirt down so that he could slip his greased palms along the base of her neck.

"Are you doing what I think you're doing?" she asked, dropping her chin.

"Depends."

"I see your point. Ahhh." She tensed, and he eased off. "No, don't. Keep going. No pain, no gain."

He smiled at the goose bumps popping out on her smooth skin. He sure liked Jordan. No coyness. Plain speaking without being in your face. He liked the way she felt, too. Soft. Satiny soft. Probably from staying out of the sun, he thought wryly.

"What is that stuff? I can already feel the heat, and yet it doesn't smell like a locker room."

"Secret recipe, made by wood elves."

She chuckled. "So, is this just part of the service?" she asked, sounding a bit breathless. "Do all your clients get this treatment?"

"Just the special ones."

She laughed softly, her shoulders beginning to relax. "I bet you say that to all the girls."

"Is this helping?"

"Oh, baby."

Zach grinned. "We still have another ten miles by kayak tomorrow. I hope you're not out of commission."

"Jeez, go ahead and spoil it."

"What?"

"I did not need to hear about your ulterior motive. Men."

He wasn't totally sure he got that. But he wasn't going to ask. His gaze caught on an inch-long scar near her shoulder blade. He guessed from an old injury because it was faint. He worked his thumb along the blade as far as the shirt would allow. "What happened here?"

"Where?" Her head came up and she started to move away, but then relaxed. "Oh. That's from when I was ten. A roller-skating accident. I came by my competitive streak early on."

"A tomboy, huh?"

"Couldn't let my brother one-up me."

"How many of you are there?"

"Just the two of us. Mom and Dad are still together. Though I can't figure that one out. My dad spends more time at the office or on the road than he does at home." She angled her head to the right and he worked the cord up the left side of her neck.

He had to move a discreet half step back when she brought her head up again and rubbed his fly. "What about you? Spend much time at the office?"

"My boss said he's going to start charging me rent."

"Ah. Like father, like daughter."

"I'm not married. It's not the same." Obviously a sore subject, judging by her tone. But then she relaxed again and leaned back too close.

"I'm afraid the session is over." He ran his palm a final time over her right shoulder. "Or dinner will be mush."

Her contented sigh sparked a highly erotic image that had him abruptly moving away from her. His entire body reacted as warmth started in his chest and spread through his belly and down to his groin. He couldn't remember when he'd had such an adolescent reaction to a woman.

Not good. "I'll be right back," he said, and trotted down to the river and splashed his face with ice-cold water.

JORDAN SLID into her sleeping bag, found a comfortable position, and purposely turned away from Zach. He was only five tempting feet away, and with the fire going and the strong moonlight, she could see way too much of him. Which meant he could see her, as well. She wished now she'd put on that sports bra, but what the heck.

Their dinner of plumped-up dehydrated pasta and vegetables, accented with snippets of beef jerky wasn't the worst thing she'd ever tasted, but it was pretty close. Fortunately, she was too tired to care. Zach apologized, claiming he'd overcooked the pasta. No wonder. He'd disappeared into the river for a good ten minutes after warning her dinner was going to be ready in five.

Her only objection was that he should have spent the time on her massage. No. No. No. She couldn't go there. Couldn't think about the feel of his hands on her skin. She had no idea how much good he'd done for the pain but the distraction worked. His touch had been the only thing that mattered. And how much she craved his further exploration.

It was only natural. Alone out here. Two normal, healthy adults. With the right chemistry. What would anyone expect? He wasn't that good an actor. Any earlier doubt she had that he was interested was gone. In fact, that might've been the reason he'd disappeared into the river. The sudden thought cheered her immeasurably. The thing was, what to do about the attraction? Who would make the first move? Just her luck he had some weird idea that it would be unethical to get physically involved because she was a client.

She rolled back over so that she could see him. "Zach?"

"Yep."

"Are you asleep?"

He chuckled, low and husky, the sound slid over her like a caress.

"The moon is almost full."

"Yep."

"Pretty, huh?"

He murmured something unintelligible.

"Do you know what time it is?"

He shifted and brought his wristwatch up. "Nine-twenty."

"Thanks."

"You should be tired."

"I am."

"We'll be getting up at dawn. Get some sleep," he said, his tone gruff, and then he rolled over, giving her his back.

She smiled and closed her eyes. By this time tomorrow evening, he'd be putty in her hands.

JORDAN FINISHED washing their two breakfast dishes, which were nothing more than light tins, and the pot. This morning's mush wasn't much better than last night's meal. She'd kill for a couple of strips of crispy bacon and a buttered bagel.

"The honeymoon is over." Zach made sure the fire was put out, dousing the dormant ashes a second time. "From now on we catch or pick most of what we eat."

She laughed, and glanced over at him. He looked yummy in his khaki cargo shorts and tight green T-shirt. Only problem was he also looked serious. "You're joking, right?"

His right eyebrow went up, making him look a tad diabolical. "You think I'd carry six days worth of food?"

"Well, yeah. That dehydrated crap can't weigh much."

"Crap?" He turned away to scoop up his pack, but not before she saw him smile. "We'll see what you think about it in a few days."

"You can't starve me. It'll look really bad on the comment card."

"You go hungry and it won't be my fault. There's plenty to eat out here. Ready?"

She struggled to pick up her pack. Her arms hurt. Her legs hurt, and so did her back. Pretty much everything hurt but her toes. "I suppose you mean, fish, which should be filleted and packaged before considered edible."

"We'll see if you feel the same way in a couple of days." He made it to the kayak ahead of her and after stowing his pack under the waterproof tarp, turned to watch her gingerly pick her way over the rocks.

She swore her pack felt twice as heavy as yesterday and each jarring step chipped at her resolve. Of course she'd make it through. She wasn't a quitter. And things had to get better. Her aches and pains would subside, and as far as meals, she could stand to lose a few pounds.

"You okay?" he asked as she approached him, stumbling the last step.

She unceremoniously dropped her pack into the kayak, not much caring where it landed.

Zach did, judging by his frown. "If you need help, just ask."

"Right. Sorry," she muttered. Yeah, over her dead body she'd beg for help. She'd signed up for this. She was seeing it through. However, she did let him arrange her pack next to his while she stretched her stiff muscles.

"Here." He offered her a hand getting into the kayak, which she didn't refuse.

She liked that his palm was slightly rough and memories of last night's massage rushed back to infuse her with a pleasant warmth.

"Wait." He squeezed her hand, and she stopped to look at him. His eyes reflected the water, diffusing the blue and adding some green. "Sunscreen."

"I forgot." Really stupid since she wore a tank top and yesterday's shorts and her thighs and arms were still a little pink. Fortunately her skin was on the olive side and a burn didn't last long.

After releasing her, he reached into one of the pockets of his cargo shorts, quickly producing a tube of heavy-duty sun blocker. "This is the strength of SPF you should be using."

"I have one pretty close."

"We'll use this for now." He uncapped the tube but instead of giving it to her, he squirted the white goop onto his palm. He rubbed his hands together and then took her right arm and worked in the sunscreen.

She could've done that herself, they both knew it. So she didn't say a word, just raised her other arm when he was done with the right. The exposed portion of her legs required coverage, too, and she held her breath waiting to see what he would do.

He hesitated, their eyes meeting, and then a slow smile lifted his lips as he handed her the tube. "You better take care of the rest."

"Chicken," she whispered.

"You got that right," he said, chuckling softly and motioning for her to get into the kayak. This time he didn't offer her a hand.

6

ZACH WATCHED her climb in by herself and then, deliberately and slowly, roll up the hem of her Spandex running shorts to expose most of her thighs. After making sure she had his attention, she took her time rubbing in the lotion.

Abruptly he looked away, untied the kayak and pushed off before hopping in behind her.

After she finished applying the sunscreen to her neck and her face, she dangled the tube over her shoulder. "Thank you," she said sweetly, and then slid on her vest.

"No problem." He took it, deposited the tube back into his pocket and then used his paddle to push them farther away from shore.

She was going to be a royal pain in the ass. She knew he was interested, and fool that he was, he kept setting himself up. Letting her bait him. It didn't matter that what had ultimately gotten to him wasn't the sweet curve of her backside. Or the softness of her skin. Not even those killer legs.

Her spunk was what hooked him. He knew she hurt but she hadn't whined once. At any time she could've asked for his help and of course he would have given it to her, but she pushed hard, refusing to ask for a pass. All that while maintaining a sense of humor. The woman was bad news. Damn it.

"So how far are we kayaking today?" she asked, keeping pace with him and doing her fair share of paddling.

"Should take us until lunch. Then we stash the kayak and hike the rest of the way."

"Until we set up camp?"

"Yes, and then for the next three days."

"What if someone steals our kayak? Then how would we get back?"

"No one's going to steal our kayak."

"What if there's an emergency? What's your contingency plan?"

He stared at the back of her head, at the ponytail sticking out of the baseball cap, amazed that her dark hair could still be so shiny. Her neck was long and slender and entirely too tempting. He had to stop looking, stop wanting. Last night had been a bitch. Had to be close to midnight before he'd finally gotten to sleep.

She glanced over her shoulder. "Did you hear me?"

"What?"

"We're going to be on foot and all alone. I want to know what the plan is in case of an emergency."

He smiled. "You're used to being in charge, huh?"

Her shoulders straightened. "So?"

"I have a satellite telephone," he said, and when she turned hopeful dark eyes on him, he added, "But only for an emergency."

"Right. Of course. I get it. However—"

"No, Jordan."

"You don't know what I was going to say."

"No?"

She shrugged a slim shoulder. "Fine."

He smiled, and they paddled in silence for a few miles. The water was calm but he knew it wouldn't be for long. He'd prepare her right before they got to the rapids, but he didn't want to freak her out. This was still a beginners' course that changed to class III rapids for a short stretch. Nothing she couldn't handle, especially with him in the kayak. Still, the first time could be intimidating.

"What is it you do again?" he asked after a while.

"Advertising. With Boyd/McCallum. Ever heard of them?"

"Sure."

"Really?"

"I've even heard of television."

She let out a sound of exasperation. "It's just that advertising is more a behind-the-scenes kind of company unless you're in the business of using us."

"You one of the bigwigs?"

"Hardly."

"Someone pulled a string or two to get you this last-minute reservation."

"That was my boss."

"Oh, right. The arm-twister."

"To be fair, his insistence had more to do with me taking a vacation, and this was available. It's company policy that every employee takes off a minimum of one week a year, two if you expect to get any raises."

"Good for him."

"Easy for you to say."

"Your boss obviously knows what he's doing. He's built a mul-timillion-dollar company."

She stopped paddling and turned to look at him. "You are familiar with Boyd."

"Yep." He smiled. "Better pay attention. About a mile ahead it's going to get rougher."

She abruptly turned back. "How much rougher?"

"Keep your eyes open and a firm grip on the paddle, and you'll be fine."

"Okay, you're making me nervous."

"I have complete confidence in you. Now reach inside the kayak and put that helmet on."

"Oh, crap," she said as she pulled out the bright-yellow helmet. She stuffed her baseball cap inside her vest, then put the helmet on. "Seriously, is this going to get hairy?"

He put his on, as well. "Just for a few minutes."

Her shoulders tensed, and he wished he'd kept his mouth shut until the last minute.

"Jordan?"

"What?"

"You're going to be okay."

"Right."

He shook his head. Nothing else to say. The next few minutes had to play out. She'd do great. In fact, she'd probably get a rush. He still did. Every time.

She remained tense, her shoulders and back rigid, and as sorry as he was to see it, there was nothing he could do. He waited until they got to the landmark mountain hemlock that grew crooked at the bend in the river, signaling the onset of the rapids.

"All right. Around this next bend—" The words were barely out when the water started its mad rush.

She gasped and jerked, and that's the last he heard from her as he concentrated on keeping them afloat and away from the rocks, the gushing white water sweeping them through twists and turns that were more exciting than any man-made thrill ride.

WATER SPLASHED in Jordan's face and she blinked feverishly, not daring to loosen her white-knuckled grip of her paddle. They bounced and swirled and more water splashed her shoulders. She wasn't one bit scared. Far from it. The last time she'd experienced this kind of exhilaration was when she'd been a kid during one of those rare occasions when her father had taken the weekend off from work.

The whole family had gone to a theme park near the beach and she'd been introduced to her first roller coaster. Her mom and brother had chickened out but her dad had ridden the beast with her six times in a row. She'd begged for yet another ride, but to her horror, she'd puked cotton candy all over her father's crisp, clean khakis and that had ended their outing. And lest she forgot that humiliating episode, her brother had made it an annual holiday reminder. Good thing the family was too busy to get together more than twice a year.

The interval seemed amazingly brief, and in minutes they were traveling relatively calm waters again. Her heartbeat started to slow, the earlier adrenaline rush subsiding. She wanted to do it again.

"You okay?" Zach asked.

"Are you kidding? That was awesome. Are there any more rapids? Are we going to do it again?"

Zach laughed. "Nope. That was your white-water highlight. You want more of that, you have to take one of our other excursions or go to Hell's Canyon up north."

"What a name."

"A lot of rafting trips up there. Popular tourist spot. So is Jackson Hole. There are a number of outfitters down there."

"So why are you located out in the boonies?"

"Remote is good. You get a true outdoor experience, and you're not running into a bunch of people."

"You have a point," she said thoughtfully, bringing up her paddle and looking up at the clear blue sky. A bald eagle soared over a granite outcropping, stealing what remained of her breath. That made three sightings since yesterday. Pretty amazing.

"Beats the heck out of rush-hour traffic."

She heard the smile in his voice and grinned, too, before returning her paddle to the water and paddling her heart out. She wanted to get to shore and pull out the small notebook she'd brought. Jot down a few thoughts before they got away. "I'm thinking there's an ad slogan here somewhere."

"Don't ruin this by thinking about work."

"Can't be helped. It's what I do. How long before we go ashore?"

"Another hour and then we stop for lunch. After that we hike until we set up camp for the night."

"Good."

"You need to stop now?"

"No emergency. I just wanted to make some notes."

"Still thinking about work," he said, sighing. "Okay, I'll bite. Would I know your work? Any jingles or slogans I'd recognize?"

She hummed a few bars of her most popular, the one that had catapulted her to early success. The slogan that had set the benchmark she could never again achieve. Shoot, why did she have to go there?

He let out a low whistle. "Impressive. You were responsible for the entire campaign, I take it."

"Yep, the commercials, the contest, the print ads, the whole thing."

"You *are* good."

"Was." She briefly closed her eyes. Too much information. Besides, she didn't want to talk about it.

He let blessed silence lapse, and then ruined it with, "Creative block?"

"You're right. I shouldn't be talking about work."

He let the subject drop, but she had a feeling he'd have questions later. God, she really, really wanted one of those candy bars.

7

THE PAIR of skewered trout sizzling over the open campfire was starting to look better and better. Zach tested one of them by forking a piece of the crisp skin and taking a bite. He made an appreciative sound and then transferred both fish onto his plate without so much as a glance at her sitting across the campfire from him.

After a five-mile hike, Jordan had decided that she'd rather paddle. Not that she'd been given an option. She'd been ready to sack out by the time they found a level place to camp, shaded by a gorgeous old spruce and an army of lodgepole pines. At least the area was near enough to a small lake that water didn't have to be lugged too far, which was pretty much her job. Not easy when her arms and legs still ached.

Aroma from the roasted fish drifted through the air around her and her stomach rumbled. He'd tried to show her how to catch her own fish but she'd refused. Screw him. The first chance she got she was sneaking off to scarf down her chocolate bars.

"Hungry?" he asked.

She didn't answer at first. Her pride still smarted. After gathering kindling and dry wood, she'd blithely agreed to start the fire. Big mistake. Three stubborn tries later she'd given up and stood back to watch Zach do it with disgusting ease. Granted that wasn't his fault, and it probably wouldn't hurt to be nice. He might reconsider and share. "A little."

"There are rabbits around here. You might get lucky and—"

"Stop." She put up a hand. "Don't even say it."

He shrugged, and after cutting open his fish, he neatly removed the bones in one piece, leaving nothing but aromatic meat. Naturally he made it look easy. But admittedly, removing the bones after it was cooked did seem more doable.

She cleared her throat and used the toe of her hiking boot to push a branch toward the fire. "You don't really need both those fish, do you?"

He nodded. "I'm starved. Besides, it's really good."

Jordan sighed. "I can't clean one of those things. I'm serious. It'll make me sick."

Zach grinned. "You catch it, I'll clean it. Come on." He took a quick bite and then licked his fingers while he rose.

"I can wait until after you eat."

"Let's do it before it gets dark. It won't take long."

"Right," she muttered, scrambling to her feet, and then following him to the lake.

"You're lucky. There's a lot of fish this time of the year." The words were no sooner out of his mouth when one jumped out of the deeper water.

The little sucker was quick, and more than the actual fish, she saw the ripple it made. She moved closer to Zach, standing at the water's edge, gentle waves lapping the toes of his boots. Now she wished she'd paid more attention to how he'd caught his fish because she didn't have a clue as to where to begin.

"I'm not sure what I should be doing," she finally admitted.

"You're going to have to wade in."

"And take off my boots?" She peered into the shallow water. There were a few rocks and plants on the sandy bottom but nothing too scary.

"Depends how far in you have to go. But they're quick drying."

"Okay," she said, deciding to leave them on because she really didn't see the point in getting too far into the icy-cold water. She took another step, suddenly realizing they had no pole or fishing line. "Then what?"

"You watch." His intense gaze stayed on the shallow water as he took a red bandana out of his pocket. "There. Look at that. They're coming right to you."

"And I'm supposed to—what am I supposed to do?" She watched him move forward at a predatory pace, while slowly hunkering down.

Suddenly he reached into the water at dizzying speed, and with minimal splashing, promptly produced a medium-size fish. He held the wiggling trout up by the tail. "Easy, huh?"

"Wow. That was amazing." Although she did feel a tad sorry for the poor thing.

He grinned and released the fish into the lake. Seizing its reprieve, the trout swam off, disappearing into the black depths of the water.

"What are you doing?" She glared at him as he retreated to the sandy bank. "That was my dinner. You can't do that."

"And deprive you of the fun of catching your own?"

"You're sick. You know that? You need some serious help."

Zach laughed. "Come on. You gotta learn. We have five more nights out here."

She hadn't realized that in her excitement she'd backed in until the water hit her mid calf. Her soaked socks and boots felt as if they weighed a ton.

"There you go," he whispered. "One's headed straight for you."

She turned sharply to him. "I'm not going to—" Stumbling backward, she lost her footing, with no place to go but down. She ended up on her backside in the awful, cold water. It only came to her waist, but she did enough splashing and flailing to get her face and hair wet, too.

"You okay?"

"Don't you dare laugh," she said, wiping at her eyes and refusing to look at him. The hell with dinner. The hell with him.

"Ah, you needed a bath, anyway." He laughed then, and it was enough to get her to push herself to her feet.

"You think this is funny?" She spun toward him, and as his gaze lowered to her breasts, the smirk left his face. She did a quick check and saw that her wet tank top clung to her hardened nipples. It didn't seem to matter that she had a sports bra on beneath the top. Everything showed.

His attention was so fixed on her chest that she caught him off guard when she grabbed hold of his arm. He backed away. "What are you doing?"

Jordan tugged hard but she couldn't budge him. "You're getting wet, too, buddy. One way or another." She used all her might but he was too strong and only laughed at her efforts to drag him into the lake.

There was no other way. She wrapped her arms around his waist, pulling him against her soggy wet shirt. He let out a yelp of surprise, and she rubbed herself against his clean dry T-shirt until she'd left her mark.

"How's that?" She moved back to survey her handiwork. The front of him was wet, all right, but her gaze went straight to the bulge building beneath his fly. She swallowed hard as her gaze traveled to his face.

"Happy?" he whispered.

"Almost." She went up on tiptoe and leaned in for a kiss.

He hesitated, and then took her by the elbow and brushed his lips across hers. Despite their wet clothes, heat emanated from his body. Warmth spread through her chest and arrowed down her belly to the juncture of her thighs.

All too quickly, he moved his head and the contact was broken. "You win," he said hoarsely and backed away. "Go eat the damn fish."

MORNING CAME too quickly. The stupid birds wouldn't quit chirping. The sun had barely made it over the horizon and still it managed to shine directly into Jordan's sleepy eyes. She squeezed them shut but since she heard Zach messing with the campfire it was no use trying to go back to sleep. He'd just make her get up in a few minutes.

She rolled over and sat up, surprised to see him making sure the fire was out. He was dressed for the day, and his sleeping bag was rolled up and stuffed in his pack. Coffee hadn't even been made.

"What's going on?" she asked around a yawn.

"Overslept."

"I didn't think that was possible on a vacation," she muttered and stretched her arms above her head. She was still tired and he looked as if he was, too.

Maybe they'd shared the same problem that had kept sleep from rescuing her last night. That one lousy kiss had hung in the air like a storm cloud threatening to explode. Then nothing happened. He'd gone to his corner, and she'd gone to hers.

The real shame was that it wasn't even a good kiss. It had happened so fast that if the tension hadn't lingered she might have thought she'd imagined the whole thing.

"We're leaving in five minutes."

"Jeez, I've got to brush my teeth," she grumbled as she untangled herself from her sleeping bag. "I'm not happy about the no-coffee thing, either."

"Next time get up earlier."

Jordan grinned. That he was cranky was the only bright spot. He'd apparently had a rough night, too. Good. She hadn't been the one who'd acted like they'd done this big bad thing by kissing. They were consenting adults, after all.

She grabbed her small toiletry bag and towel, and then headed for the lake in her oversize T-shirt and red bikini panties, smug with the knowledge that he watched her the entire way.

ZACH KNEW better. Yet last night he'd made an ass out of himself. Thirty-seven going on twelve. Yes. He'd kissed her. No matter that it was a wholly unsatisfying kiss, in fact, that made matters worse. If he was going to cross the line he might as well have gotten something out of it. Something more than regret.

"Could you slow down? This is supposed to be a hike, not a marathon," Jordan said from behind him, and then muttered something else he couldn't hear.

He did as she asked, waiting in front of a ponderosa pine that must've been there for a hundred years. They'd been hiking for four hours on empty stomachs and she had every right to be irritable. He hadn't meant to punish her for his own poor judgment.

"Why don't we stop for lunch?" he said when he saw her face flushed from the exertion of hiking uphill.

She eyed him with suspicion. "Define lunch."

He shrugged off his pack. "Will a power bar do?"

Her mouth opened in indignation, but she said nothing as she dropped to the ground and rid herself of her pack.

Guilt had him digging for an extra bar even though he liked to maintain a modest supply well into the week. "That'll hold us until I fire up the stove and make some pasta and vegetables."

"One is fine," she said when he tried to hand her both bars. "Instead of starting a fire and all that, how about we keep going and then stop early for the night?"

"Sure." He'd already planned on making it a short day for good reason. Apparently she hadn't noticed yet, but it was going to rain, which meant they had to find shelter or build one. Couldn't help but wonder why she was anxious to make camp for the night. Their kiss came to mind. Better he didn't go there. "Tell you what, you say when and we stop."

"When." She smiled cheekily and tore off the wrapper. "I think I'm good for another three hours. Does that work?"

"You're the boss."

"I do like the sound of that."

He settled down on a grassy mound with his bar and a canteen of pure, cold, stream water. His gaze went over her shoulder toward the distant summit. They were in for more than rain. It looked as if it was going to storm.

8

"TELL ME about your job."

Jordan snorted. "Gee, I get to talk about work."

"Stewing over it and describing it are two separate issues."

She bit into her bar and chewed. "The job is crazy and demanding and I love it. Except—" She shook her head and looked away.

"What?"

Hesitantly, she brought her gaze back to his. This wasn't something she normally talked about. Not with anyone. "Sometimes the pressure is a bit much."

"Especially after coming up with the Breezy slogan."

"Exactly."

He thoughtfully ate some of his bar, and she'd bet her two prized candy bars he was trying to recall how long it had been since the Breezy ad campaign had hit TV and radio.

She finished her lunch, and, closing her eyes, she crumpled the wrapper and leaned back against the trunk of a Douglas fir that had lost its bottom branches.

"Tell me," he said.

"You've got it right, you know? No setting an alarm, no deadlines, no pressure."

Zach smiled. "My life isn't always this easy."

"Yeah?" She opened her eyes. "Try having a client call you three times a day while you beat your head against a wall because the ideas just won't come." She groaned. "I was twenty-six, only two years out of grad school when I started with the company and came up with that slogan. I got lucky."

Now she prayed lightning would strike twice.

"I think talent might've had something to do with it, too." He gave her a sympathetic smile. "Maybe this trip will relax you and help free up some of that creativity."

"I don't need to relax. I need to be working. Damn it."

"Seems to me that hasn't produced any results."

"Thank you. Thank you very much."

"That wasn't a jab."

"Yeah? Well, the bruise is still there." She straightened. "If you tell anyone what I said I'll hunt you down like a dog."

"I believe you."

"Good. You should." She pushed away from the tree, got up, and dusted off the seat of her jeans. "Let's get going."

"Jordan?"

She stopped, although something in his tone made her want to run the other way.

"Don't follow in your father's footsteps."

"Don't you have a trail to hike?"

He smiled and put out his hand. She thought about ignoring it and then pulled him to his feet. Their eyes met, and for a second she thought he was going to kiss her.

Instead, he chucked her on the chin and said, "You don't always have to be tough." And then he slid on his pack and resumed the lead.

THEY'D STOPPED later than expected, and Zach decided they each needed to build a shelter. She'd gathered saplings the way he'd shown her, bending them until she saw the stress point and cutting them for poles. While he stripped them halfway up, leaving the top branches intact, she gathered large spruce swags, ostensibly for the roof, which she couldn't see.

He found a spot for each of them and stuck the poles several feet apart in the ground. "We'll finish getting more spruce branches later. Let me show you how to do this," he said and intertwined the branch tops. "We need to make a canopy and then start layering the spruce."

"That'll keep us dry if it rains?"

"Yep. Go ahead. Try it."

Jordan followed his lead but ended up yanking one of her poles out of the ground. "Why can't we share a shelter?"

"There wouldn't be enough room," he said, his eyes averted, and she smiled when she saw the pulse in his neck jump.

She stuck the pole back into the hole he'd made, and then

watched him start at the bottom and tightly layer spruce branches. By the time he was finished, he had fashioned quite an impressive little cocoon.

"See? Easy. I'll start the fire and stove while you finish yours."

"Easy," she repeated, and got to work. But her mind wouldn't stay on the project. She wasn't just distracted with work. Her mind kept going back to what he'd said about following in her father's footsteps.

It wasn't true. Not really. She didn't have other commitments, like a husband or children. She didn't depend on anyone else to pick up the slack in her life; act like her maid, as her mother had done for her dad for years. Plus, Jordan had a social life. She occasionally had a drink with friends. And here she was on vacation, wasn't she?

For the third time in an hour, her shelter collapsed. She kicked one of the poles out of the ground and stared up at the sky. It was hazy but the dark threatening clouds hung over the next mountain. Forget this. She'd take her chances.

THUNDER CRACKED directly overhead, waking Zach from a sound sleep. His arm cramped in an unnatural position, he shifted. Something pressed against his back.

"Move over, damn it."

Still groggy, he blinked. "Jordan?"

"It's starting to rain and my butt's gonna get wet."

There wasn't enough room for both of them. He moved his arm, and she snuggled close, her left braless breast weighing temptingly on his chest. Lightning lit up the sky. He listened for a moment but heard nothing. "I don't hear any rain."

"It's only a few drops, but anyway, I heard something."

"It's only thunder."

"No, it was an animal, and it scared me."

Right. He should've pretended he was still asleep. This wasn't good. "Neither of us will get any sleep like this. I would've helped you with your lean-to if you'd only asked me—"

"Shut up." She tilted her head back and scooted up until their lips met, and then slid a hand under his T-shirt.

"Jordan, this isn't a good idea," he murmured, already hard, and lying this close, unable to hide his condition.

She taunted him, trailing her fingers to the elastic waistband of his shorts.

He deepened the kiss, bringing his arm around her and finding a bare breast with his other hand. She whimpered when he lightly pinched her budded nipple between his thumb and forefinger. He plunged his tongue deeper into her mouth, exploring her sweetness.

She cupped him over his shorts, while swinging a leg over his thighs, the warm pressure almost unbearable. He pushed her T-shirt up so that he had access to both breasts. Her skin was delectably soft. Kneading and touching wasn't enough. He had to taste her.

Maneuvering himself wasn't easy, especially with the friction caused by her leg over his groin, but he managed to lower himself enough to touch the tip of his tongue to her nipple. She moved against his mouth and he suckled the crown until she whimpered.

In the next second, an awful cry pierced the night.

Jordan jumped. "What was that?"

"I don't know. An animal. It's not close." He took her nipple back into his mouth, but she wouldn't relax and he knew the mood was broken. Resigned, he drew back and pulled down her shirt. "Get some sleep. I'll be on the lookout."

"Zach." Her voice was small, apologetic.

"It's okay." He tucked her head under his chin. More than okay, she'd just saved him from making a big mistake.

WHAT REALLY upset her wasn't that they'd gotten interrupted last night, which didn't make her happy, either, but that they'd been hiking for five hours and so far he'd behaved as if nothing happened.

Oh, he'd been pleasant enough at breakfast, and had even pointed out the different types of trees and wildflowers that grew at this elevation. They might as well have been talking about the weather. The coward.

However, she did have to admit that the rainbow array of flowers was pretty spectacular and she'd been lucky enough to see three more bald eagles, two of them at fairly close range. When it had occurred to her that she hadn't once thought about the office the entire morning, she was pretty surprised.

The path narrowed and started a steeper incline, and Zach,

who'd trekked considerably ahead, waited until she caught up. "Another two miles and we'll stop for the night."

"Really?" Her heart did a flip. The sun wasn't even close to the horizon. Five more hours until sunset at least. "Why? What did you have in mind?"

He gave her a cryptic smile she hadn't expected. "You'll see."

That did it. Her heartbeat went into overdrive and if she hadn't been enjoying the view of his fine rear end, she would've sped right past him. Even so, two miles seemed interminable but then she got distracted when she heard rushing water.

"What is that?" she asked, catching up to him.

He didn't answer but led her through a thicket of trees. On the other side, about an eighth of a mile away, she could see a waterfall, gushing from last night's rain.

"Wow. Cool." She'd never seen one this close.

"We'll camp near the water."

She barely heard him. She raced ahead, the sound of the water growing as she got closer. At the first clear flat spot she dropped her pack. Next she removed her boots and socks. Mostly the ground was carpeted with pine needles, and she carefully avoided the occasional rock as she made her way to test the water. Not that she expected anything but icy cold, but she didn't care. This was the closest she'd been to anything resembling a shower in three days.

"Be careful. The rocks are—"

He stopped when she lifted the hem of her T-shirt and then yanked it off. Underneath she wore a sports bra, but that came off, too. The jeans took a moment longer to peel down. The bikini panties were a snap. "You coming?" she asked, turning to look at him.

He stood motionless. "The rocks can be slippery."

"Yes, Mom." She held on to an outcropping as she felt for her footing from one rock to the other until she was in waist-deep.

She shivered, but held her ground. Her body would adjust soon. Her pulse was another matter. The way he'd looked at her…

"You're so crazy." He had his shirt off. After unsnapping and unzipping his jeans, he yanked off his boots. In seconds he was totally, gloriously naked.

Jordan's breath died in her chest. The man was gorgeous. Perfect. Made her want to hide her not-so-perfect pale body. Too late. She watched him approach the pool, his growing arousal erasing her insecurities.

He stepped into the water, muttering a curse. "This water is going to deflate more than my ego."

She laughed. "We'll take care of that."

"Right." He winced as he slid deeper into the water.

"It won't be so bad in another minute." She couldn't get the words out without her teeth chattering.

"Whose idea was this?"

"Where's your sense of adventure?"

Before she knew what happened, he caught her wrist and pulled her to him. Her breasts made contact first, pressing against his bare chest, still dry and warm from the sun. The icy water had made her nipples harder than pebbles and she rubbed against him trying to soak up his warmth.

Groaning, he forced her head back to claim her mouth. She opened to him and he dove inside, his exploration more gentle than she'd expected. His tongue found every nook and recess, ran along her teeth and then flicked hers before it left her mouth.

He lightly bit her lower lip, nibbled at the corners, extended his quest along her jaw and then trailed his lips down the side of her neck. She arched her back in anticipation. He didn't disappoint, quickly bringing his mouth to her breasts and taking a nipple between his teeth. He bit lightly, laved the area and then drew the entire crown into his mouth.

She shuddered from the sheer pleasure of it, and he slid a hand down to her backside, molding the curve and using a handful of fleshy cheek to pull her against him. Not that she needed the encouragement. She reached for him, but with her range of motion hindered, had to content herself with gently bringing up her knee between his legs.

He moved against her, and she smiled because the cold water had indeed taken its toll. Poor guy. Hell, poor her. She'd seen what even a little visual stimulation had done. But they had time, and she had no intention of letting some frigid water ruin their day.

"You think this is funny," he whispered.

Meeting his eyes, she tried to lose the smile. "Actually, no."

He scooped her up, and with the buoyancy of the water helping his cause, he carried her to an outcropping at the edge of the water and laid her down.

9

THEY WERE close to the falls, which may have accounted for the flatness of the boulder beneath her back. Water had worn down the stone so that it was smooth and slick and even if the top were jagged she doubted she'd care. Not with Zach kissing the side of her neck and stroking the inside of her thigh with his long lean fingers. He was making her so warm and tingly, she thought she was going to explode.

"How did you find this rock?" she asked, her voice ragged and barely intelligible.

"Lucky."

"I thought it might be a favorite of yours," she said, and immediately regretted it. She knew he wasn't the type to sleep with his clients, but it was too late.

He stiffened slightly, his hand stilling, his lips leaving her skin until he braced himself over her and stared into her eyes. "It's not what you think."

"Fortunately for you, I'm incapable of thought." She slid her hands around his neck and brought his lips back to hers.

It took him a moment to relax, and then he kissed her, his tongue probing for entrance, his hand forging higher up her thigh until he found that sweet spot that had her arching off the cool stone surface. Thanks to the warm, humid air, he was hard again, and she circled her hand around his shaft, enjoying the way he shuddered at her touch.

She ran her thumb over the head of his penis, slowly, learning every groove and indentation and making him tense. He retaliated by sliding two fingers inside her and making her totally insane with need. He abandoned her mouth but found her breasts, his beard-roughened chin pleasantly scraping the soft sensitive skin around her nipples as the tip of his stiff tongue touched her just the way she liked it.

He withdrew his fingers from inside her and then used his hand to spread her thighs farther apart. She needed little coaxing. He'd been worried that with all that swimming he'd have to get creative about a lubricant, but it seemed that Jordan had taken care of the problem. But just to make sure, he moved away from her nipples and crouched before her spread thighs.

She was so beautiful. Her pale skin and the dark, close-cropped patch of curly hair that marked the sweet spot, all of it enticed him and made his already hard cock harder. He put his left hand on her hip, his right on her inner thigh and then he bent to taste her.

Cool lips held back the moist heat that welcomed his eager tongue. He moved slowly despite the urge to rush, to have everything he could as quickly as possible. One thing camping had taught him was the rewards of patience. He used the lesson now, licking her in broad strokes, brushing by the hard little nub as if it wasn't the key to making her insane.

Her hand went to his head where she grabbed hold, pulling, but not enough to make him hurry. Then her moan, just loud enough to be heard over the roar of the falls, let him know she wouldn't wait long.

He just kept up his steady pace and no sound, no yank was going to move him. The one thing that would was not something she could control. It would come, he just had to give it time.

"Zach, please."

He didn't respond except to push her thighs a bit farther apart.

"You're killing me."

He smiled at that one, but kept up the pressure, the rhythm. And he was rewarded. She trembled beneath him and he tasted a sudden rush of her tantalizing juice. That was it, she was almost ready.

He moved his right hand so his finger covered the growing nub of her clit. Moving more quickly now, he circled the bud of flesh, holding on to her tightly as she started to squirm in earnest. Alternating between his finger and his pointed tongue, he worked her into a fine madness. He wanted her to explode, go crazy, and she'd better do it soon because he had gone quite over the edge himself.

Her writhing made him abandon fingering her. Instead, he grabbed both hips. That meant he'd have to bring her off with his mouth. Not that he minded.

Only now it was sharp flicks of his tongue in combination with tight sucking, which he assumed pleasant.

Maybe *pleasant* wasn't the right word. *Pleasant* rarely made a woman scream.

She came under his tongue. It was an amazing experience to feel her shatter, but he didn't savor it for long. He stood as she still trembled, moved between her damp thighs and in one long stroke he was in her to the root.

He threw his head back at the intensity of the sensation. Not only was she hot and wet, but she squeezed him with undulating muscles. It was all he could do not to come right then, that second.

He bit his tongue, then the inside of his cheek and the pain helped him ease away from the precipice. Only then did he begin to pump.

THANK GOODNESS Jordan had found a rock and a sturdy shrub to steady her or she'd have slid away the moment he'd touched her with his tongue.

She was still trembling from her orgasm, and now that he was inside her, rubbing her so perfectly with his thick cock, it was entirely possible she was going to come again.

It was crazy. He'd done everything wrong. He'd licked her too slowly, made her wait after she was ready, ignored her not-very-subtle hints. And she'd never come like this in her life.

What was it with him? How had he known more about her body than she did?

She gasped as he changed his position and there went all coherent thought. Nothing existed except the pleasure coursing through her body. Nothing but the feel of Zach between her legs, inside her, touching her, making her lose the last vestige of her mind as she came so hard she thought her heart would stop.

"I'VE BEEN thinking about it and you might be right about my father," she said slowly as they lay on top of their sleeping bags, staring up at the stars, their legs intertwined.

Today they'd hiked to the summit, and at her insistence, they'd returned to the falls to set up camp again before heading back down toward the river tomorrow.

"What about him?"

"Sometimes I'm more like him than I care to admit." Jordan glanced over at Zach, surprised at herself for saying the words out loud.

She just wasn't one of those people who shared like that. She'd never been. Of course, she didn't have all that many close friends, and nobody from work ever breached the business wall. And yet in the last few days she'd told Zach about her personal life, about her fears and doubts, about her dreams. The way she talked to him was an anomaly but that could probably be explained by the fact that after two days she wasn't likely ever to see him again.

No, it was more than that. Much more. Making love to him had awakened a yearning inside her that was going to haunt her when they parted. Mostly sex was about release for her. Scratching that itch. Some scratchers were better than others, but none had been keepers. But Zach was different. This was about intimacy. About that warm, fuzzy feeling that scared the hell out of her because both the vulnerability and trust she'd experienced were so foreign. And the thing was, she wanted to see him again. She didn't want this feeling to go away.

"Obviously, that's not a good thing. What are you going to do to change your situation?"

She let out a strangled laugh, confused for a moment, her thoughts having derailed from the conversation. "If I don't get my act together on this new campaign, that might be decided for me."

He slid a hand under her T-shirt and gently kneaded her bare breast. "You're going to do great. But that isn't the point, either. You have to make your own decision about the path you want in life."

She touched his cheek. He was so sweet. He really was. Sweet and…amazing.

He planted a kiss in her palm. "You think I don't understand."

About to deny it, she closed her mouth again. She didn't want to hurt his feelings, but the truth was, he didn't.

"I'm not here by accident. This was a conscious choice. I used to work out here every summer to help pay for college."

This surprised her. "Did you graduate?"

He smiled. "Yep. I got a degree in business."

"But you chose not to use it."

"I've used it. I even bought this company."

She pushed up, bracing herself on her elbow so that she could look at him. "You own The Great Beyond?"

He nodded, his gaze staying on her face. "I bought it four years ago. It's small, which I like. Easier to manage."

Jordan processed the information, though she didn't feel as if much had changed. The small outfitter wasn't exactly a growing concern with all the attendant headaches and profits. He wanted to keep it small, fine. Nothing wrong with lacking ambition if your bills got paid and you were happy with the status quo, but she wasn't one of those people. She doubted Zach understood why.

"Relieved I'm not just a lowly guide?" he said, one side of his mouth lifting.

She glared at him in indignation. "That never entered my mind. I'm impressed that you found something you love and made it your career."

"Do you love advertising?"

She settled back down beside him and gave the question serious thought. "Yes," she said finally. "Most of the time. I don't even mind the pressure so much. I mean, there really wouldn't be pressure if I didn't—" She shook her head. "I'm not going to ruin my last two days by worrying about work."

Zach smiled. "Good girl." He toyed with her nipple, helping her to strengthen her resolve. Work was creeping further and further away from her mind. "I have a feeling your creativity will enjoy a resurgence after this trip."

"My, my but you think quite highly of yourself."

He chuckled. "That I do, but I can't take all the credit."

Laughing, she took a nip at his nipple, keeping the brown nub between her teeth even when he yelped.

"You wanna play dirty?" he asked, trailing his hand from her breast to the elastic of her panties.

She released him, soothing the nipple with a quick flick of her tongue. "We're supposed to be going to sleep."

"We will." He slid his hand between her thighs and touched her right where she wanted it most. "In a minute."

FOUR HOURS behind schedule, they reached their stashed kayak. Zach had planned on them getting in six hours of paddling before they set up camp for the night. That wasn't going to be easy to do before dark. Totally his fault. They'd gotten too little sleep for the past two nights and then hiked at half-speed because they were tired.

"Have you ever gotten back here and the kayak was gone?" Jordan asked, her head tipped back so she could see him under the rim of her baseball cap.

"Now, you see, only someone from the city would think of something like that."

"Well?" Her skin had turned a golden brown in the past five days, and as pretty as she was before, she was really something now.

"Once."

"No joke?" She hadn't stood back and let him move the kayak, but instead, hoisted her end into the water.

"We don't run into too many people around here. Some local kids we know were playing a prank. They left the kayak on the bank about a quarter of a mile down-river."

She laughed. "Bummer, since you didn't know that."

"That's when the satellite phone comes in handy. It didn't actually happen to me but to one of the college kids who works as a summer guide. I heard he got even."

Jordan looked at him strangely for a moment, and then smiled and slid her pack off her back.

"What?"

"Nothing."

"Don't give me that." He stowed both their packs under the tarp. She shrugged. "This is kind of a Peter Pan job, isn't it?"

"You calling me a bum?"

"I didn't say that was bad." She giggled when he caught her wrist and reeled her toward him for a quick kiss. "If you don't wanna grow up—"

"Hey, I grew up. But then I found out it wasn't all it was cracked up to be."

"I know what you mean." She sighed, her eyes drifting closed, and it made his heart swell to see her look so contented. "College and grad school were tough but, in retrospect, a lot less complicated."

"Amen."

"I think you might have the right idea, Zach Wilde."

He slid his hands down her back, cupped her bottom and

lowered his head to kiss her. Maybe this was the time to tell her about his other life. "We could always use another guide."

She stiffened and drew back before their lips met. "Right." She blinked. "You were kidding."

"No."

Her eyelashes fluttered, and she looked away, her expression that of a woman who, after the first date, was trying to decide how to let the guy down easy. "I have a life in L.A."

"From everything you've told me, you have a job in L.A. Not the same thing."

She took both his hands in hers, a kind of sad desperation in her eyes. "I have a plane to catch in thirty-six hours. Let's make the most of the time we have left."

"You're right." He forced a smile. No use telling her the full truth about himself. Tomorrow would be goodbye.

10

As soon as they'd paddled around the bend, Jordan saw the dock where The Great Beyond kept their kayaks. Through the trees she caught a glimpse of the log cabin that served as the office. A lump lodged in her throat. How had the week gone by so quickly?

She had the sudden crazy urge to keep paddling. Go right past base camp. See what was on the other side. She had another day left of vacation that she'd planned on splitting between her couch and the pool in front of her condo. Her laptop and notebooks were sitting on the coffee table waiting for her. Her plane left in three hours, but surely she could book another flight.

"What do—?"

"We have—"

They both spoke at the same time. Ironic, since the past half hour had been spent in silence, listening only to the caw of overhead birds and the splash of the paddles dipping into the water.

"Go ahead," she said, it occurring to her that he hadn't said a word about her staying longer. Maybe he had another client to meet this afternoon. Maybe he had the good sense to get that it was over. Nice while it had lasted, but no use prolonging the inevitable. She was definitely not going to be their new guide, and him, well, his life was obviously here. Still, there were those long, cold winters…He had to spend them somewhere.

"Ladies first."

"I'll give you a pass," she said and realized how much she hoped he'd ask her to stay. In fact, it was more than hope. Her palms had gotten so clammy it was hard to grip the paddle. Were his feelings the same as hers? He was a good listener, and the possessive way he touched her…

"I was just going to say that after you get changed I'll take you to the airport. Maybe we'll have time for a bite to eat."

"Oh."

With his paddle, he splashed her arm. "In a real restaurant."

The cold water startled her and she jumped. "You wanna start a water fight?"

"Let's be adult about this."

"You started it."

Zach's throaty chuckle filled her with a bittersweet longing. This really was it. The end of the road for them. And it wasn't going to be easy. Two days ago she hadn't known how she'd feel about this moment. She did now. It hurt. It hurt like hell.

She couldn't remember when it had been so easy to talk to a man. Not just a man, but anyone. Her mother was totally clueless when it came to anything outside of the newest home-decorating trends, and Sonya, well, for being a successful contract attorney, if it wasn't about her job, she couldn't think about anything much past finding a husband.

Jordan waited until they got to the dock and he'd jumped out of the kayak so that she could see his face. "Zach? Do you ever get to L.A.?"

He secured the line from the kayak to a post. "Sometimes," he said slowly. "Mostly in the winter." He extended a hand to help her out.

Ah. Winter. It was a start...

The early-afternoon sun shone directly in her eyes as she stepped from the kayak. She squinted behind her sunglasses but couldn't clearly see his face. But that his hand lingered around hers, even when he could have safely released her, gave her hope. The decision suddenly seemed easy. She couldn't just get on a plane and not tell him how she felt. Well, at least found out how he felt about her. They could meet up for long weekends. See what happened from there. Her heart started to pound.

"Zach, I have something I want to ask you, but you don't have to answer right now," she said, and when wariness crept across his face, she hurried on before she lost her nerve. "I have this industry awards dinner I have to go to next month. It's not a big deal, well, it is, sort of. One of those annual things, kind of foo-foo, you know, eight-course dinner, champagne, black-tie—"

"Look, Jordan, I—"

"No, wait, please. I wouldn't expect you to pay for your plane fare or fork out for the tuxedo. I'll take care of all of that since I'm the one asking. And you could stay with me for the weekend." She sucked in a breath. "Only if you want to, of course."

The pained look on his face made her heart sink. "You don't have to buy my plane ticket or my clothes."

"Oh, I didn't mean to insult you. Please don't take what I said the wrong way."

"Jordan, we really need—"

"Zach!" The voice came from the direction of the office.

They turned to see a short, muscular, college-age man trotting toward them. Following behind him a few yards was one of the athletic-looking blond women Jordan had seen the first day.

"You have a call. In the office," the younger man said, and when Zach started to wave him off impatiently, the man added, "It's from San Francisco, and they said it's important."

Zach's entire expression changed from annoyance at the interruption to vigilance. He passed a hand over his face and exhaled sharply. "I have to take this call," he said, holding her gaze but already backing away from her. "Go ahead and grab your shower and your things out of the locker. We'll still get something to eat and then head to the airport. We'll talk then," he added, but low enough only for her to hear.

"No problem. Go."

He left their packs and the kayak where it was, but sent a look at the other two that had them taking over where he'd left off.

"I'm Brady," the guide said, "and this is Stacy. She'll take your pack to the locker room."

"I can get it," Jordan said, feeling more buff than she had six days ago. Besides, she needed to work out some frustration. What rotten timing. The uneasy look on Zach's face when she'd offered to pay his plane fare still smarted.

"I'm going that way," the blonde said, lifting the pack with one hand and smiling, showing brilliantly white teeth against her tan face. She glanced at Brady. "Am I doing the airport run, or are you?"

"Zach's taking me," Jordan blurted.

The two exchanged glances, and Brady said, "Sometimes these calls take a while, and you don't want to be late."

Leaving without seeing him was non-negotiable, the mere

thought unfathomable. Heck, she hadn't even planned on going to the awards banquet this year. What she had to do was quit tap dancing and spit out that she wanted to see him again. "I'll wait."

"Seriously, those calls from The American Sportsman can take an hour or more."

"Stacy." Brady gave her a warning look.

"Oops." Stacy grinned. "Come on." She started toward the locker room. "If he's still on the phone after you've showered and changed, we'll figure out who's taking you."

Jordan kept pace with the much taller woman, curious as all get out. The American Sportsman was a huge sporting-goods chain. There had to be over two hundred stores. "What's going on with The American Sportsman?"

Stacy sighed. "He really doesn't like us talking about it."

"Zach?" Was he making a deal with them? Had to be. Why hadn't he mentioned it? "I'm not going to say anything."

"Well, I'm such a big mouth. Although I don't know what the huge deal is." Stacy glanced over her shoulder, but they were out of Brady's earshot. "Zach owns The American Sportsman."

Jordan stopped. "That can't be."

Stacy shrugged. "He does."

"But what is he doing here?" Pieces of their conversations over the past week flashed in her head. He had a business degree. He'd talked about growing up and it not being all it was cracked up to be… None of it made sense. The American Sportsman was a large company. Zach couldn't run a company like that from here. Why…how could he…

"He's only here about two and a half months of the year. Says he has to get away from it all." Stacy shrugged. "Don't say anything, okay? I mean, he wouldn't fire me or anything. He's really a great guy, but—hey, are you okay?"

No, she wasn't okay. She'd told him so much about herself. About her insecurities, about her father…about everything. He'd obviously shared very little. "Are you sure about this?"

"Yeah, I mean everyone who works here knows, but he acts like the rest of us so it's no big deal." Stacy slowed down, her worried gaze going from Jordan to the direction of the office and back to Jordan. "I'm so screwed, aren't I?"

"Why?" Jordan asked sweetly, her temper simmering. Hurt gripped her heart like a vice. Humiliation cut deep. She'd offered to buy him a plane ticket. He probably owned his own plane. "You didn't do anything wrong. You didn't spend six days lying through your teeth."

Stacy's concerned gaze went back toward the office. "Zach? He's not like that. He's really a—"

"I know." Jordan sneered. "A great guy."

She picked up the pace, suddenly anxious to get her things and get on that plane. There had to be a taxi, or someone else going to the airport in the next few minutes. She didn't even care if she showered. Her thoughts raced, trying to recall if The American Sportsman had ever been a client. She was pretty sure her agency had done work for them. Not her personally, but still…

What a fool she'd been. Baring her soul. Laying her emotions out like a bear rug. Shooting her mouth off the way she had, believing Zach hadn't understood what she was saying. The worst of it was the deceit. He could've told her about himself at any time. What else had he held back?

Mortified, she broke into a run. God, she wanted to scream. Mostly, she just wanted out of here. Find a nice dark corner to curl up in and have a good cry. And never see Zach Wilde again.

ZACH SWIVELED AROUND in his leather chair, tugged his red silk tie loose and stared out his office window at the San Francisco skyline. He hated days when he had to wear a suit. That didn't happen often but still too much for his taste. Hard to believe that for nine years he'd worn one nearly every day. And then at thirty-six, Jake, his best friend and business partner had done the unthinkable. He'd suffered a heart attack and died, leaving his high-school sweetheart and their two kids behind. Stuff like that just wasn't supposed to happen.

Zach sighed and checked his watch. His dinner meeting wasn't for another two hours which meant a late night again. That was the trouble with being away from the office for two months. As soon as he got back he was bombarded with appointments and dinners and…

Whose fault was that? He'd had some nerve lecturing Jordan.

His gaze went to the darkening sky. The moon was nearly full. Just like that night they'd made love under the stars. Was she looking out her window in L.A. and thinking the same thing?

Right. The woman despised him. He didn't blame her. He looked at his day planner. It had been a month since he'd seen her. She hadn't even waited for him to get off the phone so he could explain. Not that he condemned her.

But the truth was he'd never kept his life a secret. When he was in Idaho he simply wanted to be one of the worker bees. Go back to his roots. Still, he should've been the one to tell Jordan about how he spent the other ten months of his life. But he'd been selfish and hypocritical because he'd wanted her to be completely open with him. And now he couldn't stop thinking about her.

Ironic that he'd blown it by taking the call regarding the new lighter-weight backpack they were test-marketing. If Zach had been truly practicing what he'd preached to Jordan about letting go and making her own choices, he'd have never taken the call. He would've let his perfectly capable R&D vice president handle the study.

When he'd first made the decision to pull back from the rigors of running the company, he'd been ruthless about protecting his time in Idaho. He was slipping.

The intercom on his phone buzzed and he quickly pressed the button to stop the annoying noise. It was his secretary.

"I thought you went home," he said, glancing at his watch.

"I'm on my way out. But I wanted to remind you about your breakfast meeting tomorrow. Nine-thirty at the St. Francis. That should take a couple of hours, and then Mr. Yamamoto in Tokyo has asked for a conference call at—"

His fingers went to the knot at his tie. Odd. It felt tight but he'd already loosened it. "Emily. Emily," he repeated when his secretary kept going. "Tell Yamamoto it'll have to be another day." Zach's gaze was on his day planner already turned to tomorrow's appointments. He'd have to make breakfast because other people were attending and it would be rude not to show up. Everything else could wait. "I'm going to L.A. tomorrow afternoon."

"Oh. That's not on the calendar."

"I know."

Emily hesitated. "You're taking the plane I presume." The

woman had been with him for ten years, and bless her, she'd never once questioned him. "I'll make sure it's ready by one."

JORDAN SAT BACK in her chair and stared at the new Breezy campaign slogan on the wall across from her desk. Surrounding it were pictures of bald eagles soaring over tree-covered mountains, bighorn sheep scaling cliffs and, of course, a spectacular waterfall that had been photographed somewhere in Africa, all of which she'd integrated into the campaign. She'd played on the consumer's new love affair with preserving the environment, and the company loved it, Patrick loved it, and for another two years she didn't have to worry about moving her office to the basement.

Best of all, she was really proud of her work. She'd bet Zach would be pretty impressed, too. Damn it. She couldn't think about him. Why would she, anyway? He obviously didn't give a hoot about her. He hadn't even called. Not that she'd expected him to. Or wanted him to. Not really.

Okay, maybe there was a small part of her that hoped he'd call and beg for her forgiveness. That he'd come up with some totally ridiculous but plausible explanation for having deceived her. Which in itself was ridiculous and made her so darn mad. Yet she still missed him.

She jerked open her desk's top drawer where she kept a healthy supply of aspirin. The first thing she saw were the two candy bars. Sad and misshapen mementoes of that ridiculously perfect week she'd spent with a stranger. She should get it over with and eat the dumb things. Or better yet, toss them in her wastebasket. They'd been melted and reformed twice now. Leaving them tucked in the corner, she closed the drawer.

The knock at her door brought her head up.

It was Cliff from accounting, a nice guy with dark curly hair to die for, with whom she sometimes ate lunch. "You ready for a cocktail?"

"Is it that time?"

"Yep, get moving."

She should beg off. It would be easy to claim she had too much work to do. No, she'd made a deal with herself. There had to be life beyond the office. Besides, having a drink or two wouldn't kill her. She got her purse out of the bottom drawer, thought briefly about touching up her lipstick and then decided not to bother.

The lobby was crowded with people waiting for the elevator. Fridays were like that around this time of the day. People seemed to start gearing up early for the weekend and tended to leave the office by four, which Patrick encouraged. The concept was totally foreign to Jordan, but she was determined to turn over a new leaf.

An eager group from the art department commandeered the first car, but another one stopped right away. As the doors slid open, Cliff took her arm to make sure they weren't left behind. Jordan froze, and then took a step back.

"What's wrong?" Cliff tugged at her hand. "Jordan?"

Zach stepped out of the elevator. Not the same man she'd met a month ago, he wore khakis, a white shirt and navy sports jacket. He looked incredibly good.

"What are you doing here?" She pulled her hand away from Cliff and automatically smoothed her hair, which was absurd since Zach had seen her at her worst.

His startled gaze went briefly to Cliff. "I'm sorry. I should've called."

The elevator doors closed again, without a single taker. Apparently everyone preferred to find out who Zach was. It was never this quiet. Jordan pressed the button again since no one else made the effort and glared at Margie, Patrick's secretary, but the woman paid no attention. Like the rest of the staff, she looked far too interested in Zach. She was a nice woman, but the first tongue to wag over the silliest rumor.

"Cliff?" Jordan sent him a pleading look.

"I'll see you later." The elevator dinged its arrival and he made a herding motion. "Come on, ladies."

"This way," Jordan murmured, and didn't even look to see if Zach followed.

They got to her office, and she quickly closed the door behind them.

"I didn't mean to intrude," Zach said, looking uneasy.

"You didn't. We were all going to happy hour. No big deal,"

she said, her ego soothed when he looked relieved and then for good measure she added, "As a group."

His mouth curved in a smile that spread warmth through her belly, and then his gaze drew to the far wall. "Nice. Did you take those pictures?"

"No. The art department got those for me. What are you doing here?" she asked again.

"I could say I was in the neighborhood, but I won't lie. I came to see you. May I?" He gestured to a guest chair.

She gave an indifferent shrug, resisted the urge to remark about him not lying being a first, and then hurried around to her desk chair before her knees gave out.

Zach smiled as he sat. "Couldn't help but notice the new slogan. You did good."

"You're not supposed to see that yet."

"My lips are sealed."

Her gaze went to his mouth. A vivid memory of where that mouth had been had her clearing her throat. "Okay, so…"

Interestingly, he seemed a bit nervous himself, his gaze wandering to the easels set up near the window. "This is seriously good. I might have some work for you—"

"I don't need you tossing me a pity bone."

His eyes came back to meet hers. "It never occurred to me. In fact, when I decided to come here, business was the furthest thing from my mind."

Her pulse picked up speed. "I'm listening."

He smiled again. "I don't blame you for being upset."

"Gee, I'm so relieved."

"Man, have I missed that smart mouth."

She tried not to smile.

"Here's the thing. I've been divorced for five years, no children. I'm a damn good businessman, but I was a lousy husband. I worked too much. Didn't pay attention. I haven't been in a relationship since the divorce. Four years ago my business partner and best friend died young of a heart attack. It was my wakeup call. I cut back on the sixteen-hour days."

His mouth twisted wryly. "I started going back to Idaho for the summers. And lately, after giving you the you-have-to-take-charge-of-your-life speech, I realized I lost you because I just had to take that bloody call from the office. I was wrong. I was stupid. I was reverting to my old ways. And I'll probably make more mistakes, but I'm trying to learn from them and do better."

"And you're telling me all this…why?" She knew, but she wanted to hear him say it.

He got up and came around her desk. "You need to know this about me so that you can decide if you want to give us a shot." He took both her hands and pulled her to her feet. "I can't stop thinking about you, Jordan. We connected during that week. Tell me you felt it, too."

She could scarcely breathe. "It won't be easy," she whispered against his mouth when he pressed his lips to hers.

He pulled back slightly and gave her a crooked smile. "We're both tough."

She didn't feel very tough right now with his hands pressing into the small of her back. With his minty breath fanning her chin. If she could, she'd melt right into him. "I might be free tonight."

He grinned. "I was thinking I owed you a stay in a suite at the Ritz. On the beach. Think you might be able to take off the weekend?"

"Oh, yeah." She lifted up to kiss him and her phone rang. Automatically she reached over and picked it up. Of all the bad timing. And here was this gorgeous guy… Some habits wouldn't quit. She had her own crap to work on.

It was Sonya. "Hey, what are you doing tonight? Feel like happy hour at Cagney's? There's this new guy—"

Jordan smiled at Zach and ran a palm up his chest. "Sorry," she said. "I've got plans."

She replaced the receiver and turned to him. "Let's see…where were we? Oh, right." She tilted her head back and opened for him.

She didn't have to offer twice.

* * * * *

NO RESERVATIONS

Samantha Hunter

To Mike, and many more summers on the beach.

1

COMPLETE BLISS overcame Edie Stevens as she sped down the main highway that formed the spine of Cape Cod. Twelve hours from Cleveland, it might as well have been an entirely different country. Still, she was exhausted and ready to get out of the car, even if it was a very nice one.

For this special occasion she'd rented a white Mustang convertible, donned her scarf, sunglasses, and driven all day in style. At first it had been fun, zooming down Route 90 with the tunes blasting, but as the sun was setting low on the horizon, she was ready to be done with the drive.

As she turned onto a small street, she was unsure if it was the one she wanted. She looked around for a street sign, but was quickly distracted by the open vista of a quiet stretch of beach and the ocean beyond.

Her first glimpse of the Atlantic.

Pulling over, she shut off the car and got out, noticing other people milling along the muddy flats; the tide was out. A few dogs ran happily along the water's edge, sniffing voraciously, and she laughed at a small crab in a comic stand-off with one particularly persistent pooch. Her laugh drew the attention of the dog, who—soaking wet—now bounded directly toward her.

Uh-oh.

"Nice doggy, um, wait, good dog, stay, *sit*," she said rapidly, hoping something worked. She held her hands out in a stopping motion that didn't seem to discourage the dog at all.

As he stood in front of her, he seemed friendly enough, staring at her with big brown eyes and a wagging tail. She relaxed, smiling at how cute he was, when suddenly he shimmied from nose to tail, spraying water and sandy mud everywhere. Flecks of it stuck to her hands as she shielded her face.

"Oh God! Sorry about that!" a masculine voice exclaimed as she lowered her hands to see a very bronze chest coming close.

Very nice, she thought, forgetting about the ocean view for a moment.

The lines of the torso led to an equally handsome, boyish face and a friendly smile. Twenty-something, maybe? A little flutter worked its way along her midriff, and she smiled back. She was turning thirty, and dallying with a younger man just might be on her vacation to-do list.

"He got you all dirty," the guy observed with some dismay.

"It's okay. I'll wash. He's cute," she said diplomatically.

"Thanks. He's just a little too friendly sometimes, especially with women. He can't pass up a pretty face," he said in a flirty tone, and Edie couldn't believe it. This was a very good sign for her vacation. She hadn't been on the beach for five minutes and already a guy was flirting with her.

"Greg."

"Hmm?" she said, charmed by the image he made standing there shirtless against the backdrop of the sunset.

"Greg. It's my name. You have one?"

She snapped back to the moment. "Yes, Edie. My name is Edie."

"Hey, Edie. Where you from?"

"Cleveland."

"You staying here on the beach?"

"To tell you the truth, I don't know," she laughed, and blushed a little. The look he was giving her now was definitely one of male interest and a zing of excitement thrilled her. "I'm renting a beach house and I think I might have taken a wrong turn."

"Where are you heading?"

"Um, North Truro?" She blushed again, feeling stupid. "I rented a convertible, and I had my Google map, but...I lost it. I was trying to read it at a red light, and then when I took off, the map flew out of the car. So I've been more or less guessing. I had a rough idea where I was supposed to be. Guess I wasn't on target," she admitted.

"Ah, you have a little ways to go yet. I can get you back on the highway, and point you in the right direction," he said graciously, but she sensed some reluctance—or was it disappointment.

"Is it far away?"

"Not too far. But it can get a little confusing finding some of the backroads after dark."

"Oh, that's not good," she said worriedly, but he stepped nearer.

"Listen, I'm meeting some friends up at Race Point for the evening, and it's on the same route—why don't you follow us? I'll get you on your way, and maybe we can get together sometime while you're here? I know all the hot spots."

She wondered if she imagined the innuendo in his words, and then had a moment of worry. Had she been too open or too inviting with a complete stranger? As if sensing her thoughts, he reassured her with another smile, backing up a bit.

"No danger, promise. I live here over the summer. I'm a lifeguard at Chatham, and I'm a civil engineering student at BC— Boston College—so I am completely trustworthy."

College? Her interest plummeted. "Undergrad?"

"I'm just entering the first year of my Master's program."

Edie did a quick calculation. That would make him about twenty-three. Seven years—well, six and three hundred or so days—younger than she was.

She quickly dismissed her apprehensions. This vacation was for fun, for letting go of all of her responsibilities and inhibitions. Greg seemed like a nice guy. A nice guy who was *interested*. If he pushed too hard, she could take care of herself, but for the moment, he was just offering a helping hand.

"Thanks, I'd appreciate it, as long as it doesn't take you too far out of your way."

"No problem. Everything's nearby here, as you'll discover."

"You've lived here your whole life?" she asked as they made their way back from the beach, the dog at Greg's side.

"Yeah, my folks live in Chatham."

His parents. The idea that he was here, living with his parents, on a break from college, almost made her cringe. She was a dirty old lady.

"How nice. It must be great to spend all your school breaks here," she said, and groaned inwardly. Now she sounded like a prim and proper schoolmarm.

"It's my last summer doing that, so I'm enjoying it. I'm starting my own consulting company, focused on urban renewal, restoring abandoned neighborhoods, and improving ignored ones. With grad school, it's going to be a full load. What do you do?"

They reached her car, and she turned around by the driver's-side door to face him again. He was a working professional, just like her—an adult.

"I'm an accountant," she said, expecting him to give her the same pained look most people did when she made that announcement. He grinned.

"Wow. A hot accountant. Nice," he said, sharing one more long look, before turning his attention to the road. "My truck is just down the street—I'll circle back. Just follow me up about five miles up and then I'll tell you where to turn off to find your place. It will be one turn, then go a few miles down and you'll know you've found it when you hit the beach."

"Sounds good, thanks," she said, though she was still thinking about his comments from a few minutes earlier. *A hot accountant?* She was floating on air when she got back into the car.

She'd left her laptop, PDA and anything work-related at home. There was a beach bag full of magazines and books in the back seat, her hot-pink iPod, several different varieties of sunblock, and a scandalous array of condoms. Edie intended to use them all. She didn't feel guilty; she'd earned this. And if Greg wanted to ask her out, maybe she'd go. He looked as if he had a lot of…stamina.

This was *so* the right way to celebrate her thirtieth birthday, she thought, smiling back at Greg who pulled up alongside in his shiny blue truck.

It had been years since she'd had a real vacation, and with the big three-o approaching, there had been talk of a party. That was another reason to skip town. She abhorred the idea of a party, it was so…predictable.

She loved her family and friends, but for her thirtieth, she wanted something new and daring. Striking off on her own had been just the ticket, spending time with suntanned, easygoing, temporary guys like Greg if she wanted to. Perfect.

Things were different here. No one knew her, and she was free to do anything she pleased—with a handsome, younger man even. Everything the Cape had to offer would start her third decade out with an air of adventure. With any luck, maybe she'd be able to hold on to that when she went back home. Her life in Cleveland was fine, but that was it. It was just fine. Her job was okay, her friends and the men she dated were nice.

Fine, nice, okay.

The words that defined her. She needed new adjectives. Maybe she needed a new life, but for now, she just wanted a few weeks' escape.

She followed Greg until he pulled alongside, and then she parked behind him. When he jumped out of the truck and walked back, she looked at him again, and hoped it wasn't the last she'd see of him. He had amazing abs. Nice shoulders, too.

"Just take this next left, that's Beach Plum Road, and take it all the way to the water. Your place is the last house at the very end."

She smiled, deciding to jump in and go for it. "Thanks so much—maybe stop by sometime?"

Interest and a little spark of heat flew between them. "For sure. Take care," he said, backing away, and she hoped he'd keep his promise.

She felt giddy as a schoolgirl, her mood light as she drove alongside marshes and dunes. There were a few houses on the road, set back and private, and they were all lovely.

Edie's heart stopped when she finally hit the end of the road and pulled into the short driveway, the Mustang's tires crunching to a stop in front of the most charming home she'd ever laid eyes on. It was a hundred times better than the pictures she'd seen on the Web, and much larger.

Slanted dune fences latticed in vines with bright-pink flowers above the sand and grasses surrounded the house, and she couldn't have imagined anything lovelier.

A short stone path wound up to the front door, where steps led up to a whitewashed porch that wrapped entirely around the house. Cedar shingles were worn and faded by sun and salt, the roof and dormers angled sharply down in classic Cape style. Wood-framed windows were divided into eight panes each. Everywhere she looked, ocean, beach and marshlands were spread out around her. It was dusk, and a light was on inside, probably left on by the Realtor, which she found very considerate.

"Okay then, time to officially get this vacation started," she said, wondering if she would be able to take a moonlight walk on the beach later.

Lugging the bags up the steps to the porch, she searched her purse for the key sent to her, but it wasn't necessary—the door pushed open.

She hesitated for a moment. The place was probably so safe that people didn't lock the doors, she decided, and she made her way inside, though she kept her cell phone in hand, just in case.

The first thing she spotted was the unexpected sight of two other bags—and a pair of men's jeans—thrown over the sofa.

"What on earth?" she said and set her bags down, toeing the bag on the floor and taking a second look at the jeans—definitely male. The Realtor's? Caretaker's?

"Hello?" she called tentatively, the louder, "Hello? Anyone here?"

Silence answered her, and she moved through the house to the kitchen and the back door. "Hello?" she called again, checking through one beautifully decorated room after another, and finding nothing.

Relief thrummed through her. Someone had left the clothes here, maybe the previous renter, but she'd just contact the Realtor about it tomorrow. For now, she crossed back to the door to go retrieve the rest of her bags, including some groceries she'd picked up en route to tide her over.

She rushed back through the front door, humming a song that had been playing on the radio and hoping buff beach-boy Greg would come calling as he'd promised. She hadn't made it halfway inside the room when the sound of a door slamming froze her in her tracks.

"Who are you?"

They both asked the question at the same time, Edie and the nearly stark-naked, soaking wet—*gorgeous*—man who stood on the other side of the room, staring at her, both of them equally shocked.

He was tall—the epitome of tall, dark and incredibly, fascinatingly handsome. All coherent thoughts logjammed in her brain. Her heart pounded in her ears though she wasn't sure if she was frightened or just surprised. She stood staring, gaping.

"Who are you? And how did you get in here?" the man asked suspiciously, striding across the tile floor as if he belonged there. He obviously wasn't worried about his safety with *her.*

He went over to a closet where he opened a door, yanked out a towel and proceeded to rub it over his perfect torso, further distracting her. He was muscular, but not overly so. *Sculpted* was the word that came to mind as she watched him dry off.

My God, were all the men here perfect?

"I'm Edie. Edie Stevens," she managed, dragging her mind back to the moment, blinking as he reached for the jeans and hauled them on over his skivvies. "The door was open."

"So you just let yourself in?"

His sarcastic tone shook her out of her momentary halt.

"Wait. Who are *you?*" she asked more clearly, raising her eyes to his intense silver ones. The irises seemed almost transparent and his gaze was incisor-sharp. A wedge of straight black hair over his forehead added a touch of devil-may-care danger to his appearance, making her shiver. The way he looked at her—as though she'd done something wrong even though she hadn't—was so distracting.

"Well, Edie Stevens, why are you in my house?"

Her eyebrows flew up. "*Your* house?"

"Yes, my house. I live here."

A furious blush burned her cheeks as realization set in—had she screwed up again? Or had Greg sent her in the wrong direction? The door had been unlocked and the place looked so much like the one in the pictures…could she have located the wrong house? Mortified, she closed her eyes for a moment, then reluctantly opened them knowing she had to face the music.

"Oh God…I'm *so* sorry. I must have the wrong place. I got a little lost, and someone gave me directions. This was the only house on the road, and it looks just like the pictures, so I just assumed—"

"What house are you looking for?" he interrupted. He had a foot on her, height-wise, and she was face-to-face with his amazing chest. She'd always been a chest girl—nothing like a strong male torso to cuddle up on. His was fantasy material.

Edie wasn't usually flustered around men—she worked with dozens of them; many of her clients at the accounting firm were powerful, wealthy good-looking males. Being so rattled irritated her, and she drew herself up, mentally chastising herself for the flustered response.

"I was looking for 1279 Beach Plum Road. I rented the house for two weeks, and—"

"Who's your Realtor?"

"Jason Yates. Beachside Realty."

The man offered a gusty sigh, and tossed his towel on the chair by the door.

"Well, it seems you have the right address, so accept my apologies, but we've obviously got a rental mix-up. I'm Joel Roberts, the owner of the property. I distinctly instructed them not to book rentals for this month, but unfortunately, I guess someone must have gotten their wires crossed. Sorry about that."

Edie took in his conciliatory tone, but instinct told her that he didn't sound as if he was going to rectify the situation, either.

"Well, it wasn't *my* mistake. I rented this house for two weeks— I paid months in advance. I drove all the way from Cleveland."

"You'll have to find another place. I'll make sure you get a full refund of your money," he said matter-of-factly.

Edie stood her ground. "I don't want a refund—and I don't want to be stuck in some crowded motel on the highway, either. I paid in advance and in good faith for this place, and this is where I want to be. It already cost me time and money to come this far, and I want the vacation I paid for. I have my receipts," she said with conviction, glad she'd packed a copy of the rental agreement and the connected payments. In her line of work, she'd always found too much documentation was better than not enough.

He seemed momentarily taken aback by her vehemence, but shook his head.

"I'm sorry, I really am. I understand you're in a spot, but I'm here for the next few weeks, and this *is* my home. I have contacts around the Cape— you can stay here tonight. I'll make some calls in the morning to find you another comparable house, maybe even someplace better, okay?"

"You want us to stay here in the same house? Together?"

He smiled, but it didn't reach his eyes. "Don't worry. It's just one night, and you're not in any danger from me."

"Oh. Thanks. I think."

She supposed he was being reasonable about it, and if he could find her a nice place, she couldn't really argue with that.

Normally, she would never have agreed to spend the night in the same house with a strange man, but it wasn't as if they were sharing a room, right? And what other choice did she have? It *was* his house. She couldn't exactly ask him to leave. And sharing a house with a handsome man, even for a night, piqued her sense of adventure.

Edie wasn't a risk-taker, but this was her chance. She could spend the night with this guy, right?

"There are four bedrooms in this house—and I assume the doors close. I think we can both tough it out for a night, assuming you stay on the right side of yours." She figured a little warning never hurt. Better to be direct.

He raised his eyebrows. "Don't worry about that. Pretty as you are, I'm not interested in that particular kind of trouble."

Just what did he mean by that, she wondered? She was tempted to ask, but the way his expression turned carefully neutral as he said the words discouraged her from doing so. None of her business.

She grimaced and grabbed her bags, frustrated that her perfect vacation wasn't exactly getting off to a peaceful start. Who knew what tomorrow would bring, where she'd end up, or how long it would take to find a new place and settle in?

Mind over matter. She was here. She was on vacation, and she had a place to stay for the night. It would all work out. Vacation was about adventure, and adventure wasn't always safe and predictable.

Hoisting her bags, she nodded.

"If you can tell me which room is mine, I'd appreciate it, and we'll get this settled in the morning, I guess."

Upstairs she walked into the first room she passed and fell in love with the place all over again. Setting her bags down with a decisive thump, she walked over to the window and looked out at the sunset, the sky and the ocean seeming to darken at once, closing in on each other. It was soothing, so different from the noisy, bustling suburban neighborhoods she was used to. She smiled as a silver-white bird cut through the scene, diving for its dinner.

The room was so pretty with its practical and sturdy furnishings and nautical colors and themes. It was perfect. She didn't want to give up her vacation dream. Maybe she could use feminine wiles to convince him to let her stay...?

Her shoulders slumped and she leaned back against the wall. No, she wanted some adventure, but she wasn't *that* daring. Besides, he'd hardly looked interested, and her feminine wiles were out of practice.

Still, she had to find a way to convince him to let her stay. It was a big house, and why not? Edie was an optimist—they could work it out.

It was too early to go to bed anyway, and she was hungry. Maybe she'd go downstairs and wow her temporary host with her culinary skills, a much safer way of getting on his good side.

As she changed her clothes, however, she strategically chose a particularly sexy black tank top that she'd bought especially for the trip. It revealed more cleavage than she usually did, but if she was going to persuade Joel to let her hang around, she had to use every asset she had available.

Taking a deep breath and planning to put her best foot forward, she headed downstairs and hoped for the best.

2

JOEL SAT on the deck listening to the sounds of the waves splashing up on the shore and tried to find a solution out of this situation. He'd made a few quick phone calls while his new guest was upstairs, but it was a no-go. It was high season, and there wasn't a house rental or even a hotel room to be found.

He was here to relax, to get back in touch with what mattered in his life. And he had intended to do that alone.

A failed marriage had been the last straw in his life, and he had to make some changes. He owned a successful law practice, and it had taken everything he had for the last ten years. He'd finally stopped handling it all himself and had added two partners who could run things without him for periods of time. But it was still *his* firm. However, he was planning to reprioritize a little. Women were not a priority except in the most casual way, and having one living in his house was very inconvenient. Especially a blond bombshell who made it difficult to Zen out and remember he was here for a higher purpose.

His rumbling stomach put an end to his brooding thoughts for the time being. Right now he should put something on for dinner and play the host, at least for tonight. Pushing out of his chair, he went back inside, and, as he rounded the corner, the sight of Edie Stevens in a pair of barely-there white shorts and a sexy black tank top stopped him in his tracks. Guilt and lust assailed him all at once. He wanted her to go, but he momentarily forgot why.

Reining in his libido, he ruthlessly reminded himself that the same reaction to another beautiful woman had landed him in a marriage that never should have happened. His romantic impulses weren't very reliable.

All the same, he was almost incapable of dragging his eyes away from Edie as she bent to tie her sneaker. Her skin was pale, but it was classic peaches-and-cream. With loose blond curls, blue eyes and Daisy Duke legs, she was a midwest-farmer's-daughter fantasy walking around his house.

She saw him and straightened, facing him. "I, uh, settled in, but wondered if I could make you something for dinner? I'm a decent cook, and I wanted to thank you for letting me stay tonight and trying to find me another place."

He decided to break the bad news directly. "Actually, I'm not sure this will work out. I made some calls, but I couldn't find you another place. I'm sorry, I really am. I will refund your money and in addition, I'd even be willing to rent you the house another time. You can come here for another two weeks we mutually agree on, no charge."

She looked at him, her soft blue irises turning steely as slate in spite of his more-than-generous offer. She wasn't happy, but it was the best he could do. He was taking a loss on negotiating with her, and Joel rarely lost.

"Listen, I rented this house, and I'm staying here if you can't find another place," she declared stubbornly. "My contract is signed and paid in full. I have all the paperwork with me, and you haven't even considered the four-hundred-and-fifty-dollar car rental, one hundred dollars of gas and the twelve-hour drive here. I am not turning around and driving back now."

He hadn't expected that reaction, he had to be honest. She had grounds, literally, but he'd expected her to jump at his offer and couldn't believe she was pushing the issue.

However, she had a point. He'd drawn up the airtight rental contracts himself, and he couldn't ask her to leave when she had a signed agreement, not to mention her other expenses. There were a few cancellation clauses in the contract, but "the owner wants the house to himself" wasn't one of them.

"I was just hoping that you'd understand, and that we could work something out," he said lamely.

"I see. You live here. I came here for my vacation, and that's all I want. I suggest we just keep doing what we're doing now. Share."

"Share? As in live here? Together?"

"Sure, why not? We're adults."

"It won't work," he stated flatly.

"Why not?"

"It won't work because I'm a man and you're a woman—a very sexy, hot woman, and if we're in the same space, we're going to end up in bed, and though I'm quite sure it would be great, I don't need that kind of trouble."

She narrowed her eyes. "Well, aren't we just sure of ourselves?" she said sarcastically, but her cheeks turned pink, and he knew he'd hit a nerve.

He ran a hand through his hair, realizing he had sounded just a bit full of himself. Finding women willing to spend time with him had never been a problem, but Edie Stevens didn't look like she was one of them. He tried a different tack, if appealing to her money sense wouldn't work.

"I'm sorry. But you see, I came here to be alone, to reflect on life after my divorce, and I don't really see how I can do that with company. Especially company as distracting as you are," he said, meaning it.

She blinked, and he knew she'd been thrown by the compliment. Score one for him. It wasn't enough to throw her off her game, though.

"I'm sorry about your divorce, that sucks. But I'll be gone a lot, at the beach, shopping, relaxing. I don't expect you to entertain me, or even talk to me if you don't want to. We could just share the space. There are two bathrooms, so we should be fine."

She made it all sound so easy, so practical. He stood silent, unable to come up with any more objections, except that looking at her made him hot. That was going to make it difficult for him to relax, but he didn't think she'd be sympathetic to the point.

Being a lawyer, he couldn't deny the logic of her argument. She'd rented the place, and what harm could it do? She seemed nice enough, and it was only two weeks, right?

He was nodding before he had really finished the thought, and her smile was so wide he felt the flash of it right down to his feet. Edie might not be interested in him, but Joel could find himself in a cold shower a lot over the next two weeks.

"Oh, good! Thank you!"

Suddenly she was sweet as sunshine, and Joel knew he'd lost— and lost soundly.

She opened a few cupboards and pulled out a pan. "Let me make you dinner, okay? We can just talk and get comfortable with each other, and as of tomorrow morning, you'll hardly know I'm here."

Joel blankly watched Edie plunge into the refrigerator and start making dinner. It was disconcerting, but he was just going to go with the flow. He could sit tonight and share a meal, and hope she'd hold to her word that in the morning, they'd live like two strangers in the same house. It was just two weeks, he reminded himself.

He choked off a groan as she bent to grab some vegetables out of the lower compartment, the white shorts riding up even higher. He closed his eyes, hoping the next two weeks would pass very quickly.

EDIE GASPED, walking forward into the dark gray-green water until it was up to her knees. It was bitterly cold; she hadn't expected the warmth of the Caribbean, but her toes were already numb. Was it safe to swim in water this cold?

About twenty yards down the beach she saw two young children run into the rolling surf, laughing and screeching as their mother looked on. The fearless children made her ashamed of her shivering hesitation, and she took a deep breath and dove.

Oh. My. God.

Her body sliced through the icy water, and she surfaced with a laugh, quickly breaking into a strong crawl to get her body moving before she froze into place. The sun was baking down on her back, the cold water sliding along her front, her body hugged between bracing cold and burning hot.

Edie was a good swimmer, a credit to daily laps at the gym and parents who insisted their children learn to swim well at a young age. Cleveland sat on the edge of Lake Erie, which seemed as large as an ocean and was certainly as dangerous.

Stopping for a moment to gauge how far she'd gone, she could still see the beach house to her left, and she spotted a boat moored in a small cove to her right. Someone walked on the deck—Joel. It had to be.

He was definitely incredibly hot and she was quite sure he'd know what he was doing in bed. He had that confident air that said he liked to be in control, and no doubt he knew how to satisfy. Maybe she'd like to find out, but he'd also made it clear he wasn't interested. Besides, he had too much emotional baggage, coming off of his divorce. Handsome as he was—and as curious as she was—she wasn't here to get weighed down by guys with issues. *Fun* was the operative word.

True to her word, she'd gotten up, taken herself out for breakfast, bought enough groceries to last her two weeks, and then come back and gathered all of her things for the beach, planning to stay here the entire day. Joel wouldn't even know she was around, and she wanted to put him out of her thoughts, as well. Maybe she'd even meet some other hunks out on the sand. It was still early.

She swam along, not realizing how far she'd gone until a sudden pull grabbed her out of nowhere. She tensed, missing a stroke, and the next thing she knew, she was underwater, and her mind blanked with panic—*shark!*

No…no biting, she sighed with relief. However, she was being dragged out at a good speed. She was caught in an undertow, and knew if she was going to avoid drowning, she had to relax. Within moments the drag lessened, and she saw that she was quite a distance from the shore.

She could still spot Joel's boat, and that was good. She tried swimming parallel, the only way to really get out of an undertow, but the current was too wide. She was stuck. It was damned cold. Treading water, she could see the speck of Joel's red baseball cap on the deck of his boat. She shouted, choking down several mouthfuls of water, and she spat, trying again.

He stood in place, and she hoped against hope that he saw her. Unsure if her voice was carrying, she reached back and undid her top, lifting her arm up as high as she could and waving the bright-yellow bra in the air like a flag.

Two seconds later, to her immense relief, the red cap waved back. Help was on the way.

She just had to keep moving, so she started swimming in slow circles. She hoped to God there were no sharks in the water with her. Or jellyfish. Edie really hated the idea of big, gloopy, stinging jellyfish.

Her fingers were so stiff from the cold water that it took her several tries to get her top back on, gulping several mouthfuls of salt water as she did so.

A moment later, she heard a humming noise. A hundred feet or so ahead of her, Joel and his red hat bobbed over the swells in a small Zodiac, heading right for her. She was so relieved that she cried out, choking on another mouthful of water, but she waved her hands and did what she could to make sure he didn't lose sight of her.

The craft pulled up beside her, and before she could say so much as much as one word, she was grabbed, hoisted fully out of the water and plopped unceremoniously in the bottom of the boat. It took a second of Joel staring at her in disbelief before she realized she was nearly topless, her swimsuit bra sliding every which way.

"Oh!" She coughed, still spitting out water, covering herself with one arm while she pushed her hair back and pulled herself into a more normal position, trying to adjust her top.

"Here. Wrap up—your lips are turning blue," Joel said gruffly, tossing her a towel from where he sat as he restarted the motor and turned back to the cove.

He sounded cranky, but she barely noticed. She was freezing, exhausted and just so happy to be out of the water that nothing mattered as long as he got her back to terra firma. Wrapping up in the towel, putting her face to the sun, she still couldn't seem to feel any warmth, and she shivered uncontrollably.

They pulled up beside the larger boat, and Joel attached the Zodiac quickly, reaching down and helping her to her feet. Her knees gave way at first, but then, embarrassed, she held her own as he supported her from the back, getting her up on deck.

"C'mon, brisk walk, jumping jacks, whatever you have to do to get the blood moving."

"I'm so tired, my limbs feel like spaghetti," she said breathlessly, but did as she was told, making a few small hops and shaking out her arms. She started to feel more normal, if still cold and exhausted. She walked toward the bench along the rail of the boat, but tripped, her knees like rubber, gasping as Joel caught her. His hands moved over her briskly, rubbing warmth into her skin.

"Thank you so much," she whispered, leaning into his warm chest and closing her eyes for a moment. His hands gripped her shoulders. Her eyes shot open to see Joel's stark ones staring into hers.

"Okay, you look better. We can go to the doctor if you want to."

"No, I'm okay. I just have to get warm."

"How did you end up out there? You would have been dead if I hadn't seen you."

She was too tired to be indignant at his tone as his chin brushed her forehead. "I got caught in a rip—could happen to anyone."

"You shouldn't have gone out there alone."

She didn't look at him, knowing she'd been stupid and impulsive, and that he was right. Yet, she felt stubborn. "I'm a good swimmer. I would have made it back, just a hell of a lot slower."

"Hypothermia sets in fast. I didn't think to warn you about the currents, so I'm sorry, too. At least you didn't panic," he said, continuing to hold her close. His skin was so hot next to hers, she felt as though he was transferring heat directly to her. She cuddled in, seeking the heat.

"My father drilled this stuff into us since we were kids, but you know, you never really think it will happen."

"Smart thinking with the bathing-suit top. That yellow stands out. Though I have to say, you look pretty great without it, as well."

She heard the smile in his voice, and relaxed. Joel was warm and solid, and he smelled great. She sighed and rubbed her cheek against his shirt like a cat.

"You sure you're okay?" He slid one arm around her shoulders, and tipped her chin up so he was looking right into her eyes.

"More than," she said, looking into his eyes and not bothering to hide that she was completely turned on. Maybe it was the near-death experience, but she wanted Joel to keep warming her up—and then some.

His eyes narrowed, watching her, and drifted down to her lips. "I see," he murmured, his mouth next to hers. A second later he was kissing her, and then it was like being hit by several hundred volts of electricity. She went from cold to warm to hot in seconds, and moaned, wrapping her arms around his neck, arching closer.

She'd been right. Joel was definitely a man who knew what he was doing.

His lips were hard, hot and insistent, prying her lips apart as he invaded her, tasting her deeply. He kissed like a man, like a very hungry, determined man. There was no introduction or hesitation, just raw passion between them.

As his hands moved to her breasts, she hesitated for a split second. What was she doing? She was out in the middle of the morning, with a strange man, half-naked….

Her hesitation passed as his hands slipped over her. It was *wonderful*.

"Damn…you're just as soft as you look," he said, lowering his head and drawing a hard, eager nipple into his mouth.

Sensation ripped through her and she pressed into him, letting him tease and suck, passion spiking. Sexy and bold, she could let loose and do whatever she wanted. Then remembering they were out in the open, she looked around.

"Maybe we should check out the…"

He drew away, looked up at her, his breathing faster, his cheeks ruddy, eyes darkening.

"I have a small cabin below, but I've been remodeling it. There's no bed."

"Don't need a bed, just some privacy," she said playfully.

The few men she'd been with, it had always been at night, in a bed, sometimes with the lights on, but that was the limit of her sexual craziness. The idea of no bed at all was exciting, and being here on Joel's boat, she couldn't wait to see what they would do to improvise. The way he was looking at her was enough to convince her she was doing the right thing—his eyes were devouring her, and she felt like the sexiest woman on earth.

She leaned in and kissed him again, becoming the total sex kitten she'd always wanted to be.

"What are we waiting for?"

Luckily, Joel wasn't content to wait, either, sliding his arms under her and lifting her up, nibbling her shoulder as they walked down the narrow steps.

"You're delicious," he said, and she smiled.

"You don't know that yet, but I wouldn't mind you finding out."

"Jesus," he said gustily, and she was fascinated as she watched his pulse pound visibly in his neck. A riff of excitement thrilled through her as she watched him shuck his shorts and shirt, seeing he had nothing on underneath.

He leaned down, kissed her without preamble, and the kiss was even hotter than before. She covered his hands as they worked her breasts. He was obsessed with her breasts, and she didn't mind one bit. She slid her hands down his body exploring every glorious inch of it, then closed her hand around his cock, stroking, loving how large and velvety he was. He broke away from her, his breathing hard.

"It's been a while, I'm afraid, and I don't know that I can last too long if you keep stroking me like that," he said raggedly.

"There's no need to wait," she said sincerely, so turned on she wanted him inside her now and wasn't coy about losing her own bathing-suit bottoms. He pulled his wallet out of his shorts, removed a condom and sheathed himself, his eyes fixed on her the whole time. She held his gaze, the tender spot between her legs aching and wet, needing what he was promising. She'd never been this hot, this ready, for any man.

"That table is sturdy and bolted to the floor," he suggested, nodding to a small square table in the corner. Edie walked to the table and turned, looking at Joel.

She ran a hand over the table's surface, which was polished, but still could leave a sliver in her backside—not terrifically sexy—and opted to lean. The notion of Joel standing behind her blinded her with lust. She'd never been *done* that way before, and so she planted her elbows on the table, peeking back at him sexily.

"This work for you?"

"You couldn't be more perfect," he said admiringly, massaging her bottom and exploring all the soft skin open to his touch. She shuddered with pleasure as his fingertips prodded at forbidden spaces, testing her, excitement making her fingers form into fists on the cool surface of the table. She planted her feet wide, adjusting to the movement of the boat, and moaning when the slight rocking motion just added to the heat of his touches.

It was like being lifted out of herself into a dream, into the sexy, incredible life of someone she'd always wished she could be.

"I'm *so* ready, Joel," she said, unashamed of the raw need in her tone, and lifted her hips slightly, issuing a blatant invitation. He took advantage, sliding one, then two fingers inside her. She knew she was completely open to him from his vantage point, and it excited her more than she could stand. She pressed backward, seeking the motion and the satisfaction she craved.

"Oh!" she gasped as her inner muscles coiled, tightening almost painfully around his fingers. She'd never been penetrated this way, so surely, so…completely. His thumb sneaked forward to press on the hard, hot nub of her clit, and she cried out, pushing back harder.

"Come for me, sweetheart," he ordered sexily, inserting his fingers a little deeper, rubbing a little more insistently, and she was happy to comply as shocks of pleasure rippled through her, everything falling away from her in several long seconds of ecstasy.

She stilled, held her breath as he nestled close behind her, withdrawing his fingers and bending over her, his strong, slick hands closing over her breasts as the end of his erection nudged her opening.

"Your breasts drive me wild. Hearing you come drives me wild," he said against her skin. She couldn't hold back a whimper of need, the rush of heat liquefying into a torrent of pleasure at the contact. Holding herself steady, she moaned as he buried himself deep with one masterful thrust and a masculine groan of satisfaction.

"You are so damned tight," he murmured, sliding his tongue over her back and leaving wet kisses all over her skin as his hands clamped down on her breasts. He withdrew, then drove home again, hard and long, making her entire body convulse with sensation.

Whispering hot words and encouraging her to come for him again, he slid one hand down to massage her intimately, which also served to push her pelvis up and back so he could enter her even more deeply.

His long, hard thrusts became faster and harder, his skin slapping against hers, the butterfly motions of his fingers creating a delicious contrast with the way he took a nipple between his fingers, pinching until it was almost painful, but not quite. The onslaught of his touch inside and out ultimately catapulted her over the brink. She swore she could feel his orgasm pulse inside her as he came right after she did, his groans of pleasure sweet against the skin of her shoulder.

It was the only time she'd ever come so hard she couldn't remember anything but the orgasm. It had been…surreal, like being lifted out of reality and then set back again.

"Joel…my knees are shaking," she said, huskily. He straightened, moving out from between her legs to draw her back against him, supporting her.

"You are…incredible," he said, tasting her, kissing her so sweetly she felt the desire building again, and wiggled against him. "I want to say we shouldn't have done that, but I'm very glad we did."

"Me, too. It was so good, Joel," she said dreamily. "Fun."

He turned her around and tipped her chin so she could see him. He looked like a Greek Adonis in the sunlight streaming through the porthole, looking down at her, his eyes lazy from satisfaction. "No regrets?"

"There's no way I could regret *that*." She shook her head, letting it rest on his shoulder. "I have to admit, I've never even slept with a man on the first or second date, let alone doing what we just did within hours of meeting, but that's what vacation is for, right?"

She was saying it for herself as much as him. She'd remember this moment until her last day, in fact, she was quite sure it might come back as her final thought. She'd die with a smile, for sure.

He grinned and her heart tumbled in her chest. Had a man ever smiled at her and made her entire reality crash around her like that?

"Yeah, I guess that *is* what vacations are for."

"You know what?"

"What?"

"I want to do it again," she said mischievously.

"Wildcat," he said approvingly, but then turned serious. "I just don't want there to be any misunderstandings. Temporary fun is all I'm up for, Edie. I really don't want to get involved right now. I did come here to be alone."

She nodded, the warm afterglow hanging on and making her mellow. "I can understand that, and our original deal holds as far as I'm concerned. We can go our separate ways and enjoy our time, but if we decide to do this again, I wouldn't argue."

He looked at her as though she'd given him the most amazing gift, quickly followed by a flash of disbelief and doubt.

"I promise, no strings, Joel. I want the same thing you do, just some summer fun."

She slid her hand around the back of his neck, drawing him down and kissing him with every ounce of desire inside her. She was quite sure this would be the best vacation of her life, even as her heart made her question how sure she was about what she'd said to Joel.

She'd never had really casual sex before, sex that she knew wouldn't lead anywhere, but she would stick to her word, no matter what. As Joel gathered her up and covered her lips with his, he proceeded to erase any nagging worries from her mind.

3

JOEL HUNG OVER the side of the boat, leaning awkwardly down over the rail to sand a patch of fiberglass that needed to be resealed and painted. Sweat dripped down his brow, and he paused for a moment, getting a breath.

In four days he'd gotten a lot done, working on the boat most of the day and catching up with Edie when she was home. As promised, she was gone a lot, too—at the beach, down in town, shopping and keeping herself busy.

After that first time on the boat, they'd kept to the plan and spent their days on their own, but at night, in the house, they couldn't keep their clothes on for more than five minutes. It was hands-down the best sex he'd ever had. She had no reservations, no inhibitions, and he showed no signs of being tired of it, either.

That was worrisome.

Make no mistake, Joel liked sex, but he'd never craved it the way he did lately. He wasn't getting involved with this girl and compounding the mistakes he'd already made in life, he told himself, starting to scrub at the boat's surface again with renewed energy.

Something landed on his backside, and he jerked and hit his head before he saw it was Edie. Her thighs straddled his butt, and she slid her palms up his back, massaging aching muscles. In his dangling position, she had him trapped. He wouldn't mind except that he went rock-hard immediately, and being sandwiched between her and the hard surface of the deck was a little uncomfortable, though in the best possible way.

"Hey," he said, shifting beneath her, "let me up, you hussy."

She laughed, lifting up a little and letting him slide back fully onto the deck. He didn't get up, but he did roll over. She lowered back down, settling the warm valley between her thighs over the bulge in his shorts, her eyes going wide as she wiggled her eyebrows comically.

"And you're calling *me* a hussy?"

"Men can't be hussies," he said, stretching his arms up above his head and lacing his fingers behind, enjoying the view. She looked good enough to eat in a flirty sundress that left very little between them except her panties and his jeans. Those could be very quickly disposed of, he thought.

Hands planted on his chest, she pressed down just right and closed her eyes. A rosy tint of excitement infused her cheeks, slightly tanned after a few days in the sun.

"Ohhh, you feel good, and this is tempting, but I was heading into P-town for some shopping and lunch. Want to come with me? I read something about a beach club and a band playing tonight. Sounds fun."

He hesitated for a minute, wanting to spend some time with Edie, but that time was about them having sex, not going on a date. Even a casual date was risky. One thing could lead to another and before he knew it, expectations would be formed and he'd be in over his head, digging his way out of another relationship. No, thanks.

"Sorry, babe." He shrugged, lifting his hips and rubbing against the hot junction of her thighs. "Have to get these spots painted—can't leave them exposed to the elements. You have fun, though."

Disappointment flickered briefly in her eyes, but she rebounded so quickly he thought he might have imagined it. A second later, she was up and off him, smoothing her dress and smiling brightly.

"Okay, then. I'm gone. I'll probably be late."

"Wish I could join you, but," he said with a nod to the area he'd been sanding, hoping he sounded sincere.

"No problem. I just thought I'd ask." She smiled promisingly. "Maybe we'll bump into each other later tonight."

"You can count on it."

She waved and blew him a kiss, and left.

That was it. No guilt, no histrionics, tears or pouting. Not what he was used to, and he wasn't sure why he felt strange that she so easily walked away. It was stupid, since he'd turned down her invitation, right?

Joel had to admit, Edie was the most straightforward, least manipulative woman he'd ever met. He enjoyed her company, she stayed out of his way, and they had great sex. Sex that she was apparently still interested in, even when he declined to spend the day with her. It was all good. He'd been handed every man's fantasy: a beautiful woman who enjoyed hot sex and didn't place any more demands on him than to satisfy her in bed.

So why was he less than motivated to work on the boat now? Partly because he was so achingly hard he couldn't turn back over, but also he felt a sense of disappointment. He couldn't figure it out.

"I'm just hungry," he said to the stark blue sky, glancing at his watch. He walked to the cooler on deck, grabbed a beer and sat, looking out at the water.

He was doing the right thing. What he and Edie had was good, clean fun, and would end in about nine days. Then they'd go their separate ways and that would be that.

Peering down into the cooler again, he cursed, he'd left his food up at the house, in the fridge. Ah well, he wanted a break anyway.

When he got home he saw the message button blinking on the phone. He pressed the button as he went to the fridge, but was stopped in his tracks by what he heard.

The messages weren't for him, but for Edie from her girlfriends. One after the other they had sent happy wishes and some things he wasn't sure he should have heard—her girlfriends were obviously curious about whether she was "hooking up" for her…birthday. It was clear that Edie had hoped to spend her vacation doing, well, what she and Joel were doing—and her friends knew it. Did they know about him? No doubt they would. Deep down, that bothered him, though he couldn't imagine why. Guys bragged all the time if they bagged a sexy girl—he'd done it himself—but it was a little different, he'd admit, the shoe being on the other foot.

"Happy Birthday," her family sang in one message.

To Edie.

He didn't mean to listen to her messages, and was saved cutting it short as the song was cut off in midchorus. He couldn't help but smile when a two-part message picked up where the first left off, finishing the tune on a hysterically loud and off-key note, several members of her family offering birthday wishes along with condolences—she was thirty today. Not just a birthday, a milestone.

Joel blew out a breath, feeling as though he'd been socked in the gut. She was alone on her birthday. She'd had on a nice dress and had asked him to go into town with her, to spend an evening at a club, and he'd blown her off.

But he hadn't known—and even if he had, wasn't that even more reason to not go? Birthdays meant something, and being Edie's birthday date might create connections he didn't want. Besides, if she wanted a party, why wasn't she home? She'd made it clear she'd come here to find casual sex and party. She had no expectations of him.

But she'd asked him to go out with her, his conscience nagged.

He didn't want to, and he shouldn't, feel guilty about this.

But he did. Dammit!

He finished listening, and was envious of all the people who so obviously cared for Edie. His own family didn't tend to make a big fuss over birthdays, even though his parents always sent him a gift and his brother never failed to at least call. It was Joel who'd always been busy, who'd always been working. To be honest, he couldn't even remember what he'd done on his thirtieth birthday. His friends were all business acquaintances, and he couldn't remember the last time anyone had sung the birthday song, not since he was a child. Listening to Edie's messages, though he didn't mean to, reminded him again of everything he'd lost touch with over the years, and intended to fix.

He hovered, unsure if he should go change and catch up with her, or go back to the boat. Finally deciding it was best for both of them in the long run if he just returned to working on the boat, he headed for the kitchen to grab his lunch.

He made it as far as the front room before he detoured upstairs to shower and get dressed.

EDIE WALKED along the crowded, narrow streets of Provincetown, gripping several shopping bags. It was her birthday and she'd celebrated by making liberal use of her credit card, buying some beautiful locally made jewelry, a painting of the shore and several items of clothing. She'd picked up some souvenirs and funny items, as well, taking her time and picking through the gift shops.

She loved it here—for such a small town, it was bustling and hip. Locals navigated the streets expertly on bicycles, winding in and around tourists browsing from shop to shop.

It was a little strange being completely alone on her birthday, as if she had a secret as she walked among the passers-by, but she was proud of herself that she was actually enjoying it. It would have been very nice if Joel had come along—she'd felt a little let down that he hadn't—but they didn't have that kind of relationship. Actually, they didn't have a relationship at all, and she had to be sure to remember that. She frowned.

She was enjoying him—he was the perfect summer fling, and boy, was he good at it. In four days they'd flung each other in just about every way she could think of, and just thinking of it made her slick. She loved what he did to her, with her, and what he encouraged her do to him. She was making up for a lifetime of boring sex in a short period of time, and she was sure she'd never settle for less in the future, now that she knew how adventurous sex could be. A few of the items she'd picked up reflected her newfound sexual prowess, and she couldn't wait to wear them for Joel and see his reaction.

Still, while he'd actually fallen asleep in her bed the night before, and she'd awakened to watch the sun kiss his face right before she did, she had to squelch any of her more tender feelings. What she didn't want for her birthday was to get hurt. She'd enjoy what they had, and that was it.

"Hey, Edie from Cleveland," a male voice called out, and she looked up into Greg's smiling face.

"Greg. Wow, this is a surprise," she said, smiling back, vaguely relieved to meet someone she knew.

"I planned to look you up, you know, and now you just pop up right here in front of me. Must be fate," he teased, standing a little closer than a casual acquaintance might. Edie told herself it was because he was moving out of the way of the stream of people behind him, but she couldn't help her heartbeat picking up a little, her new adventurous self not backing away.

He was so handsome, if in a way completely opposite to Joel. The undisguised, boyish pleasure in his expression as he looked at her made her blush, and she smiled, flirting right back.

"I've just been shopping, and thinking of what to do next," she said lightly, feeling as if she'd stated the obvious.

"Are you hungry? We could grab some lunch—I know the best spots, if you're interested."

She put a hand to her stomach and nodded. "I'm starving—lunch sounds perfect. I wasn't sure which place to choose."

He slung his arm around her so easily, they might have known each other for years and they merged back into the throng of people.

"Let me lead the way—not only do I know where you can get the best lobster roll around, but I'm friends with the hostess so we won't have to wait forever for a good seat," he said.

"Sounds perfect. A lobster roll is a pleasure that I still needed to check off on my vacation must-do list," she responded.

Greg leaned in close to her ear. "Let me know if there's anything else on that list I might be able to help you with."

She chuckled, feeling her cheeks warm again, and just nodded, a few suggestions popping in her mind.

What was the proper protocol here? She'd never been interested in two men before in her entire life, and was this okay? Was it okay to be sleeping with Joel, but flirting with Greg? Even thinking about maybe doing a little more than flirting?

Would Joel care? Did Edie care if he cared? He hadn't wanted to come with her, and she was enjoying herself—and if she wanted to enjoy herself with Greg, why not?

So why did she feel as if she was doing something illegal?

"Here we are. After you." Greg gallantly led her through the door of a small café that sported the same ocean-weathered shingles and wood planks as every other building on the strip. The interior was small, no more than a diner counter, really. Edie was fine with that, though she'd been looking for something a little fancier for her birthday lunch.

"Through here," Greg instructed, leading her by her hand out onto a small deck that was propped up over the water, a square holding about ten tables that looked out over the ocean and allowed a view of the street. Colorful umbrellas protected each table from birds and sun, and flower boxes surrounded the deck. Edie relaxed, sighing in pleasure.

"This is so beautiful! What a view."

"And the food is not only fresh and delicious, but relatively inexpensive, as well. No tourist pricing here," he added.

As a waitress took their order, she smiled and settled more comfortably in her chair.

"This is ideal. Thank you. I'm so glad we bumped into each other again. I hope I'm not derailing your plans."

"Had no plans, was just walking around, hanging out. Can't think of a better way to spend my afternoon than with a pretty accountant from Ohio," he said, then faltered, grinning in a shy way she found utterly charming. "That is…not to assume you want to spend the afternoon with me. I was just…I mean, you know—ugh, let's try again," he cursed softly, and she laughed.

"No, that's fine—to tell you the truth—" she leaned in conspiratorially "—I am very happy to have someone to spend the day with because…it's my birthday."

"Whoa! Seriously? And you're all alone? Well, then I'm doubly glad to be here. May I ask what birthday it is?"

"You might change your mind about hanging out with me if I tell you," she teased.

"Not much chance of that," he said, reaching over and letting his fingers lie on hers.

"Okay, prepare yourself—the big three-o."

To his credit, he looked astounded. She wanted to kiss him for that alone.

"No freakin' way! You're lying."

"Nope. I can even show you my driver's license."

He slid his chair over a little closer to hers, lifting his glass up. "Well, damn. Here's to thirty. I think I'm suddenly *very* into older women," he said sincerely, and she laughed, clinking her glass to his.

As their meals came and they continued to chat, Edie found she was enjoying Greg's company very much, and yet…yet Joel was still at the edges of her mind. It made no sense. They had no connection other than sex, no promises, no obligations. Why should she be thinking of him while she was sitting here with Greg?

And why wasn't she responding at all to the obviously sexual signals that Greg was sending her way? Maybe she should experiment, really let go, and if she wanted Greg, and he wanted her, what was the harm, right? She was here to have fun, and she was pretty sure Greg would be a lot of fun.

Still, as much as she wanted to be a liberated, *Sex in the City* type of gal, the truth was that she was Edie, and she was more comfortable with one man at a time. Even if she and Joel didn't have anything resembling a relationship, she was with him at the moment, and she had…well, some feelings for him, even if they were casual ones. The chemistry she had with Joel was different from anything she'd known before. As cute as Greg was, she just couldn't do it. Or him.

She looked up, almost as if something tangible had interrupted her thoughts.

Joel.

He stood on the sidewalk, dressed in khaki pants and black cotton shirt, looking so handsome her heart plunged. He strode by, then paused, as if looking over the crowd. Looking for her?

"Something wrong?" Greg asked.

"I just, uh, I see someone I know," she stuttered, having completely forgotten about Greg for about thirty seconds.

"You've made friends fast, I see," Greg said with a smile, reaching to take the check from her side of the table and brushing his hand along hers in the process and lifting it to his lips—just as Joel turned. His stare locked on to them, and Edie stared back, fighting the urge to stand up and run out to meet him, to tell him it wasn't what it looked like….

But wasn't it exactly what it looked like?

She'd been sitting, flirting and having lunch with another man. *Another* man? How could there be another man, when Joel wasn't *her* man in the first place? Joel hadn't wanted to come with her today; he'd been working on his boat. He was only interested in sex, right? It wasn't as if they were exclusive; it wasn't as if they'd shared anything more than orgasms. They'd made no promises.

So why was he twenty feet away, looking at Greg as though he wanted to kill him? What was Joel thinking? Would he cause a scene? Why on earth would he? Her pulse leapt with a little zip of hope.

Greg, completely clueless about the drama playing out around him, paid the check and spoke briefly to the waitress. Edie couldn't take her eyes off Joel.

"Hey, happy birthday," Greg said as they stood. Edie wasn't prepared, wasn't paying attention, as Greg swooped in for a kiss. She turned to him quickly, smiling, murmuring a thank-you, aware she was being very rude to the man who *had* wanted to spend time with her on her birthday. Shouldn't she be focused on him, and not feeling so guilty? Putting Joel out of her field of vision, she reached up and kissed Greg back—on the cheek.

As they left, walking out on the sunlit sidewalk, she looked over to where Joel had been standing. He was gone.

4

I HAD A good time, and I deserved it, Edie repeated to herself for about the hundredth time as she drove up to the beach house and parked. She and Greg had gone on an afternoon whale watch, and after dinner, went over to the beach club where the band was playing.

While her thoughts had drifted to Joel now and then, she had been having too much fun to care. Greg had been a wonderful date. He'd called some of his friends to meet them at the club, and it had been an enjoyable impromptu thirtieth-birthday party. Edie couldn't have asked for anything better, though she'd quickly felt out of place among the younger crowd, and left much earlier than she'd planned on. She'd had a good time, but something had been missing. Namely, Joel.

Before she even stepped out of the car, she heard the hard-rock music blaring loudly from the boat, and saw the lights Joel had set up down there shining brightly in the dark. He sometimes worked until early evening, but never this late.

Her first instinct was to just go to bed—it was still her birthday, and she didn't want to ruin it with any more awkwardness. However, she'd never be able to sleep with that loud music playing. Besides, it was probably better to ask him now what had happened in town than wait until later. She didn't have anything to be guilty about, and he didn't have any right to be angry—she just had to remember that.

Walking down the path and hoping she was imagining problems where there weren't any, she resisted the urge to cover her ears with her hands. Shirtless, Joel was stretched out, wielding a small sander at a hard-to-reach spot. He was covered with sweat. He didn't notice her, and he certainly couldn't hear her over the sound of the sander and the music.

She shouted, but he didn't respond, and she was reluctant to nudge him and startle him while he was handling a power tool so she did the next best thing. She turned the music off. Blessed silence surrounded her, only to be followed a split second later with a bitten-out curse as Joel yanked himself up from the side of the boat, and swore again as he hit his head. Only then did he see her, and his angry eyes cooled before they broke contact with hers.

"Sorry—I called out to you but you didn't hear me."

He just nodded, picking up a rag and wiping his hands very thoroughly before shooting it back over the rail and looking at her impatiently. "Do you need something? I was hoping to finish this before bed."

Flustered for a moment, she remembered she had nothing to feel bad about, and took a deep breath. Her father always said confronting a problem directly was the best approach, and she was going to test out that advice.

"Why did you come to town today? And why did you just leave without a word?"

He was quiet for a moment, then shrugged, but she knew his body well enough to sense the tension in it. "No big deal. I came in to find you for lunch. I felt bad about not coming along," he said shortly.

"Why would you feel bad? I was okay with you staying here to work," she reminded him.

"It was your birthday. I didn't think you should spend it alone. But I see that you didn't, so no problem," he said casually, but maybe a little too casually, betraying the fact that he was really upset. But why? She resisted the impulse to bite back.

"How did you know it was my birthday?" she asked instead.

"There are a couple of messages on the machine back at the house—I listened in by mistake—sorry. I figured you shouldn't be by yourself, and went to find you."

Her heart softened a little more. "That's nice of you, Joel. You should have said so and joined us—you would have been welcome. The band was fantastic tonight. For such a small town, there's a lot of nightlife." She smiled, the pleasure of the day not quite diminished.

He seemed deflated, and turned back to pick up some of his tools. "I'm glad you enjoyed yourself. I wouldn't have wanted to interrupt your date."

"It wasn't a date—not the way you mean, anyway—I met Greg

when I first arrived here, when I stopped for directions, and he helped me find your place. We bumped into each other completely by accident today, and yes, we had a nice time. I didn't mind going to town on my own, but it was good to have company, too, and I'm not apologizing for that."

"Listen, you don't owe me anything, and you certainly don't have to lie or apologize."

"I'm not lying!"

The doubting look in his eyes made her want to scream.

"He's obviously more than a friend. I saw him touch you, kiss you. But hey, you have a right to do whatever, or whoever, you want."

Edie knew rationally that she didn't have to explain anything to Joel, but she wanted very badly for him to relax, to know that she and Greg had shared a pleasant day, and that was all.

Joel's words might be casual, but his tone, the look in his eyes and the tension that clutched his body, wasn't. He obviously didn't like seeing her with another man, and that warmed something deep inside of her.

"Joel, he touched my hand accidentally when he was reaching for the bill, and the kiss was innocent. That was the sum total of our contact all day, except for dancing. Really, that was it," she said softly, coaxing him to listen, to believe.

Why would Joel be so suspicious? He'd said he was divorced, and she figured that didn't help—obviously his previous relationships hadn't gone well, but she didn't care to be measured by the yardstick of women he'd known before.

She continued, "I'm not saying more wouldn't have happened if I'd wanted it to, but I didn't want it to. I don't go around dropping into bed with every man who happens to ask."

"He asked?" Joel's eyes narrowed, his lips tightening.

She stepped closer, wanting contact, wanting to reassure him, and following her instincts.

"Yeah, he did. But I think he knew what my answer would be— it was pretty clear my mind was elsewhere for the rest of the day after you made your appearance. I wish you'd come to join us. I missed you," she admitted, hoping she wasn't crossing a line, but Joel had a right to his emotions, and she had a right to hers. He wanted honesty, so she was giving it to him. "I came back early because I wanted to spend some time with you on my birthday. Maybe dance?"

She touched his chest tentatively, laying her hand over the spot where his heart was beating hard, even if he was trying to deny his response to her. He sucked in a breath as she resumed her exploration, clamping his hand over hers, looking down at her intently.

"I wanted to throw him over the side of that pretty little deck when I saw him touch you—so I left," he said, the admission seeming to erupt, and the confusion she saw in his eyes alongside the passion made her step in closer. She framed his face with her hands.

"I know. I saw. You have any idea why?"

"Yeah. I don't like sharing. Even if it's for a short time, even though it's temporary, while you're here, you're with me."

She rubbed a thumb over his lips, simultaneously thrilled and disappointed at his declaration. She liked the idea of being his, though not just temporarily.

That wasn't fair. Joel wasn't in a place for commitments, but for the moment, she *was* his. Wanted to be his, couldn't help being his. Whatever came after would have to take care of itself. She swallowed her disappointment, concentrating on the moment, since it was what they had.

"You should have said so, then," she said huskily.

"I'm saying so now." He caressed her cheek with the pad of his thumb in a gesture more tender than she'd experienced from him so far. There was more than sex in his touch, and she wondered if he knew it. "I wish I'd danced with you, too."

She glanced at her watch. "I have an hour left to my birthday. Want to go back to the house and celebrate with me?" She smiled. "We can always put some music on. Have that dance."

"Yeah. I'd like that."

She nearly squeaked with happiness as he picked her up in his arms, and strode off the boat, toward the house.

JOEL KNEW he was behaving a little like a caveman picking Edie up and carrying her back to the house, but he wanted her, needed to be with her, inside of her, as soon as possible—to touch her and wipe the thoughts of any other man except for him from her mind. They wouldn't have made it past the door except that he was covered in sawdust and paint, and he needed a shower. He carried her into the bathroom with him, hoping they'd share.

He loved how her eyes didn't disguise anything, openly revealing her desire as she let her dress fall to the floor and stepped past him. With Edie, there was no subterfuge, no games. He wouldn't have believed there was a woman on the planet like her, but he knew as he watched the emotions play over her face that she was the real deal.

He stripped his shorts off and didn't wait for her to remove hers, pulling her up against him for a deep kiss, breathing in her scent, his hands roaming over all of those fantastic, soft curves until they were both panting with excitement.

"Let's get this sawdust off you," she said.

"Couldn't agree more," he answered with a chuckle, helping her into the shower with him, never breaking contact.

Warm water sluiced down over their bodies and he took the soap from its ledge, wrapping both of their hands around it as he washed the sweat and sand from his body.

"I want your hands on me, Edie," he said roughly.

"Happy to oblige," she said breathlessly.

Her small, smooth hands worked butterfly caresses over his skin, washing away wisps of soap, and she followed her hands with her lips. As she lowered, closing her mouth over his shaft and taking him deep, he moaned, planting one hand on the tile wall for balance, and one in her hair.

The play of her lips over his skin was heaven, and when she raised her hand to cup his balls with her feather-soft fingers, he nearly lost it and tried to pull back, letting her know he was close. He'd been selfish enough today; he wanted to make up for his stupid behavior however he could.

She peeked up at him, her cheeks flushed with passion, her lips wrapped around him as she closed her eyes in bliss and took him even deeper. He wrapped his fingers in wet blond curls, knowing he couldn't hold on much longer. She seemed intent on making sure of it. He'd wanted to take her, and instead was being taken, thoroughly possessed, by her. And he loved it.

His head spun and the breath whooshed from his body as the rush of release poured through him. He fought the urge to close his eyes, caught instead by the vision of her in front of him, doing for him what no one had ever done quite so lovingly.

As his mind cleared he ran his fingers along her cheek, tenderness he'd never experienced before overcoming him. He reached down, tugging her up next to him, and she didn't resist this time, cuddling against him. The water turned cool, and he shut it off without putting any space between them.

Out of the shower, he grabbed thick towels from the rack and neither one of them said a word, not breaking the spell.

He dried her off first, leaving kisses along the way until he saw her hands tremble when she lifted one to balance on his shoulder. He swept the same towel over himself in a quick, cursory movement and dropped it to the floor, taking her hand in his and leading her out into the main room.

"Joel?" She said, pausing for a second, gazing around at the open windows.

"Shhh. We're fine. No one's around to see," he reassured.

He led her to the sofa, intent on pleasing her the way she'd pleased him, on giving as much as he had received. It was her birthday after all, and he hadn't given her a gift.

Joel didn't question the emotions coursing through him, the feeling of affection and caring that softened the edges of need and desire. It was just sex, but sex could be special. For Edie, he wanted it to be memorable.

Lowering her onto the huge sofa, he levered over her so that he could kiss her deeply, plundering her mouth until she moaned in need. His cock responded by twitching against the creamy softness of her skin. Amazing how intensely she turned him on, giving him the stamina he'd had when he was ten years younger. Right now, though, he was focused only on her.

He ran his fingers over her hardened nipples in a way he knew she liked, causing her to arch underneath him. He caught them and pinched, drawing yet another throaty moan. When his fingers found their way to the thatch of downy-soft hair between her thighs, he groaned back at how slick and hot she was—ready for him.

He brought her close several times, swallowing her moans and delighting in her gasps as he pushed her to the brink and then denied her satisfaction. She was trembling, flushed and writhing beneath him when he slid down, parting her thighs with his shoulders and settling down in between.

She tasted like sex, salt water and honey, and he lost himself in the intimate kiss, sucking and sweeping his tongue over her, finding out which spots made her quiver and which ones made her body tighten with need. He discovered that when he nibbled at her clit, she made the most beautiful sounds deep in her throat. He couldn't resist drawing them from her time and again, until the sounds turned into breathless pleas.

Burying his fingers inside her and finding yet more sensitive flesh that sent her skyrocketing, he kissed and licked, hypnotized by the rhythm they'd found and experiencing a joy he wasn't quite sure he'd ever known as she cried out his name, over and over, her inner muscles clutching, her body pouring forth its own honeyed pleasure onto his hands and mouth.

He was burning up, and she was ready, so he reached quickly to find his wallet on the table where he'd left it, sheathing himself and entering her with no preamble. He was so hot, it didn't take much. A few quick, hard thrusts and they both burst in one more sparkling explosion of pleasure, leaving them spent and tangled around each other.

He didn't know what time it was when he woke up, lying over her, although to the inside of the sofa, most of his weight off her. She was out like a light, sleeping, and he chuckled. She was so beautiful, and hot and so giving of herself. He moved a hand over her breast, watching her nipple peak, her mouth form an "Oh" in sleepy response to his touch. It was all he could do not to take her again, to love her until the sun came up.

Love?

No.

Joel wasn't about to confuse love with what was happening. He liked Edie—a lot—but in just over a week, she'd be gone, and he'd be back to his life. And that was how he wanted it. It was sex—warm, fantastic, incredible sex—and that was all he was interested in. He was almost completely sure that was true.

5

THE NEXT MORNING Edie was floating on air. She'd always thought she had a happy life, but now things were different. Last night with Joel, something had changed, at least for her. The warning bells were ringing, but she was intent on ignoring them. When they'd awakened, entangled and hot for each other, he'd made love to her slowly, turning her inside out, pleasure saturating her soul. And more.

It seemed that his previous distance was all but erased, and he was as interested in being around her as she was in him. His touch was never far away, nor his kiss. She loved it, and that was big trouble.

Her old life felt so far away. And she didn't miss it.

Joel, stretched out on the sand alongside her as the afternoon sun passed over them, toyed with her fingers and asked a question out of the blue, seeming to read her mind.

"So, how did a sexy chick like you end up being an accountant, anyway?"

"What, accountants can't be sexy?"

"None of mine are." They laughed, but he pressed on. "Seriously, do you love it?"

She sighed. "I don't love it, no. I like it, but it was never as if accounting was my grand passion or anything. I was good at math, and I wanted something steady, something sure, so that I knew I'd have a job and income after college. I'd always taken care of my family's finances, so accounting seemed like a natural fit. I like the people I work for, though."

"That's always a plus. Weren't you a little young to be running the family finances?" He propped up on one elbow, impossibly handsome, looking down at her. "Tell me to mind my own business if you want."

"No, it's fine." She touched his face gently, secretly happy he wanted to know about her life, though there wasn't much interesting to tell. "I inherited the only practical gene in my family, is all."

"And that means?"

"My parents are kind of hippies—my mom was an art teacher who left teaching to try to be a full-time artist, and my dad was on disability from his job and so he started sculpting. They do okay, and they're happy, but it was never a big-money operation. They're not really clued into keeping track of things—they get into something they're working on and lose track of time, other things."

"Like paying bills on time?"

"Exactly, or buying groceries. My younger sister is an aspiring actress, and my brother is in college, drifting from program to program, trying to figure out what he wants to do."

"So you shoulder all the responsibility?"

"I don't think of it that way. They're my family, I love them, and I don't mind helping out."

"By helping out, do you mean you needed a reliable career so you could support them?"

"No, no, not like that. They actually do pretty well on the local art scene, and have even had a few studio showings. My mother teaches, though she does it on a part-time basis. My sister supports herself, though I do help with my brother's tuition a bit."

Joel paused, and Edie sensed he was holding back what he wanted to say—not that she hadn't heard it all from her friends. Cutting the apron ties, and all of that. Her family was important to her, and she was happy, more or less. She still had her own life, and being here with Joel proved that. Didn't it?

He didn't say anything, but he just ran his fingers up and down her arm. "It's nice that you all take care of each other. If you hadn't become an accountant, what would you have been?"

She wasn't sure she wanted to say. She was living one fantasy right now, why think about others?

"Edie?"

She gave in. "Well, this was a long time ago, but I always thought I'd like some kind of business of my own. You know, a bakery or bookstore, that kind of thing. Maybe a bakery that's also a bookstore," she quipped, joking. Suddenly, it hit her with a sinking feeling how long it had been since she'd given up on that idea. She'd gone as far as shopping for locations once in college, but it didn't take much studying to know how difficult and risky starting her own business would be.

"As an accountant, you have the financial skills to support a business plan—why don't you do it?"

She shook her head and sat up, staring out at the ocean. "Too risky, and doesn't everyone on the planet think of that? You know, owning their own shop or bed and breakfast, but very few people actually do it, and probably fewer make it work."

"Sounds like you've given up before you even tried."

Anger sparked. Why were they talking about this? Real life wasn't part of their deal.

"Joel, I know you mean well, but not everyone can be as successful at their own business as you've been, and look what you lost in the meantime. Your marriage. My family is important to me, and going off and starting my own business would just be risky and selfish."

She expected him to draw away, or snap back, but instead he drew her tight against his chest.

"You're right. I'm sorry."

Now she felt terrible. "No, I'm sorry for saying something so mean about your marriage. I didn't mean it. It's just, well, I've made different choices."

"You didn't say anything I don't know. Thing is, I love being a lawyer, but I ran my marriage into the ground because I didn't know how to balance things. It was selfish. Even getting married was selfish, when I knew I didn't have the energy to put into a relationship. Which is why I don't want to make the same mistake again. My mother and father built the family business together, and I think it brought them closer—I didn't know how to do that. The firm was something I was married to before I got married, I guess."

"What kind of business do they run?"

"They have a chain of popular seafood restaurants."

"Do you have any involvement?"

"I handle a few cases and contracts for my father. I really wanted to be a lawyer since I was about ten. I don't know, I saw something on TV that was very exciting, a lawyer giving a big closing argument, winning a case, saving the day. I wanted to be that guy."

"And you are."

"No. I have a very successful corporate law firm that spends its time protecting the money of some very important clients, but it's not what I envisioned."

"Why so different?"

"There's not a whole lot of money in public defense and criminal law."

"And money matters?"

"Sure—think about what you just told me. I guess in my own fashion, I was bent on success to show my father I could do it, but also to show him I was right to not just inherit the family business. I wanted a certain lifestyle, and I went after it single-mindedly. I lost sight of important things in the process."

"You said you came here to think, to reprioritize?" As he kissed her hair, his hand circled tantalizingly on her bare midriff.

"Yeah. The firm is doing well, and now I have to figure out what else I want. Take more time for life, and maybe even start taking some criminal cases on."

"So you will pursue your dream!" she said, pleased.

"I'm thinking about it. I want to try to focus on what matters."

"That's wonderful, Joel."

"You're wonderful," he said, dipping his lips into the curve of her neck, making her shiver with desire.

A WEEK LATER, Edie knew she was definitely in trouble. They'd been out sailing all day, and it was like a movie, every moment perfect as she drifted through scenery that she'd only ever seen on postcards and calendars.

With only a few days left to her vacation, neither one of them had expressed any inclination for anything more than the temporary affair they were having. Back at the dock, as she watched him gather up the ropes and tie the boat securely, her heart beat faster. Her fingers stretched and relaxed, recalling every inch of him that she'd gotten to know so quickly and so intimately. Had she ever known any man so well?

No.

At least, not physically. With Joel, she'd memorized the strong lateral muscles of his back, the chords at the back of his neck, and the lovely play of biceps and other muscles in his gorgeous arms. She knew the dip where his flat stomach transitioned to his hip, and the strong thigh and leg muscles that brought her so much pleasure. She knew he was ticklish behind the knees, and what spots could turn laugher from tickling to moans of desire.

He looked back and caught her stare. "Hey."

"Hey, back," she said happily.

"You have lust in your eyes," he teased.

More than that, she thought, but said instead, "Can you blame me?"

"Well, I can't say I mind, as long as you're looking at me," he replied, crossing to where she sat. When he slid his hand back around her neck, she winced at the unexpected pain. He froze, drawing his hand away gently.

"What? Oh, no." He looked down more closely, and winced. "You got a bit of a burn."

"But I used sunblock!" she protested, touching exposed spots and finding she had more than one that felt hot to the touch and hurt when she prodded.

"You're so fair, and being out on the water is a whole different ballgame—I should have known better and reminded you to reapply," he said with a note of self-recrimination. "Let's get you up to the house. I have some lotion that works wonders."

"You'll put it on for me?" she asked flirtatiously.

He grinned, seeking her hand as they walked along the well-worn path. "I will, though I think you should take it easy tonight, drink lots of water—take some aspirin. We'll see how serious it is when we get in a better light."

Edie shivered as the cool night breeze wafted over her hot skin. Unreasonable tears formed, not from pain, but from regret that she'd been thoughtless, and that her sunburn could keep her from Joel for even one night. Their time was short as it was. She swiped the tears away before he could see.

"I'm sure I'll be fine. It's just a sunburn."

"You don't feel sick or have a headache? Dizzy?"

"No, just a little tingly. Hot, but shivery."

"Hmm." He sounded concerned as he opened the door and ushered her in.

He flicked the light on and turned to inspect her shoulders—when he inched the material from her shoulders, she shivered again, for an entirely different reason.

"You're pretty red—good thing you were wearing a hat. It protected your head and your face, but your arms, shoulders and neck are going to smart for a bit. Let's get something on them before it really kicks in. It'll probably feel worse before it gets better."

"Okay," she said, not about to argue. The lack of the cool breeze that had been tickling her skin outside intensified the heat that suddenly seemed all-consuming over her tender flesh, and she followed willingly to his bathroom where he took a bottle of green gel from the cabinet.

"It's a special aloe lotion—it will cool your skin and anesthetize the burn, and moisturizing will reduce peeling. I've had a few bad burns, and this will help a lot, with a few aspirin."

"Thank God…I don't think I've had a burn since I was a kid, and I'd forgotten how lousy it is," she said, sighing in relief as he gently smoothed the cooling gel over her skin. Further investigation showed some redness on the backs of her legs, as well, and the tops of her feet were red—she hadn't even thought to put sunblock on her feet. Stupid.

By the time Joel had finished layering the soothing gel all over her, she was caught between relief and wanting him so much she wasn't sure which way to go. Joel made it clear he was only providing comfort, and deep down she appreciated his solicitousness.

Normally, she was the one who took care of everyone, the steady rock in her family upon whom everyone depended. It was nice to be coddled. It also reminded her how near she was to the end of her time here. Soon she would be back to her job and her family. A normal, boring person among a family of artists and free spirits.

She loved them dearly, and knew they loved her, too, but nonetheless, it often landed on her shoulders to be the responsible one, the one who planned, the one who took care of mundane, everyday things like bills and doctor's appointments. She thought of her conversation with Joel on the beach. Of how Joel was thinking about what he had given up, and of going back after his dreams.

What had she given up? Was she wrong not to pursue her own

dreams? Did her family really need her that much, or was that a convenient excuse not to take risks in her life? She feared the latter.

"Feel better?" he asked, looking up at her with silvery eyes that pierced right through to her heart. She loved his eyes.

"Mostly," she answered.

"You sound tired. Let's get you something to drink, some aspirin, and we'll hit the sack early."

No, she didn't want to sleep. Didn't want to lose a single second she could have with him.

"Could we just watch some movies or television for a while, or talk? I'm not tired. I feel much better. I promise. This salve is a miracle."

He looked at her skeptically, and she almost laughed, feeling like a child asking to stay up after bedtime. She shut down that thought a little too late for comfort. It wasn't too big a leap to think of Joel looking at his own children with those wonderful eyes. He'd be a fantastic father—she was certain of it.

Oh, she was in *sooo* deep.

"Sure we can watch some TV. There are a ton of DVDs, as well—why don't you pick something?"

"How about a chick flick?"

He smiled in a sideways, sexy way that melted her heart. "I'll suffer through it. I have you to watch."

He turned away and she raised a hand to her throat, where sudden emotion choked back words. She hoped there was an action-adventure in there somewhere, because she couldn't stand to watch someone else's happily-ever-after when she knew she wasn't going to have one with Joel.

6

JOEL SET the book he'd been reading aside, yawning. Edie had fallen asleep halfway through the movie. He'd let her rest there on the sofa because he knew how difficult it could be to fall asleep with a bad sunburn. He also enjoyed watching her sleep. He enjoyed just about anything with Edie, maybe a little more than he should.

In the days since their fight—and their making up—on her birthday, he'd decided to throw himself in and savor his time with her; the boat could wait. However, in doing so, he might have gotten in deeper than he'd anticipated. He reassured himself that it was just a rebound thing, a summer romance, but deep down, a little voice told him differently.

Could he be falling for her? How was that possible so soon after the divorce? Wasn't it smarter to wait and get some distance before jumping into another relationship? Not that Edie had given even one clue that she wanted more. As far as he knew, she'd be packing up in a few days and returning to Cleveland.

The idea left him feeling hollow inside. Not good.

Joel jerked when the phone rang, nearly dislodging Edie from her nesting spot. She moaned and turned over, allowing him to jump neatly from the sofa and leap toward the phone before it woke her—who the hell would be calling this time of night?

He vaguely recognized the number on the caller ID, but when he heard the voice, it definitely rang a bell: Edie's mother, who didn't seem at all thrown that a man was answering the phone her daughter should have answered. The fact that she seemed to know him threw him even more.

"Joel! Is that you? Is Edie there?"

Momentarily shocked into silence by the unexpected familiarity, he paused, and then it hit him that Edie must have told her family something about him.

"Yes, this is Joel," he said more formally. "Edie is here, but she's sleeping."

"We need her, there's been an accident. Can you put her on, please?"

Joel put the phone down and shook Edie gently awake. Though he was trying not to panic her, she rushed over to the phone when he told her it was her mother, and they needed to talk to her.

Joel watched the color drain from her face as she spoke in calming tones to her mother, assuring her she would be home right away.

"My sister was in a car accident," she whispered to Joel in a quivering voice, covering the receiver for a moment.

Joel put a hand on her shoulder and made her sit as she spoke with her mother, then her father. She kept trying to get off the phone, telling them she had to get on the road if she were going to get home quickly, but it appeared they all wanted to talk to her as he heard her reassuring them. Joel grabbed his cell phone. There was no way he was letting her drive this way.

When she finally hung up, she lifted a trembling hand to wipe away one tear, and Joel hauled her up close, holding her tight.

"How serious is it?"

"It's hard to say—my mother said the doctor was in with her, and hadn't come out to talk to them yet. I—I have to get home."

"I know. We're going."

She pushed away, looked up at him, bemused. "What? We?"

"While you were talking I called and booked a water taxi to Boston and flights out of Logan. We're on the next plane to Cleveland, so pack something and let's go now."

"But, you don't have to go, I can go, I have my c-car…."

"It will take too long, and you're not driving when you're so worried."

"But Joel, you shouldn't have to pay for all of this—"

"Shush. We'll work that out later."

She was quiet while they got ready and got to the airport, but not one more tear had fallen. She'd made some other calls, attending to details, making sure things were taken care of, and asking a friend to check in on her parents.

Through it all, he hustled her along, and before long, they were standing in line at the gate, ready to board. He had the feeling Edie was the backbone of her family, that this little blond bombshell of a woman was the one who held it all together. He'd heard as much in her mother's desperation on the phone, and in how she talked to all of them, attended to what needed to be done without complaint.

Who looked out for Edie? Protectiveness, concern and other emotions swamped him as they took their seats.

For the moment, he would.

"OH, EDIE…we're so glad you made it home! How did you get here so fast?"

Her mother wrapped her in a tight hug, looking stressed.

"Mom, why aren't you at the hospital? Where's Katie?"

"She's here. She's fine."

Edie took a full step back. It was just 7:00 a.m. and she'd been running all night on fear and caffeine. "Fine? But you said she had an accident—what did the doctors say?"

She didn't know she'd raised her voice until she felt Joel's hand on her shoulder. Joel came forward, quietly introducing himself. He'd offered to drop her off and go to a hotel, but there was no way she'd hear of it when he had paid to get her home so quickly. And if she were completely honest, she'd been anxious, and had wanted him with her. Having him with her on the plane had kept her imagination from taking over by picturing everything terrible that might have happened to Katie. He'd kept her talking, distracting her, and she was so grateful for everything.

Though right now, at this moment, she was just completely stymied. Her mother, presently calm and very taken with Joel, seemed far away from the hysterical woman on the phone,

"Mom—really, please. Joel rushed us home on a plane— where's Katie? What's going on? I've been worried sick—you were a wreck on the phone."

"Oh, I'm so sorry, honey. We tried to call you back but your cell phone was off. I left messages."

"I didn't check. When we hit the ground, we just got here as fast as possible."

"Yes, of course, I didn't think of that. Katie is fine. It wasn't that serious."

"But you said the doctors were in with her, and no one had said anything… It sounded so bad…."

"I know, but we were so upset, I may have just been too worked up. I'm so sorry, sweetheart. There was a car accident, and Katie was hurt, but it was just a bump on the head—she has a concussion and some cuts and bruises but that's all, thank God. I'm so sorry we worried you. I called you as soon as we knew, but your phone was off, and…" Her mother shrugged and pulled Edie into a hug that she returned limply.

"I guess waiting to call me until after you knew whether it was serious didn't make sense," she said vaguely.

"I know, we should have done that, but we were so upset and we just thought you had to know. But everything is fine. You should get back to your vacation."

Edie just couldn't believe it, but then again, she could. In the end, Edie was still thankful they'd called. Exhaustion caught up with her as she swayed a little, and Joel's body provided a solid wall of support.

"You okay?" he asked, looking down into her face.

"I—I'm fine. I'm so sorry…we came all the way here, and you didn't need to."

"I'm glad your sister is okay. These things happen. Coming here was the right thing to do."

She lifted her gaze to his, almost completely missing her mother's watchful eyes, which were dancing with interest when Edie looked back at her.

"Mom, I'm glad everything is okay, but my vacation is almost over, and I'm exhausted—we both are. I need some sleep, then I'll need to go back, get my things and return the car to the rental agency, I guess. Maybe I can get an extra day off."

"Oh, honey, I wish we'd been able to get hold of you sooner. Joel, it was so good of you to rush her home—a white knight, I think, yes…with those clear, penetrating eyes…maybe a painting instead of clay."

Edie almost laughed in spite of her exhaustion—had Joel just blushed? If anyone could make that happen, it would be her mother. As they went inside, Joel hung back. Edie turned to him.

"Joel?"

"Edie, since everything is good, I should probably leave. I don't want to impose on your family."

Edie and her mother objected at the same time, and Edie watched her mother step forward and wrap Joel in a tight mom-hug—Joel was definitely on her mother's A-list.

"Joel, don't leave. At least not without me. Let me see Katie. We'll stay at my apartment, and head back tomorrow."

She saw him soften, nod, and her heart warmed. Edie knew the adult thing to do was to part ways with a kiss and forget the whole thing, but she couldn't let go yet. He was her vacation lover, and technically, she was still on vacation. She planned on spending every second they had left together, and didn't think about anything after that.

A FEW HOURS later, Joel was seeing double by the time he and Edie left the house.

"Sorry that went on so long—I really thought we'd just stay a few minutes," Edie said to him as they walked down the sidewalk, peering up at the night sky. "You were a big hit. When they like someone, it's hard to make them let go."

"They're a great bunch, Edie."

She shook her head, smiling, as they walked in the direction of her apartment.

"Here's my building," she said, navigating a turn around a wrought-iron fence. "I should apologize, again. I could have waited and not jumped the gun, bringing us out here so quickly."

"Maybe they just wanted you here. Maybe you wanted to be here. Nothing wrong with that," he said as they entered a small, well-designed apartment, painted with bright colors and accented with eclectic furnishings that should have clashed, but didn't. Edie clearly had more of her parents' artistic sense than she thought. She hung their jackets on the rack and he set their bags down.

"Do you want anything? A drink? I have a halfway-stocked bar, though to be honest, I'm not sure what's in there."

He answered honestly, unable to take his eyes away from her. "Only you. I just want you." His voice was ragged, maybe with desire, maybe with emotion or exhaustion, but all he knew in his heart was that he'd uttered the truth.

All he wanted was Edie. It seemed very simple. He was reordering his life, changing his priorities. Edie was very clearly becoming a priority. He wanted more time with her, a chance to see what they could have together. However, the woman of his dreams was standing right in front of him, and he didn't know what to do. She hadn't shared anything that would make him think she was open to more than a fling.

Was that really what he wanted? Was he just tired and mixed up? Was it another mistake to be paid for later down the line? All he knew was that when she'd gotten that call, he'd wanted to protect her, to be at her side and to make sure she was okay. He wanted to be with her even when they weren't just having fun—or sex. That meant something, right?

She walked up to him, shadows under her eyes, no makeup, her hair tossed and road-weary, but he thought she was completely gorgeous. Emotion such as he'd never really experienced washed over him. Scared him.

She slid her hands up his chest, linked her arms around his neck, and cuddled in.

"You feel so good. I just want to sleep right here. Can we just catch a quick shower and go to bed?"

"Sounds perfect," he said, realizing it did as he scooped his arms around her in a hug. The desire was there, muted by their sleepiness, but there was also comfort. He wasn't sure he'd ever felt comfort—not really, not in just this way—with a woman before. And while he still had questions, he wasn't sure he was ready to let it go.

EDIE WOKE FIRST to the strange feeling of being in her own bed, but not alone. That wasn't a usual occurrence in her life. And yet, it felt great—normal. Right.

She snuggled into Joel, wrapping arms and legs around him, finding him hard and warm against her stomach. They hadn't bothered dressing after their showers, but had just dried off and fallen into bed, passing out almost immediately.

She was awake now, and so was he—at least parts of him. Desire spiked as she pressed against him. She didn't hide the surge of emotion that gripped her as she watched him sleeping, and lifted her hips up gently, lowering until he was planted deep inside.

Feeling so connected to him was becoming second nature, as if her body sought out its natural connection to his. Was that possible, in such a short amount of time?

He moaned, arching up slightly, eyes still shut. She knew he slept like the dead, and smiled at the intimate knowledge. She pressed gently against him once more, sighing at the perfection of it.

Desire drizzled through her like warm honey, melting her from the inside out. *I love you,* she thought, the emotion carrying her through her climax, enjoying the expression of her feelings, even if it was a silent declaration.

"Are you sure about that?" Joel's voice was rough with sleep and desire.

She nearly fell to the side, startled, but his hands gripped down on her hips, steadying her as he thrust up once, then again, his head arching back as he pushed her toward another, fuller orgasm. The pleasure was so mutual that they rose and fell back together, words forgotten for the moment.

Collapsing against his chest, she sighed, her heartbeat echoing his. He wove his fingers through her hair, and reached down, tipping her chin up so it rested on his sternum.

"Did you mean it?"

"What?"

"What you said. That you love me. Or was it just the moment, the sex?"

His eyes held hers and she wanted to bolt when she realized that she'd actually said out loud what she'd believed she'd only thought. Oh God…how could she have made such a stupid mistake? Was there anything that would send Joel packing faster? Granted, what they had was pretty much over anyway, but she didn't want it to end on this note.

"Edie? Look at me."

She'd closed her eyes, squeezing them tight, afraid he'd see the truth. For better or worse, the deed was done. She did love him, so much it hurt, and she couldn't lie to his face.

"Yes, it is. I'm sorry, I didn't plan on it, and I don't expect anything, I just…I got carried away. But I know how you feel, what we have, and that's okay, I—"

"Edie. Stop."

He sat up, pushing pillows behind his back. She slid to his side, kneeling on the mattress and tugged the sheet around her—she was feeling too vulnerable, too exposed, to really *be* exposed. He yanked the sheet back down.

"Don't ever cover up in front of me. Don't cover anything. Especially how you feel."

"But—"

"No, listen. I know. I'm glad you said that. I know we had an agreement, that all we had was sex, but—" His gaze held hers, and he paused for a long moment before he spoke again. "Nothing was put in writing, was it? Things can change. I want more, too. I think I love you, too, or I'm well on my way to it."

"But—"

"No, I know. It's a fling and a rebound fling at that, and I don't blame you if you don't trust my emotions, considering what I've said and where I'm coming from, relationship-wise. But if you give me a chance, Edie, I want to give us a chance."

"But, I—"

He held a hand up. "I know—you have your life and your family here, and that's hard. I can't move my firm, but maybe we can meet each other halfway and see what happens. Maybe I could open a Cleveland office, maybe they could specialize in criminal cases, who knows?"

"That's a really big step, Joel," she said cautiously.

"I'm not saying tomorrow, or even next month, but I'm open to the possibilities. Are you?"

He reached out, pulled her down so that her face was close to his, his heart practically stopping when he thought she might say no. Never had his life seemed so precariously balanced on such a small word.

"Edie, I love you—and I think I can prove it in all the ways you deserve. Will you take a chance? Can we see if our fling could end up being a whole lot more?"

She smiled, lifting a hand to his face, her eyes spilling over with tears. His heart hammered in his chest; he didn't know if the tears were good or bad. "Are there any more 'buts'?"

She laughed, shaking her head. He leaned in, kissing tears away.

"I do love you, Joel. It's scary, the idea of having just met you, but loving you, and seeing how this adventure has changed my life, it makes me think maybe I should think more about pursing my dreams, maybe not play it so safe all the time."

"But?"

Her smile was brilliant, and his hopes soared. "No buts. I think it feels right. My parents always say time means nothing, that when something is right, it's right. That you have to trust your heart. I trust my heart, Joel. And most of all, I trust yours."

She laid her hand on his heart, and he laid his over it, more moved than he'd ever been in his life.

"I think we're probably going to stay a few more days here, then, right?" he asked, breathless, as she kissed his lips, then his neck, and lower.

"Mmm. If you can stay, that would be wonderful. You can meet my friends, and I can show you around town. Maybe I can pick your brain on running my own business."

He smiled in pleased surprise. "Edie! That's amazing!"

"Well, it's just a notion still. One thing at a time. You're inspiring me, I guess."

"Whatever I can do to help."

"Well, I'll take you up on that, but for the moment, I'm still on vacation."

As her kisses drifted lower, utter happiness stole over him, and he knew—he just knew—that all was right in the world. Love, passion and happiness formed a trifecta of bliss. *She loved him.* As he loved her. Edie was his, and nothing else mattered. The rest was details.

He looked deeply into her eyes, making sure. "Are you sure? You want something more serious? I have to be sure, Edie. No reservations?"

"No, no reservations, but I plan on sticking around, anyway," she said confidently, and showed him how certain she was for the rest of the morning.

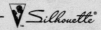

SPECIAL EDITION™

NEW YORK TIMES
BESTSELLING AUTHOR

DIANA PALMER

A brand-new Long, Tall Texans novel

HEART OF STONE

Feeling unwanted and unloved, Keely returns
to Jacobsville and to Boone Sinclair, a rancher
troubled by his own past. Boone has always
seemed reserved, but now Keely discovers a
sensuality with him that quickly turns to love. Can
they each see past their own scars to let love in?

*Available September 2008
wherever you buy books.*

REQUEST YOUR FREE BOOKS!

2 FREE NOVELS
PLUS 2
FREE GIFTS!

HARLEQUIN®

Blaze™

Red-hot reads!

YES! Please send me 2 FREE Harlequin® Blaze™ novels and my 2 FREE gifts (gifts are worth about $10). After receiving them, if I don't wish to receive any more books, I can return the shipping statement marked "cancel". If I don't cancel, I will receive 6 brand-new novels every month and be billed just $4.24 per book in the U.S. or $4.71 per book in Canada, plus 25¢ shipping and handling per book and applicable taxes, if any*. That's a savings of 15% or more off the cover price! I understand that accepting the 2 free books and gifts places me under no obligation to buy anything. I can always return a shipment and cancel at any time. Even if I never buy another book, the two free books and gifts are mine to keep forever.

151 HDN ERVA   351 HDN ERUX

Name	(PLEASE PRINT)	

Address		Apt. #

City	State/Prov.	Zip/Postal Code

Signature (if under 18, a parent or guardian must sign)

Mail to the **Harlequin Reader Service:**
IN U.S.A.: P.O. Box 1867, Buffalo, NY 14240-1867
IN CANADA: P.O. Box 609, Fort Erie, Ontario L2A 5X3

Not valid to current subscribers of Harlequin Blaze books.

Want to try two free books from another line?
Call 1-800-873-8635 or visit www.morefreebooks.com.

* Terms and prices subject to change without notice. N.Y. residents add applicable sales tax. Canadian residents will be charged applicable provincial taxes and GST. Offer not valid in Quebec. This offer is limited to one order per household. All orders subject to approval. Credit or debit balances in a customer's account(s) may be offset by any other outstanding balance owed by or to the customer. Please allow 4 to 6 weeks for delivery. Offer available while quantities last.

Your Privacy: Harlequin Books is committed to protecting your privacy. Our Privacy Policy is available online at www.eHarlequin.com or upon request from the Reader Service. From time to time we make our lists of customers available to reputable third parties who may have a product or service of interest to you. If you would prefer we not share your name and address, please check here.

HB08R

Romantic
SUSPENSE

Sparked by Danger, Fueled by Passion.

Cindy Dees
Killer Affair

Seduction in the sand…and a killer on the beach.

Can-do girl Madeline Crummby is off to a remote
Fijian island to review an exclusive resort, and she hires
Tom Laruso, a burned-out bodyguard, to fly her there
in spite of an approaching hurricane. When their plane
crashes, they are trapped on an island with a serial killer
who stalks overaffectionate couples. When their false
attempts to lure out the killer turn all too real, Tom and
Madeline must risk their lives and their hearts….

**Look for the third installment
of this thrilling miniseries,
available August 2008
wherever books are sold.**

HARLEQUIN®

Blaze™

COMING NEXT MONTH

#411 SECRET SEDUCTION Lori Wilde
Perfect Anatomy, Bk. 2
Security specialist Tanner Doyle is an undercover bodyguard protecting surgeon
Vanessa Rodriguez at the posh Confidential Rejuvenations clinic. Luckily,
keeping the good doctor close to his side won't be a problem—the sizzling
sexual chemistry between them is like a fever neither can escape....

#412 THE HELL-RAISER Rhonda Nelson
Men Out of Uniform, Bk. 5
After months of wrangling with her greedy stepmother over her inheritance, the
last thing Sarah Jane Walker needs is P.I. Mick Chivers reporting on her every
move. Although with sexy Mick around, she's tempted to give him something
worth watching....

#413 LIE WITH ME Cara Summers
Lust in Translation
Philly Angelis has been in love with Roman Oliver forever, but he's always treated
her like a kid. But not for long... Philly's embarking on a trip to Greece—to find her
inner Aphrodite! And heaven help Roman when he catches up with her....

#414 PLEASURE TO THE MAX! Cami Dalton
Cassie Parker gave up believing in fairy tales years ago. So when her aunt
sends her a gift—a lover's box, reputed to be able to make fantasies come
true—Cassie's not impressed...until a sexy stranger shows up and seduces
her on the spot. Now she's starring in an X-rated fairy tale of her very own.

#415 WHISPERS IN THE DARK Kira Sinclair
Radio talk show host Christopher Faulkner, aka Dr. Desire, has been helping
people with their sexual hang-ups for years. But when he gets an over-the-air
call from vulnerable Karyn Mitchell, he suspects he'll soon be the one in over
his head....

#416 FLASHBACK Jill Shalvis
American Heroes: The Firefighters, Bk. 2
Firefighter Aidan Donnelly has always battled flames with trademark icy calm.
That is, until a blazing old flame returns—in the shape of sizzling soap star
Mackenzie Stafford! Aidan wants to pour water over the unquenchable heat
between them. But that just creates more steam....

www.eHarlequin.com